Angel and the Deadly Secret

ANGEL AND THE DEADLY SECRET

Anthea Cohen

Constable • London

First published in Great Britain 2003
by Constable, an imprint of Constable & Robinson Ltd
3 The Lanchesters, 162 Fulham Palace Road,
London W6 9ER
www.constablerobinson.com

ISBN 1–84119–480–8

Printed and bound in Great Britain

A CIP catalogue record for this book
is available from the British Library

Chapter One

The amber lights of the street lamps lit up the white fronts of the houses, now divided into expensive and much sought-after flats. The façade of each one was unblemished. White, carefully and expensively maintained.

Four steps led up to the wide glass-panelled front door of each block. There was a row of half a dozen names denoting who lived in the flats above. The hallway, lit from dusk till dawn, threw a discreet golden light down the steps to the pavement below.

Lights too were showing in the windows above. Some curtains were drawn, some were still open, partially revealing the interiors.

Famous people lived in one or two of the flats, well-known names and personalities. The rows of cars, each in its own parking area, matched the class of flat. BMWs, one or two Rolls, large Rovers, some chauffeur-driven. Also here and there a high-seated Range Rover, almost always looking clean and shining, showing no hint of ever being driven through muddy rain-soaked country lanes. Perhaps they never were. They were merely a fashion, a whim.

Even the road running by the flats looked cleaner than other parts of this huge coastal town. No crisp packets blew about, no food containers littered the pavements or gutters. No children ran about to scatter the crisp packets. The flats were too small to house families. The inhabitants were mostly retired, late middle-aged and wealthy or at least comfortably off. One could almost hear the conversation that might go on inside. Talk of concerts, latest West End plays, galleries, racing perhaps? Horses, not dogs!

This rarefied atmosphere was valuable. Not only to the flat dwellers, but to the estate agents who grew fat on the commission they received when the flats changed occupants, as they frequently did, with the prices usually rising.

The cold February air had, one could guess, no effect upon the rooms behind the lighted windows, no effect at all. Central heating, double glazing and, in some cases, air-conditioning were all playing their expensive part in keeping the sea-chilled winter at bay. Just as the warm sea breezes of summer could be let in at will, or kept out at will!

The only thing that couldn't be held at bay was the constant stream of traffic along the lighted sea front. Cars, lorries, motor bikes – the traffic flowed by these expensive well-kept flats relentlessly. One reason perhaps why the flats were not quite such a frightening price as they once were, why the glamorous names were giving way to the ordinary unknowns.

This had, to some extent, wiped off the smug smiles from the estate agents' faces.

Not completely, though.

The flats still sold like hot cakes!

Agnes slid the Porsche neatly into her usual parking space outside the flats. As she locked the car and heard the reassuring 'clonk' it flashed across her mind that by now she certainly should be able to park expertly in the space provided. It was a year and nine months since she had moved into one of the two top flats in the building. Parking the car was almost a reflex action. She dropped the locking device into her handbag and took out her front door key.

Pausing on the top step, she looked across the road to where the amber lights shone on the green railings that separated the Esplanade from the drop down to the shingle below. Little beyond the railings could be seen, but the waves as they met the shingle made a noise like applause – a thousand hands clapping.

Agnes glanced at her watch. Twenty to nine. The February night was chilly and foggy. The mist rolling across the road from the sea looked like smoke and added to the chill.

She opened the front door, sending a stream of light down the four white-painted stone steps. The flats' central heating was welcoming. Agnes was about to shut the door behind her and make for the lift when a voice, calling from the street below, stopped her. She opened the door wide and peered down into the misty dimness.

'Please, Mrs Turner! Mrs Turner, don't close the door. Wait for me, please!'

It was Amy Horrocks. She lived one floor below Agnes. She was hurrying, almost running, which was not easy for her as she was not young and suffered from back trouble. She reached the steps, leant for a moment on the white-painted pilaster, then began a laboured climb up the steps, still talking, almost crying.

'Thank you, thank you! I was being followed all the way from the church!'

'Are you sure, Amy? Why should anyone follow you? Were they muggers or what?'

Amy had not the breath to reply.

As Agnes turned to shut the door, two people passed the bottom of the steps. A man and a woman. They were talking animatedly, and did not even look up at the open door directly above them.

Agnes watched them go by, then closed the door. She turned to Amy Horrocks who was leaning against the mail shelf, trembling. Agnes noted the sweat on her top lip and forehead. She was deathly pale.

'They've found out where I live, or were trying to. Now they know, Agnes, now they know!'

Agnes put the front door key into her bag and, taking

7

Amy Horrocks firmly by the arm, propelled her into the lift. As she pressed the button for the top floor her companion protested.

'Oh, please don't worry about me, Mrs Turner – Agnes. I'm all right, really I am!'

'Amy, I'm taking you up to my flat. You certainly don't look all right.'

After they had been greeted by an ecstatic Polly, Agnes sat Amy Horrocks on the settee, went to the kitchen, and came back with a small glass of brandy. She drew up a table and pushed the glass towards her still shaking guest who, though protesting, picked up the glass and took a sip, a very small sip, hardly wetting her lips.

To Agnes's surprise, Polly, not normally a great greeter of guests, jumped up on to the settee and sat close to Amy, leaning against her, as if to comfort.

'What makes you think you were being followed, Amy? Did they, or he or she – or whoever it was – speak to you or try to stop you, or catch hold of you?'

'No, no. It started just as I left the church. There were two of them, just behind me. When I hurried, they hurried. When I slowed down because I was so breathless they did the same.'

She took a little more brandy.

'But what did you mean when you said, "They've found out where I live," Amy? Who has found out where you live? And what if they have?'

At this question Amy Horrocks appeared to become more agitated. She got up, pushing away the still affectionate Polly, and in spite of Agnes's offer of more brandy she would not stay but crossed the room, opened the door and made her way across the small hall and opened the front door of the flat. She turned then and stammered out her thanks.

'It was good of you, Mrs – Agnes. Thank you. I was very unnerved, very. I hardly knew what I was saying – just nonsense, I am sure!'

Agnes shrugged her shoulders and watched Amy walk

8

down the stairs, not bothering to use the lift just to go down the one floor. She walked carefully – favouring her back, Agnes supposed. Or because she was still shaking from what Agnes felt must be an imagined threat.

Back in the flat Agnes fed Polly and noticed the brandy still on the draining board. She poured herself a brandy and ginger ale, one of her favourite drinks, and sat down in front of the television.

Ten o'clock news, then Polly's short stroll and bed. Agnes had been to a drinks party and the nibbles had been very good, more than adequate to take the place of supper.

Yes, Polly's walk, then bed if there was nothing on television. That was the routine. One year and nine months of it.

Oh, there had been breaks, one or two. One weekend, one week abroad . . .

The death of her friend Madge Hillier had been a great blow to Agnes, who was not one to make new friends easily. She was finding life much lonelier in this flat, once the door was shut. It was turning out to be a solitary place in spite of there being other residents around. The few sounds she could hear around her, doors shutting, windows closing, the click of an electric switch being turned on or off, seemed to add to her sense of alienation.

Was she restless enough to think about moving again? The flat would sell easily enough. Probably make money. Property was going up and up these days. But where to go!

Agnes switched off the television. Her thoughts had almost obliterated the news on the screen.

'Come on, Polly, walkies, walkies!'

During the short walk she always took Polly for before bedtime, her thoughts of moving did not go away.

Indeed they had been a bit persistent lately. Maybe . . .

Back indoors she took Polly's collar off and gave her her night-time biscuit. Agnes then made herself a hot drink

9

and sat down to watch the later news, determinedly concentrating on what she was seeing and not letting her preoccupation get in the way of the newsreader or the pictures on the screen. Polly jumped up and cuddled up beside her, warm and lovable.

As Agnes got ready for bed her thoughts veered away from herself and returned to Amy Horrocks. Had she really been followed? Those two people, the man and woman who she had seen walk by, certainly had not looked as if they were following anybody.

But the things Amy had said, her obvious state of shock! Agnes's curiosity was certainly stirred. As she turned on her side, nestled her head into her pillow and murmured a 'Goodnight' to Polly, she felt she would like to know more about quiet little Amy Horrocks. As always, gathering knowledge about other people's secret lives fascinated her.

Chapter Two

The next day, the day after Amy's little drama, was wet and windy. Polly had to make do with a short walk in the afternoon and Agnes was home, glad to be out of the driving rain, just after three. Even Polly didn't appear to have enjoyed the weather much and showed her pleasure in being home by drying herself on the carpet before Agnes could get at her with her rough towel. She did manage to dry her feet and legs and rub the mud off them before Polly took a flying leap on to the settee.

Agnes changed her slacks and shoes and hung her short mac in the bathroom. She was just going into the kitchen to make herself a cup of tea when the telephone rang. It was Amy Horrocks, asking Agnes if she would like to come down and have tea with her.

'Please do, Agnes. I felt I was so rude to you after all your kindness. I should have explained – I mean, told you what it was all about, why I . . .'

Agnes was quite willing to go down and take tea with Amy. Indeed she rather looked forward to hearing whatever story she had to tell. Maybe it would be interesting, give her something to think about, take her mind off her own boredom.

'Please bring little Polly. I do like her, Mrs Turner, I mean – Agnes.'

Amy Horrocks always had difficulty over using first names with all the residents of the other flats. Agnes felt it was probably due to a lack of confidence, low self-esteem.

She would persist in the application of Mr, Miss or Mrs long after they had addressed her as 'Amy'.

Agnes was pleased Polly was asked. Polly loved exploring new rooms and it would be nice not to have to leave the little dog on her own. Polly was a very sociable creature and, judging by her behaviour yesterday, had taken to Amy.

Half an hour later Agnes was sitting in Amy Horrocks' flat which was directly under her own. Polly, let off her lead at the request of her host, had followed Amy into the kitchen, from where Agnes could hear noises of tea being made and a lively conversation taking place between the two. When a few minutes later a trolley was wheeled in Agnes was pleased to see a plate of dainty ham sandwiches and a selection of cakes. Because of the intermittent rain and Polly's delayed and shortened walks while the rain held off, she had not managed to get herself a proper lunch and had had to manage with a glass of milk and some biscuits. She said this to Amy Horrocks, whose face lit up with a relieved smile.

'Oh, I'm so glad! I never seem to know about tea, what to give people, not that I ask many.'

She flushed with pleasure.

Neither Amy nor Agnes broached the subject of yesterday's little drama while they were drinking their tea and Agnes was eating most of the sandwiches. Polly caused a diversion by jumping on to the settee next to Amy and pinching her ham sandwich. Normally Agnes would have given her a good scolding for such bad behaviour but Amy seemed so delighted and amused that Polly got off with a caution only.

It was Amy who brought the matter up. She began with more apologies for her behaviour. In fact, she rambled on for so long about how she had not explained to Agnes why she had been so upset that it seemed the reason for it all would never be explained. Again and again Agnes tried to steer the flow of words, to make more sense of what had triggered off the incident the evening before. Amy's hands were now clasped in her lap, the half-empty cup of tea growing cold in front of her.

'You will hate me when I tell you what I've done, what I did. It was a terrible thing to do.'

Agnes tried to reassure her.

'Of course I won't hate you, Amy. Of course I won't.'

She poured Amy another cup of tea and put it in front of her. Polly still sat beside her.

'Drink that. It's still hot. You must try to calm down. What you did, or think you did, can't be so terrible. It's probably just in your mind.'

Amy put the cup and saucer down with a clatter.

'It was so terrible! More terrible than you can imagine – and I *was* being followed, Agnes. I know I was. I know I was!'

She looked at Agnes, her eyes red-rimmed, her expression tragic.

'I killed my mother, Agnes. I did. I killed my own mother, I murdered her and they know I did!'

Agnes put her teacup down with almost the same clatter as Amy had. There was a moment's silence. Agnes put out a hand, and took Amy's.

'Who are those people you thought were following you? Do they know you feel you were responsible for your mother's death?'

'I don't *feel* I killed her. I *did*, Agnes, and the people are my brother and his wife! They have been trying to find me. Now I believe they have.'

'Perhaps you had better begin at the beginning, Amy. Tell me the whole story.'

Amy looked at her, leaned back and closed her eyes for a moment, then looked down at Polly, still close at her side. She stroked the little dog's head gently. Polly gazed up at her. Agnes knew her brown eyes would be full of animal sympathy. Amy drew a deep breath, sat up, straightened, and started her story.

It took an hour. Agnes listened and tried to ignore Amy's need for unnecessary explanations and tearful excuses.

Her story ended with entreaties to Agnes to tell her what to do about her brother and his wife who obviously were intent, she was sure, on seeing how much money they could make with their accusations. Rather than going to a lawyer or seeing that justice was done, even perhaps going to the police!

What to do! Agnes, at the end of the story, had no advice to offer.

'I must think it all out if I am to help you, Amy. They are blackmailers, no less! That is, if they are accusing you of influencing your mother to change her will when she was mentally unstable.'

Agnes left to give Polly a run. Amy wanted to come out with her, but Agnes needed to be alone in order to think out the cold facts of this horrendous tale, without any emotional interruptions. She had at the moment no idea what advice to give Amy as how to handle her relatives, or what to do about the frightening position in which she found herself.

The skeletal outline of the whole thing was to Agnes fascinating and rather thrilling.

Amy Horrocks had a brother who seemingly had been his parents' pride and joy. Three years younger than his sister, he seemed to have completely stolen her limelight and, although they were not unkind to their daughter, the parents had little or no time to listen to her plans or ambitions. When she announced that she was going to train as a nurse, it raised no objections from either of them and very little interest, though Amy remembered that her mother had remarked, 'Nurses come from all classes nowadays and, if the television is anything to go by, the majority can't speak the Queen's English.'

Amy had trained in London and over the years had gradually achieved promotion. Apparently she loved nursing and was happy in all her posts. One sad little remark, almost as if Amy were making a confession of her own

14

shortcomings, particularly struck Agnes with its similarity to her own youth.

'I never had boyfriends. The others in my class always seemed to have dates. I didn't, but I didn't mind, Agnes. I loved my work and it was enough. It satisfied me. Anyway, I was too shy to . . .'

Her brother married, divorced, then married again. An Australian girl. Amy's father died and her mother, without her husband and her beloved son, seemed to lose interest in life and became more and more depressed.

At last Amy had to stay at home to be with her. Giving up her post as Surgical Ward Sister was a terrible and totally unappreciated sacrifice. It was her son, now living in Australia, that Amy's mother missed and grieved for. Amy seemed to be classed as a necessary evil. She suggested again and again that her mother sell the big house, buy a small bungalow, or even that she might be happier in a hotel or a residential home.

Nothing would move the old lady and at last, after a few years of boredom and misery, Amy had an idea that might at least solve some of their difficulties. If her mother would not move from her big house, Amy would make it a suitable place for herself to live in. She would turn the house into a residential home. Money was getting tighter and tighter. This would, if carefully run, bring in enough to maintain the house and keep the two of them financially secure.

Agnes, as she had listened to Amy's story, could not help but admire the way she had tackled the task, dividing some rooms into two, making the large sitting room a double-bedded ward. One bedroom for her mother, one for herself. Alterations to the kitchen, additions of bathrooms, showers, lavatories. Permissions from the Council, fire precautions, ramps for wheelchairs, a thousand things to cope with.

Agnes realized, as she listened, that Amy's enthusiasm was kept high by the hope that her plans would enable her to return in some degree to her great love which would

15

always be, as Agnes's love had been long ago, nursing. Her mother too would be looked after if she became more difficult. Maybe the other residents would raise her spirits?

For about three years all went well. There was room for eight patients. The home became well known in Esher and its reputation for good care, good food and general value for money ensured that Amy never had an empty bed. She managed with one retired trained nurse on night duty and two semi-trained during the day, with Mrs Meaner and a help in the kitchen. Mrs Meaner was Amy's prop and stay – fat, jolly, a good plain cook who could turn her hand to any invalid diet directly it was explained to her. Amy's brother was kept informed of all the arrangements.

Then the double blow fell on all her aspirations. Amy's mother had never been enthusiastic about the home, but suddenly she developed a hatred for it. From being quiet and reticent, grumbling occasionally, but reasonable to a degree, she became extremely aggressive and bitter.

Word spread about her mother's behaviour. Soon there were several unoccupied beds and the home was in danger of closing down. Her mother's attitude made the other guests feel that Mrs Horrocks was against the whole idea of changing her house into what she called a 'boarding house' with paying guests.

During her tearful and sometimes rather muddled explanation of what had eventually led to what she considered her 'terrible crime', Amy related an incident which to her seemed of little importance and which she only mentioned in order to highlight her mother's ability to handle her own affairs when she, Amy, had been working at the hospital and had merely used her mother's house as a place to live outside the hospital in order to keep her mother from feeling too alone after the death of her husband.

Six months after her father's death Amy had arrived

home at about seven o'clock in the evening. She was ready to spend it, after supper, either talking to her mother, telling her about the day's happenings on the ward, or watching television.

Her mother rarely showed much interest in her daughter's work, but this evening she had done so, even asking questions. Amy remembered all this because her mother's attitude had been so unusual. Then the reason had bubbled over. Mother's Day had come and gone. Amy had taken her mother out to dinner to mark the occasion, sent her a card by post, but . . .

'Do you realize I didn't even get a card from your brother, nor any flowers! Nothing! It's that new wife of his. She doesn't like me.'

Amy had tried to placate her mother, give some excuses. He was busy or had muddled the dates. Mrs Horrocks would have none of it.

'No birthday card either. Nothing. Well, after all I have done for him – loving, forgiving, financial help – that's it, that's absolutely it!'

Outbursts like this from her mother often took place. Amy was used to them. They could be aimed at the grocer for not delivering on time, the local postman, anyone. And these people were never forgiven.

Amy could not believe she would act this way about her beloved son. Surely it was a storm in a teacup. Amy decided she would write or telephone him to see if she could prompt him to make up for his forgetfulness. She had telephoned Australia, but had got short shrift from her brother.

'Well, I can't remember her all the time. She's got you, for goodness sake. We are busy here! I've plenty on my plate, believe me, Amy!'

His wife had started a beauty culture shop. Amy had let it go. What could she do anyway? Then later another small incident had occurred that stuck in Amy's memory, even through the trauma, guilt and fear of her final and terrifying act.

She had come home from work ready for another boring evening. She cooked supper and brought in two trays: plaice and chips and peas for her mother who would not eat alone during the day and sandwiches for herself because she took advantage of the hospital lunch, which was usually very good. She was just settling herself on the settee with her tray. The television was on and her mother was watching *Coronation Street*, her favourite programme, with her usual rapt and undivided attention.

Amy was just about to start her meal when she noticed a gold gleam in the crack of the cushions beside her. She put her tray aside and stuck her fingers down beside the seat and picked up a Parker pen, a gold Parker pen. She placed it on the table and waited for the end of the soap opera. Her mother would not take at all kindly to being interrupted then.

'Mother, look. Whose is this? It's certainly not mine. Is it yours? It looks like gold. Probably is!'

She handed the pen to her mother who obviously recognized it at once and was not best pleased.

'That's Mr Robinson's. He must have left it.'

Amy had been surprised. Her mother had given no hint that she had seen her lawyer or wanted to see him. Amy had asked her but had got a brusque reply that it was none of her business and that if she wanted to see him she would do so, wherever and whenever she wished. They must return the pen.

Amy must see to that.

The situation in the residential home became more desperate as Amy's mother's behaviour became increasingly bizarre and unmanageable. Amy was at her wits' end. Then something happened to help Amy and what she now thought of as 'her poor demented mother', culminating in the – to Amy, dreadful – result that was eventually revealed at the end of the teatime story told to Agnes Turner, with so many emotional interruptions.

A man and a woman arrived unannounced one morning, bringing with them an elderly lady. They introduced themselves as Mr and Mrs Bennett and the elderly lady as the woman's mother, Mrs Coleman. They had been rather diffident in their request, obviously under the impression that Amy's residential home would probably be full up and they would be very lucky if she had a vacancy. They wanted a single room for their mother for three weeks while they were away on holiday in Athens, the daughter explained.

'My mother is quite sprightly and able to do everything for herself, but she hates being alone in our rather isolated house.'

Amy had been delighted and even more so when her fees proved acceptable. Mrs Coleman moved in on the following Friday and seemed to be of no trouble, cheerful and independent.

One thing she asked Amy to do was to put her pills out for her in the morning. Two blood pressure pills, one aspirin and one small white pill she laughingly referred to as her 'pee pill'. She had handed the little bag containing the bottles and boxes to Amy who doled out the first morning's medicine and discovered something else in the bag which had rather surprised her.

A brown glass bottle, unlike the modern plastic ones, containing about eighty Nembutal tablets, or rather capsules, yellow in colour. The ancient label read in letters almost obliterated by time and usage: 'One or two to be taken at night.'

She had not put this bottle back in Mrs Coleman's bag. Nembutal was almost never given now, the barbiturates were no longer used as sleeping tablets. The quantity of yellow capsules in this container could be considered lethal so Amy locked it up in her drug cupboard, intending to give it back when Mrs Coleman was discharged from her care in three weeks' time.

Unfortunately, or perhaps fortunately, she forgot to do so. A very pleased and grateful Mr and Mrs Bennett called for their mother and departed, saying that she had been so happy here at Homewood. They hoped that Amy would accept her as a resident when and if they wanted to go away again. Though three weeks' fees was only a drop in the ocean, it had boosted Amy's morale a little.

A few weeks went by fairly quietly, as far as her mother was concerned, and four paying residents were just keeping the wages paid. Amy still had Mrs Meaner, who had agreed to take a little wage cut. She was a kind soul, who confessed to the age of sixty-five though Amy had her doubts and thought seventy-plus would be nearer the truth. However, she lived in a small house about five minutes' walk from Homewood, up one of the small streets that ran at right angles to the High Street, so no transport was needed.

As Amy narrated to Agnes, things were quiet. Her mother did not get up or dress, just lay in bed, sometimes sleeping, sometimes gazing vacantly across the room. Her hands, which were becoming more and more deformed by arthritis, picked and pulled at the sheets. Her life seemed without purpose or reason. Then one day her behaviour changed.

Amy was downstairs working out the week's menus with Mrs Meaner when there was a loud crash from her mother's room. She dashed upstairs and burst into her mother's room to find her stark naked, blood running down one arm. The window was shattered. She had used her white china water jug to break the window. She still held the handle of the jug in her hand. Her mother turned and with all her might threw the piece of jagged china at Amy. It just caught her face. She felt a slight pain as it hit her, and a little blood ran down her cheek.

The auxiliary nurse was behind her. They had rushed in and grasped the old lady's arms and after a monumental struggle had managed to get her on to her bed. By this time she was screaming and shouting out swear words which Amy did not think her mother even knew, much less would utter. The cut on her arm was superficial. Amy had cleaned the wound and bandaged it. In answer to the auxiliary nurse's question, 'Shouldn't we call a doctor?' she had answered a firm, 'No.'

This incident was the first of many. Amy knew her mother was getting more and more violent and she dreaded to think of having to put her somewhere where restraint would certainly be used.

It was after several of these awful scenes that, while cleaning out the drug cupboard where all dangerous drugs were kept under lock and key, Amy came upon the bottle of yellow capsules left by the mother of the holiday pair. The Nembutal. As Amy reached this part of her story, she broke down completely. Agnes had to wait while Amy sat forward, her elbows on her knees, hands over her face, the tears running through her fingers. Agnes sat beside her and, in an uncharacteristic gesture, put her arm around Amy's shoulders. She was curiously excited by the build-up to what she could see was an inevitable climax.

Amy managed at last to continue. Her mother was now incontinent and could barely be left for even minutes at a time. Amy managed to get a bed with cot sides from the local Red Cross but this was not safe. Restless, inarticulate, violent, Amy's mother managed to climb over the cot sides when she was left for a few minutes and took a bad fall to the floor which luckily only resulted in a few nasty bruises. The doctor when called was as helpful as he could be. Heavy sedation was really all he had to offer and this often only worked for a short time. A locum was taking Dr Harris's place for three weeks while he was away on a course and Amy had great hopes that he might have more to offer her mother than Dr Harris.

Alas, he did not. Indeed Amy told Agnes he simply dismissed the problem as almost inevitable at the patient's great age and said they must handle the situation as best they could. He saw another patient before he left but did not mention coming to see Mrs Horrocks again. 'Call me if you want me,' had been his message, though Dr Harris had at least called in weekly to see Amy's mother.

21

It was after a truly awful night that Amy finally began to feel that her mother's quality of life was nil. She lay on her back screaming all night. Nothing would stop her. Amy called the locum doctor. It was very early in the morning. He was not best pleased. Amy, almost as distressed as her mother and worried sick, had asked him, almost beseechingly, 'Is she in pain? Why is she screaming?'

He had made a cursory examination and shaken his head impatiently.

'No, no. Your mother is suffering from senile dementia, Miss Horrocks. She will be noisy. There is little one can do in these cases.'

He had left and Amy had sat with her mother, thinking she could not stand another night like last night. She found herself thinking, then leaning over the cot side and saying, 'This is not fair, Mother. I can stop all this for you and I will!'

Amy had been calmer then, looking at Agnes as she talked and not crying any more. Her eyes were wide open and red-rimmed.

'I opened the capsules one by one into her milk. Thirty tablets I stirred in. I think they were one and a half grains each.'

Agnes looked down at Polly, thinking of Amy confessing her guilt. Thirty tablets. That was enough to finish the old lady off and quite right too. What a life! Poor Amy.

According to Amy, and Agnes had no reason to doubt her, her mother had become quiet and peaceful and after a few hours had died. Agnes knew how powerful Nembutal could be. Long ago, when she had started nursing, barbiturates, of which Nembutal was one, had been given to make people sleep, to cure insomnia. Soon after she had started training, all the barbiturates had disappeared. Seconal, Nembutal, Sodium Amytal, no longer used. Was it fate that had made Mrs Coleman leave that bottle behind? Amy believed so and, as she finished the long and painful story, Agnes believed it too. But then, in Amy's place she would have done exactly the same, but a good deal sooner – of that she was very sure!

Robert, Amy's brother, did not come to his mother's funeral. Excuses poured down the phone. His wife's new venture, he couldn't leave her, not at the moment anyway. Later perhaps. He was inquisitive about the will and it was obvious that he still thought of himself as his mother's favourite, as Amy did until Mr Robinson produced the will and she found that her brother had been cut out entirely. Everything was left to her. The house, whatever money her mother had left. When he heard, Robert was beside himself.

'You knew she had changed her will, you must have. Perhaps you did it yourself, got her to do it. That's it, isn't it?'

Agnes felt that Amy Horrocks was overreacting quite considerably.

She felt the story Amy had dreamed up about being followed by her brother and sister-in-law was pure nonsense.

If her relatives had really been searching for her to seek revenge, surely they could have found out where she had moved to from the buyer of Homewood, or from Mr Robinson. Presumably he had negotiated the sale of the house, either as a dwelling place or, perhaps even more advantageously, as a residential home.

Amy seemed genuinely to feel that she was being threatened by her brother, and, with her imagination running riot, she had really believed she was being followed. Her nerves and anxious manner could be symptomatic of some mental condition.

However, the fact that it was all in Amy's imagination was proved a few days later when she told Agnes that her brother had telephoned her from Australia saying he was coming over to England as soon as they had enough money for the fare, emphasizing the fact that his mother

23

appeared to have left him nothing at all and he wanted, as he put it, 'to look into this'. His wife's beauty venture was not doing at all well and Amy would have to 'cough up', as he elegantly put it, or they would never be able to scrape together the money.

'Anyway,' he had added, 'some of her money is mine, if not all of it!'

'So, it couldn't have been them, Agnes. I must have been stupid to think it, but I was a bit frightened and felt guilty too, and you never know with my brother what he will do.'

The usual facile tears followed this remark as Agnes agreed.

'I never dreamed, Agnes, that Mother would alter her will and leave everything to me. Robert was always her love, her favourite.'

'Well, she did leave everything to you, Amy, so be thankful and enjoy it, for goodness sake!'

'But I killed her, Agnes, I can't forget that. I gave her those tablets and I killed her.'

'Think of it this way, Amy. You put the poor old lady out of her misery. Think of it like that.'

Amy nodded tearfully, perhaps realizing from Agnes's tone that she was getting a bit tired of going over the matter again and again.

A week passed and Amy stopped talking about her 'terrible crime'. Agnes noticed she was regaining her small amount of self-esteem. She was managing to address the other residents by their Christian names and dropping the nervous 'Mr' and 'Mrs' as she had used before. Maybe telling, confessing the whole affair to Agnes, had helped her more than she realized. Gradually she stopped talking about her past until something dramatic happened that brought the whole matter back again with a bump.

Chapter Three

One rainy afternoon, Agnes came in with Polly and found Amy standing outside her door waiting for her. Her face was tense and pale. She burst out with her news almost before the lift doors had closed behind Agnes and Polly.

'I *was* being followed that night, from the church, Agnes. I really was – and who do you think it was?'

Agnes did not even hazard a guess. Indeed Amy Horrocks gave her little time to.

'It was Mr and Mrs Bennett, you remember – the daughter and son-in-law of Mrs Coleman, the lady who left the Nembutal behind.'

Agnes's boredom with the story was for the moment arrested. She led the way into her flat, took Polly's collar and lead off and turned back to Amy.

'Whatever did they want and how come they were following you? What for?'

'They told me on the telephone that they had tried to get in touch with me before, they didn't say why.'

'Didn't you ask them, for goodness sake?'

Amy Horrocks shook her head.

'I asked them, but they didn't want to talk about it on the telephone, so I asked them to tea tomorrow. They seemed eager to come so I . . .'

She looked pleadingly at Agnes who guessed what was coming.

'Do please come to tea with them, Agnes. Suppose it's the Nembutal, suppose they want to ask me something about it?'

'But what could I do to . . . what could I say? I only know what you have told me. I'd be of very little help to you.'

'Yes, but you'd give me support, just being there.'

'All right, I'll come, Amy.'

Agnes was not quite as reluctant as she made herself sound. There was a tiny tinge of intrigue here. What could these people want? Was it something to do with the drug? Could they have heard of Amy's mother's death so soon after their mother's stay and put two and two together?

Amy's face was bright with relief because Agnes had agreed to come, to be there to support her, whatever the Bennetts' questions were about. Perhaps it would be another matter entirely. Perhaps the old lady had left something else behind, some jewellery maybe? Agnes dared not suggest this to Amy in case she started another state of panic. Panic was something always lurking just round the corner with Amy.

Agnes took Polly on their walk a little earlier than usual the next day and afterwards left Polly in her own flat. After all, Agnes reasoned, perhaps Mr and Mrs Bennett might not be dog lovers, and anyway Polly would create a diversion that would probably help Amy but not the visitors. She rang Amy's doorbell at a quarter to four. Amy's face lit up when she saw it was Agnes waiting to come in.

'Oh, Agnes, I am so glad. I thought you might change your mind and decide you didn't want to come after all. I would have understood, but I . . .'

Agnes walked through to the kitchen where Amy was putting cups and saucers on the tea trolley. She looked at the little repast Amy had laid out.

'Oh, Amy, not sandwiches, just a plate of biscuits. That looks too much for such a visit. I should just have biscuits. After all, it's not a party.'

'Oh, do you think so? I'll take the sandwiches away then.'

She lifted the plate of dainty sandwiches and put them on the working surface, covering them with another plate, then changing her mind said, 'I'll cover them up, Agnes, and we can have them for our supper if you like.'

She tore off a strip of Clingfilm from the roll in a plastic holder on the wall and neatly covered the plate of sandwiches.

'There,' she said and looked at Agnes, her face anxious.

Her hands were trembling a little, Agnes noticed, as she put the plate down.

'Oh dear, Agnes, isn't it all awful. If only . . .'

Agnes caught herself almost smiling as she followed Amy back into the sitting room. After all, in spite of Amy's timid manner and wide-eyed look of innocence, she had taken the old lady's Nembutal and killed with it. Not bad going for such a mouse-like little woman. She composed her face and sat down in an armchair. The doorbell rang. Amy cast her an anxious look and left the room to go and greet the dreaded guests.

There was nothing at all 'dreadful' about the two people Amy guided into the room to introduce to Agnes. Mrs Bennett was what Agnes always thought of as a 'saucy' little woman. Inclined to plumpness, white softly curled hair that looked natural, shiny and healthy. No make-up – perhaps just a trace of pink lipstick. Her husband, a prosperous, quite good-looking man. They were, Agnes guessed, in their early fifties.

Everybody sat down and there was some overlapping conversation until Mrs Bennett turned to her husband, laying a hand on his arm. They were sitting together on the settee. She smiled.

'You explain, dear, you're so much better at explaining things than I am. I never know where to start or finish!'

'Well, as to following Miss Horrocks, as I explained on the telephone, or rather tried to . . .' He put up a hand and smoothed back his rather thinning brown hair. 'That was a coincidence. We've bought a house in Lewes with a granny annexe for my wife's mother. Your new vicar here is a friend of ours. We came to the evening service, just to support him. We are not churchgoers. Then we saw Miss Horrocks.'

Mrs Bennett broke in. 'We had tried to contact Miss Horrocks but she hadn't left a forwarding address, and we couldn't –'

'Yes, dear, that's right. I was going to say that. Anyway, we followed her to her flat, decided it was too late to call and that we would telephone.'

Amy turned to Agnes in triumph.

'You see, I was right, I said I was being followed from the church that evening. Agnes didn't believe me.'

Mrs Bennett's rosy little face looked quite concerned.

'I do hope we didn't frighten you, Miss Horrocks?'

Rather to Agnes's amusement and surprise, Amy shook her head and smiled reassuringly.

'Oh no, not at all, Mrs Bennett. I just thought . . .'

She did cast a rather apologetic look towards Agnes. She got to her feet and made for the kitchen.

'I'll just make us all a cup of tea.'

When Amy was in the kitchen Agnes took great trouble to steer the conversation into general topics. The weather, the difficulty in parking . . . She was glad when after what seemed like ages Amy wheeled in her squeaky tea trolley and started dispensing cups of tea. The biscuits were waved aside by both Mr and Mrs Bennett. Agnes felt pleased she had vetoed the sandwiches.

Mr Bennett, having sipped his tea, decided to adopt a more direct approach to revealing the real purpose of the visit. It was at first unclear what he was talking about but eventually the dreaded word 'Nembutal' was mentioned. He took quite a time to reach this point because there was much to be told before the drug loomed in the story and its importance became apparent to both Amy and Agnes.

The previous year they had decided to move house and find something to accommodate Mrs Bennett's mother who was becoming lonelier and disliked living alone. All her friends were either dying or going into homes and generally disappearing from her circle, leaving her more and more isolated. The house they found was ideal. Mrs Coleman did not want to move in with her daughter and son-in-law, but just be near them. The granny annexe seemed to be the perfect answer but alas, after being in the little annexe for a few months, Mrs Bennett had to admit that her mother was showing more and more signs of depression.

'It was really quite worrying, Miss Horrocks. We called in two or three times a day, had her in for meals whenever she felt like it, but it was no use. When she started talking about taking her own life, well, you can imagine how we felt. Then we remembered the Nembutal.'

Agnes noticed Amy stiffening. Her teacup was half-way to her lips and she put the cup back in its saucer with a little clatter. She drew her feet back from their formerly relaxed position. Her back straightened.

'The Nembutal, Mrs Bennett? That is a sleeping pill?'

Agnes felt sorry for Amy, whose voice had failed her as she had started the question. She had to stop and clear her throat. Agnes could imagine how nervous she was feeling. Mr Bennett nodded and explained himself, while his wife also nodded in agreement. She left the explanation to her husband.

The situation had worsened and though both Mr and Mrs Bennett had tried to comfort themselves with the adage that people who threaten suicide don't usually carry out their threats, they also reasoned – as did Mrs Coleman's doctor, whom they consulted frequently – that a lot of elderly ladies became depressed as they aged. Their loss of looks and increasing disabilities with hearing, sight or memory all played a part. The psychiatrist was not very helpful except to say that there was no sign of deterioration in their mother's brain, she was simply depressed. He gave her some Prozac to be doled out by Mrs Bennett. As she was so depressed, he did not think it advisable to give her the opportunity to take more than the prescribed amount.

It was about then that Mrs Bennett remembered the

29

Nembutal. She had known that her mother had a large bottle of the yellow capsules in her toilet bag and had never thought much of it. She knew that they were very old, given to Mrs Coleman by her doctor years before when she had had some difficulty in sleeping. Obviously, the insomnia had improved for she had kept the pills.

Mrs Bennett seemed a little reluctant to confess the next part of her little story, but she had to tell Amy that she last remembered seeing the bottle in her mother's toilet bag when she packed her soap and flannel, toothbrush and paste, Aspirin and one or two other little bottles and potions.

'I didn't like doing it, Miss Horrocks, but I felt if the doctor thought she should not have the Prozac – I mean, I should be in charge of it, just in case she . . . well, you know!'

She hesitated. Agnes could tell she was a nice woman, who hated invading anyone's privacy. Mrs Bennett took another sip of tea before she resumed, looking sideways at her husband, obviously for his support. He smiled at her.

'I searched, first her toilet bag, then her bedroom. It was horrible doing it. She was visiting a friend. I hated searching but I felt I had to continue when there was no sign of the Nembutal anywhere. I got really quite anxious. Where could she have put them?'

Mr Bennett broke in at this stage.

'Then we thought of you, Miss Horrocks. We were relieved. We knew that you were a trained nurse, you told us. Nurses never let patients keep drugs with them, so we realized you must have taken the Nembutal, locked it up and perhaps forgotten to give it back when Mother left after her three weeks at Homewood.'

They both looked at Amy expectantly. Agnes waited for her reply, curiosity tinged with amusement. This was a tricky question for Amy Horrocks to answer. How would she handle it? There was what is commonly referred to as

30

a pregnant pause. Amy glanced at Agnes: her face had gone rather pale, her fingers twisting together.

There was a moment's hesitation on Amy's part. Agnes hoped that whatever she said, she wouldn't give the impression of reluctance, of not knowing quite what to say. Amy dropped her eyes and put out a hand and moved the plate of biscuits an inch or two nearer to her guests, then cleared her throat and looked at Mr and Mrs Bennett. Her eyes were direct and candid.

'Oh, no, Mrs Bennett, I couldn't do that. You see, your mother was not my patient. She was just staying in Homewood as a resident while you were in . . . Athens, wasn't it?'

Mr and Mrs Bennett nodded in agreement.

'So, you see, it wasn't my place to look in her washbag, or indeed in any part of her luggage. That would have been a gross invasion of privacy. Had she been admitted as my patient, then of course I would have asked what medication she had been prescribed and taken charge of it.'

Agnes applauded Amy's composure and the way she had stated her case. She had lied very well, but with good cause. The introduction of a large bottle of lethal drugs, followed pretty conveniently by the death of Mrs Horrocks, was not something that needed investigation. Mr and Mrs Bennett looked very disappointed and upset. They had obviously pinned their hopes on the capsules being safely lodged with Amy.

'Oh dear, Miss Horrocks, it was silly of us. I suppose you were really our last hope. Her threats to . . .'

Mrs Bennett broke down and her husband put his hand over hers as it rested on her knee. Agnes broke in.

'Perhaps it's just her state of mind at the moment, Mrs Bennett. When she makes some new friends and settles down in her new home her spirits may improve.'

'You haven't heard her or seen her, Mrs Turner. She has changed so much since she stayed with your friend.'

Mrs Bennett rose and Amy fetched her light coat, helped her on with it. Mr Bennett stood beside her, his look gloomy. They moved into the hall, both bidding a subdued farewell to Agnes, who stayed at the little tea trolley and let Amy see them out. She heard Amy say as they got to the front door:

'Please keep in touch, Mrs Bennett, and let me know how Mrs Coleman is, won't you? I really feel quite anxious about her, but I am sure . . .'

Amy did not finish but Mrs Bennett answered her very positively, thanking her at the same time and apologizing for following her from the church that night and frightening her so much.

'I will tell you how my mother gets on, Miss Horrocks. You are the only person I have been absolutely frank with, except my husband and the doctor.'

There was a little more murmured talk and then the sound of the lift door closing. Amy must have taken them to the lift before saying goodbye. She came back into the sitting room after a few seconds. She did not look at Agnes or speak to her.

She picked up the teapot and walked toward the kitchen.

'We can eat the sandwiches now and I'll make a fresh pot of tea for us.'

Agnes said nothing, merely watched her host disappear into the kitchen. She felt Amy would now have to attempt to justify her adroit lies. She was prepared to listen and most certainly would not judge. She popped up to her own flat, leaving Amy's door on the jar, and fetched Polly. Amy and the little dog seemed to get on so well together. Perhaps, Agnes thought, it would comfort Amy a little. Also relieve the situation for herself. She knew that Amy Horrocks would not be able to justify the lies she had told about Mrs Coleman's sleeping capsules and would probably become very boring in her efforts to do so. Agnes would much rather have stayed in her own flat and made her own supper and watched television, but she could not disappoint Amy. She would have to listen and put on an air of sympathy and understanding.

Chapter Four

Two weeks passed. Agnes was hoping that Amy was now thinking of other things and at least beginning to block out her past misdeeds, but one morning there was a ring on Agnes's doorbell and there she was, with an apologetic tear-stained face and, as usual, a screwed-up tissue in her hand.

'Something's happened, Agnes. Could I just have a word with you? You are always so sensible and calm and really I've no one else to talk to.'

In her other hand she clutched a letter from the Bennetts. In fact it was mostly a thank-you letter saying how much they had appreciated Amy's interest and help. However, it was the last part of the letter that had disturbed poor Amy's fragile peace of mind.

Amy read it out:

'"We let Mother go off with a trusted friend on a shopping trip. She didn't want to go but at last we persuaded her. Whilst she was out we did a thorough search of all her three rooms. She has a nice bed-sitting room with her television and her own furniture. Also a small kitchen and a bathroom. We searched everywhere for the pills and even went through her desk, various handbags – everywhere. But again, there was no sign. We now think she probably keeps the Nembutal with her, for safety's sake.

'"My mother's depression remains just as deep and frightening even after the shopping trip. The friend who took her said she was constantly threatening to 'end it all'."'

When she had finished reading the letter, Amy sat down on the settee and wept some more.

Agnes shrugged her shoulders. When she was invited to discuss the letter she was not very sympathetic and she knew it.

'Look, Amy, you can at least comfort yourself that you still have the rest of the Nembutal, so Mrs Bennett's mother can't use it to do away with herself. Your mother is no longer suffering. She is no longer demented, incontinent, with absolutely no quality to her life at all. I am sure she must have hated not being in control, having to have everything done for her. You only did good, Amy, for goodness sake. Try to forget all about it!'

The next upset was Amy's brother telephoning again from Australia, insisting she send the money for his air fare so that he could talk it all over with Amy and get the will and everything else sorted out.

This set up a new galaxy of fears. What would he do? Would he contest the will? Should she send him the money or refuse?

Agnes was getting very bored with the whole of what she termed in her mind 'the Nembutal incident'. She tried to comfort Amy by telling her that people who talked about killing themselves usually didn't and were only trying to bring attention to themselves. Amy, being a nurse, could contradict this statement with facts, with which Agnes had to agree, in some cases anyway.

Agnes then said, perhaps rather hard-heartedly, 'Well, at least if the old lady tops herself, it won't be with the Nembutal. You've seen to that, Amy!'

That remark had not, to put it mildly, gone down very well and Agnes had regretted making it and tried to gloss over it. After all, Amy had no one else to talk to, no one else who, as Amy put it, 'knew her awful secret'.

In a way it made her feel responsible, closer to Amy.

Perhaps it was because long ago she herself had unlocked the same door for a friend and had never felt a shade of regret.

Agnes would never tell Amy what she had done. She was a person who kept her own counsel. Amy was not like that. She was unable to carry things alone. Did this fact make Agnes impatient or sympathetic? She was not sure. In a way it bored her. In another way it made her feel needed, more powerful perhaps, to have someone more ineffectual relying on her. Like Polly, in a way, but the feelings were different.

She loved Polly but certainly did not love Amy Horrocks.

Agnes was puzzled by her own reactions. Perhaps even tearful, inadequate Amy was better than nobody at all. Anyway, Agnes decided to be more sympathetic to Amy if she came to her again.

Amy heard no more from her brother and Agnes began to believe the threat was just a threat and that he wanted to frighten Amy. She managed to dissuade Amy from even thinking about sending him money to pay for his fare to come over to 'have it out with her'.

Could he contest the will? She was not sure – but while he was in Australia he would at least be less able to intimidate his sister.

Anyway, he seemed all talk and no 'do'.

Chapter Five

It was partly the constant appearance of Amy Horrocks with her various problems and worries that was responsible for Agnes coming upon the house she wanted to own. As she drove along the quiet lane where it stood, all by itself, surrounded by rather rough small hedged fields, it stopped her in her tracks. The front door and all the windows were shut and the curtains drawn. A 'For Sale' notice lay on the path just inside the gate, which had only one hinge and was tied up with white, new-looking string.

The house attracted Agnes in such a way that it seemed to call out to her, 'Buy me.' She noticed the name of the estate agents, half covered with mud, and thought perhaps it was already sold. Surely the agents would have replaced the fallen sign with one saying 'Sold' if this were so? Anyway, she would go and see.

When Agnes talked to the young man at Watkins and Bull, the estate agents, she could understand why the board had been left on the ground half covered with mud. Watkins and Bull had obviously been trying to sell the house for so long without success that they had lost interest. When she enquired about it he tried to hide his surprise and searched his files for the brochure. At last he found it and handed it to Agnes with a slightly apologetic smile.

'It's rather an unusual property as you no doubt noticed, Mrs – er – Turner. It's been on the market some time. The owner has been in hospital. He's back home now, in a wheelchair, I'm afraid, waiting to go into a home.'

Agnes made sympathetic noises and asked, 'He won't be able to show me around the house very well, will he? Can you meet me there?'

He motioned with his hand as if to dismiss that idea, picked up the telephone and, referring again to the particulars he had given Agnes, dialled a number. The ringing went on for some time without being answered and the estate agent looked at Agnes and then shrugged his shoulders, raising his eyes heavenwards.

'You have to wait, you see. Major Hayward doesn't always have the telephone by him, unfortunately – not that we have to ring him very often, I'm afraid.'

At last the receiver at the other end was picked up.

'Ah, Major Hayward, I have a client here who would like to look over your house . . . Yes, a lady, sir.'

Agnes could hear a loud rather hoarse voice on the other end of the phone. The voice suggested three o'clock. Agnes looked at her watch. It was half-past two. She nodded at the agent in agreement and he covered the telephone receiver with his hand. She nodded again and tapped her watch with her finger, smiling.

'Make it three fifteen, then I can give my dog a walk and leave her in the car while I view the house.' Major Hayward agreed to this, then the receiver went down with a bang.

The estate agent, still smiling, handed Agnes the brochure describing the house. He looked slightly anxious in spite of his smile. He also handed her a card bearing his name – Mr Wilson.

'Would you be kind enough to ring me when you have seen the house, Mrs Turner? Perhaps tomorrow, if it would be convenient. I hope you will like the property. It's really quite unique in its way.'

He walked to the door with her. His face changed a little when he saw the Porsche standing outside. Agnes got in, spoke to Polly then drove away.

*   *   *

37

The estate agent was in Brighton, and she had quite a way to go back to the house which had so appealed to her. As she drove, the prosperous-looking houses on each side of the road on which she was travelling began to thin and become further and further apart until eventually there were no more dwellings at all and the road was lined with rather run-down fields and small copses. Agnes wondered why the fields had not been sold for future development and she determined to ask Major Hayward if building on these fields was something that might happen in the near future.

At last she approached the house on the left side of the road. It was situated well back from the road, surrounded by a brown fence, badly in need of repair. Agnes gave Polly a short walk and put her back in the car, poured a little dish of water and put it on the car floor. Polly, ears pricked, seemed always to understand that she was to stay in the car when the little dish of water was in evidence. She settled herself in the passenger seat on the small rug which was her special property. Agnes locked the car and made her way to the rickety brown gate, tied up with string that she had noted before. She untied the string and entered. With some difficulty she tied it up again, wondering as she did so why the piece of new-looking string was there, to keep something in or something out? Anyway, the gate would do neither.

Agnes stood for a moment on the rough neglected lawn inside the gate and looked at the house. The estate agent, Mr Wilson, had been quite right, very right in describing the house in front of her as 'unusual'.

Painted white, its roof beautifully and newly thatched, it was built in a circle. The whole house was completely round. Agnes moved forward and sideways to confirm the photographs in her hand. The thatched roof followed the circle of the walls, its apex decorated by a small ball of thatch, again beautifully crafted.

Whoever had been the thatcher had loved his work, had taken great pride in it. Agnes approached the front door. It was open. She used the knocker and the small incongruous bell. Someone called, 'Come in.'

Agnes stepped forward into a little round hall, the walls as white as the outside of the house. On the floor was a grass green carpet so that she did not see at first the huge wolfhound in front of her, the sound of its approach completely silent on the thick carpet.

Agnes put her hand out, lower than the dog's grey muzzle.

'Don't worry, she won't hurt you. She likes visitors.'

Agnes looked up. Standing in the doorway, leaning on the frame for support, was a tall white-haired military-looking man. Agnes smiled. This was obviously Major Hayward.

'I'm Mrs Turner, Agnes Turner. I telephoned, at least the agent did, for an appointment to see over your house.'

He nodded, turned round with difficulty, using a stick in each hand, walked stiffly over to a settee in the room to his right and plumped down. As he did so he winced and gave a little grunt of pain and made an apologetic gesture towards Agnes.

'Hips, that's why I've got to leave here, can't cope. Had them done, you know, replaced. Didn't work with me. Total failure.'

'I'm so sorry. It must be dreadful to have to leave this lovely place. How long have you lived here?'

A stick clattered to the floor and he attempted to lean forward to pick it up but gave up. Agnes retrieved it and placed it with the other against the settee arm beside him. Major Hayward gave a little gesture of thanks.

'Damn things are always falling down. I used to leave them behind, but now I'm not able to walk without them.'

He sounded so bitter, but then remembered Agnes's last question.

'Thirty years. My wife and I couldn't resist it. It's hell to furnish and not easy to decorate but we loved it, my wife and I. Alice. She died two years ago.'

Agnes suddenly laughed, a very hearty laugh for her.

'Well, Major Hayward, I've got to say you do a first-class selling job on your lovely round house. Is it called that, by the way? There's no name on the gate, is there?'

He shook his head, laughing a little to himself.

'No, Alice named it, but the name fell off after she died. I didn't bother any more. I felt . . .'

Agnes nodded. She understood completely. And as she sat in the charming room with its curved outer wall, she wanted the place more than ever.

'Tell me what your wife – Alice, if I may call her that – named the house. I would really like to know.'

He smiled a little for the first time, a real smile.

'It was called Kitten Cottage. Alice wanted it to be an animal sanctuary, and it was. We took in cats and later dogs, that's where Wilma came from. Alice loved her. Now if I ever sell the place she'll have to be put down. She's too big, people always say she's too big.'

He smoothed his moustache with his finger. He was embarrassed by his own emotion. Agnes tried not to notice the tears in his eyes. Wilma came and sat beside him, leaning on the end of the sofa. Both the sticks fell down and the dog came over to Agnes looking mournful, resting her grey muzzle on Agnes's knee.

Agnes surprised herself. She was not one for acting on impulse but in that moment all logical thought and common sense flew out of the window. Maybe it was the name Kitten Cottage. Maybe it was the thought of the animal sanctuary, now no more.

Major Hayward started to struggle to his feet.

'I'd better show you round the place, hadn't I?'

Agnes couldn't stop the words. 'Major Hayward, I will buy Kitten Cottage!'

Agnes carefully tied the gate into place with the piece of white string. She looked back at the house. The front door was still wide open and Wilma sat just inside watching

Agnes get into the car. The wolfhound's expression was as mournful as ever, but the brown eyes did not waver, watching as Agnes let Polly out on to the grass to have a little smell round and sit down to 'relieve herself', as Amy Horrocks always rather delicately put it.

One more look and a glance at her watch. Five to five! She had been at Kitten Cottage for almost two hours. She wanted to catch the estate agent to have a talk with him. She thought the office might be closed by the time she got back to Brighton – half an hour's drive, perhaps more if the traffic was congested.

She drove fast but carefully. She felt exhilarated, excited, as if a new era in her life was about to begin.

Polly, always able to sense her moods, looked at her, bright brown eyes gazing up into hers, tail wagging, looking rather as Agnes felt. She smiled at the little dog by her side and grimaced.

'Nobody could ever have called me an impulsive buyer before, Poll, not until today, this very afternoon.'

This was true. Agnes always gave careful thought to any purchase or any change in her way of life that might cost money, whether it was something trivial like clothes or make-up or a new place to live. Perhaps that was because in her youth she had been very poor and when money came to her suddenly and unexpectedly, she had felt the need to husband it carefully so that she would never find herself poor again.

But today, this afternoon, her customary prudence had been swept away for better or for worse!

Agnes drew up outside the estate agent's. The door was open and Mr Wilson was just ushering an elderly lady out. As she arrived at the door she heard him say goodbye to his client.

'Thank you, Mrs Yates. Two o'clock tomorrow then?'

Agnes approached him, the Kitten Cottage brochure in her hand. He stood back to let her enter, a curious expression on his face.

'Do come in, Mrs – er – Turner. I didn't expect to see you

41

so soon. No, no. We are not closing,' he added hastily as Agnes enquired whether she was too late. 'We are open as long as anyone wants to see us.'

Agnes felt this was probably a slight exaggeration but let it pass as he closed the door behind them and pulled forward the chair opposite his own at the desk, his face expectant.

'I have been over the property, Mr Wilson. Kitten Cottage. Major Hayward showed me the ground floor, the adjacent grounds and outhouses. I explored the upstairs part of the house by myself because, as you probably know, the owner is chair-bound.'

'Yes, I do know that, Mrs Turner, but Major Hayward prefers to show the property himself. We always offer to accompany any would-be buyer, not that anyone's asked to see the property for some time.'

Agnes then proceeded to take the estate agent's breath away. She had agreed to buy it with the surrounding ground and outbuildings. Also she had agreed to the owner living in the house as at present for the two months he had to wait for the room in the residential home he had chosen. She understood from him that the room would become vacant when its present occupant went to Australia to live with his son.

She paused. The young estate agent closed his mouth which had fallen open during Agnes's account of her discussion with Major Hayward.

'You will need a lawyer for all this, Mrs Turner.'

He handed her a form to sign.

'Of course, and I have agreed to buy at the asking price. Also I have agreed to buy much of the furniture and outhouses as they stand. They are in a very poor condition actually – the outhouses, I mean, not the furniture.'

Mr Wilson was busy making notes on the pad in front of him. Obviously the potential sale pleased him. Agnes had found out from Major Hayward that the house had been on the market for two years.

The agent was not the only person pleased by Agnes's

decision. Major Hayward seemed to have shed so many of his worries and grief during her visit that Agnes felt she had done something really worthwhile. Furthermore, this was something she hoped would alter her own life completely once again and alleviate that growing feeling of boredom. She knew only too well, in her case, that boredom could lead to a return of the depression which had once put her in a psychiatric ward for some weeks: a frightening experience she had no wish to repeat.

'I will go to see my lawyer tomorrow, Mr Wilson.'

She handed back the form he had given her with her address, telephone number, bank and other particulars.

'By the way, Major Hayward has a dog. He tells me if he goes into the residential home the dog might – would have to be put down. This upsets him as it was his wife's dog. I told him I would take the dog on when he leaves. Is that all right?'

'Yes, indeed, Mrs Turner. Very kind-hearted of you.'

Mr Wilson stood up and accompanied her to the door. His attitude was quite different. His eyes followed her out to the Porsche.

Agnes was sure he would think the sale of Kitten Cottage was a big feather in his cap. She felt quite pleased about this. Indeed, she felt very satisfied with her afternoon's work.

Chapter Six

The purchase of Kitten Cottage went ahead more smoothly and quickly than Agnes could have dared hope. Perhaps this was thanks to the fact that it was not dependent on a chain of would-be buyers and sellers; there was no lack of ready money or need for mortgages or borrowed money. Agnes had also entrusted the sale of her own flat to the same estate agents. This made the whole exercise more efficient.

Her lawyer too could not have been more speedy and helpful. When Agnes explained the rather complicated problems which Major Hayward had, he revealed he was a friend of Major Hayward, a friend of very long standing, although he was not his lawyer. All went well until a slight snag appeared regarding the Major's move to his room in the residential home. The present occupant could not take the flight to Australia for at least another two months, maybe a little longer.

Agnes was slightly put out, as the couple who had bought her flat intended to move in on the very day she had hoped to move into her new cottage. However, she would not let the matter affect Major Hayward, who had been most co-operative in letting her have workmen in to do some upstairs decorating and allowing her to move in her own bedroom furniture before the sale was completed. This had been a tremendous help.

Through all the form signing, the driving back and forth to Kitten Cottage, the business with the hold-up in the residential home, which literally made Agnes homeless for nearly three weeks, the moving and storage of her furniture, arranging for an upholsterer to re-cover the chairs and sofa, which needed doing – through all of this – which could have been a horror – Amy Horrocks proved herself a true friend and helped with everything.

When she heard there was a delay over the move into Kitten Cottage she immediately insisted that Agnes should stay in her spare room with Polly. She also took over Polly's walks while Agnes was involved with the agent and her lawyer. Most surprisingly to Agnes, Amy took over Wilma's walks too, gradually introducing the two dogs, thereby alleviating one of Agnes's anxieties. She was worried that Polly, being young, energetic and pretty vocal, might irritate the big old wolfhound.

During this time, however, Amy was not without her own worries. She had received a letter from her own lawyer – a rather frightening letter for Amy. The lawyer informed her that he had received a letter from Mr Robert Horrocks' legal adviser saying that his client was considering contesting his mother's will. The reason given was that he did not think she was of sound mind when she made it. The lawyer suggested Amy should come to see him, or he come to see her, so that they could talk over the matter before he replied.

'He wouldn't want to see me unless he thinks there is something in what Robert says, would he?' Amy wailed.

Agnes tried to reassure her but felt that, if nothing more, the final meeting between old Mrs Horrocks and her lawyer, Mr Robinson, would be raised. She remembered the incident Amy had told her about: the gold pen being left behind. Certainly, according to her daughter, Mrs Horrocks had been quite lucid. Although she had altered her will in Amy's favour, this had been justified in her own mind. She felt her son had changed. He no longer telephoned her or sent cards on her birthday or Mother's Day. She did not forgive him for this; in some ways she blamed it on his wife, saying she was turning him against her.

Agnes had taken Amy to see Kitten Cottage and introduced her to Major Hayward. In spite of Amy's usually shy manner, she got on very well with the old gentleman. Agnes encouraged her to go to the cottage to take Wilma out for short arthritic walks with Polly, who danced around the old dog on her extending nylon lead. She noted too, as did Major Hayward, that Wilma looked far less mournful and even started to play with an old rubber ball that he said she had taken no notice of for about a year.

Agnes's promise to him that she would look after Wilma until she no longer enjoyed life had done so much for Major Hayward. He was devoted to the old dog.

'She really belonged to my dear wife and at first she seemed to miss her sorely. She was always trying to find her, then she settled down but she always looked so sad. Alice always said animals grieved just as much as humans. I didn't believe her but I do now, I'm afraid.'

At last the day came when Major Hayward could be admitted to the residential home. A very large taxi came for him. 'Very large' was his request and, when his baggage was packed into it, one could see why. Two large suitcases contained his clothes. Amy and Agnes had helped him pack, suggesting now and again that perhaps he wouldn't need this or that suit or extra bathrobe, etc. But no, he felt everything must be taken with him, including his entire military uniform! They could both see it was useless arguing with the old gentleman. That was how he wanted it and that was how he was going to have it. He was adamant.

Another slightly smaller case was to be placed in the back of the car. This, Agnes knew, contained at least a dozen silver-framed photographs of his wife Alice. Also photos of the cottage, of various animals they had rescued, and of Wilma – Wilma playing with a ball, or trying to climb on his wife's lap and disguising her large doggie self as a 'lap dog'. There were several of children and their parents (carefully vetted) who had adopted animals from the sanctuary. Also lots of small ornaments he could not visualize life without. The taxi man carried this one to the car. He looked at Agnes as he lugged it along the garden path, pretending to puff and pant with the effort.

'*Queen Mary*'s anchor in this one, miss?' he said, raising his eyes to heaven and making a dramatic fuss carrying it.

Wilma sat in her usual place on the front doorstep, looking slightly worried and getting in everyone's way. The wheelchair was stowed in the boot, along with three framed oil paintings, carefully wrapped in brown paper and yards of Sellotape keeping it in place. At last Major Hayward, having carefully supervised the packing of all his worldly goods, got into the car.

All the furniture that Agnes had not wanted, some of her own from the flat and some from Kitten Cottage, had gone to the sale rooms for auction, so this really was the final goodbye for Major Hayward.

He wound the window down. Agnes and Amy stood on his side of the car saying 'Good luck.' Very formally he shook hands with both of them, but the formality was slightly softened by the tears in his eyes, tears he was obviously deeply ashamed of. He turned his head away. 'Couldn't have done it without you two to help,' he said almost gruffly. 'Thank you both.'

The Major took one more look at the cottage, white and pretty in the morning sunlight. Then at Wilma framed by the front door of the house. That was about as much as he could bear, Agnes felt.

'Don't worry, we will take good care of Wilma and we will come to see you when you have had time to settle in. After all, Major, it will take you a bit of time to unpack!'

This brought a smile to lighten his face a little.

'I know you will. I hope Alice knows Wilma is not to be despatched just because I've got to leave.'

The taxi moved away from the gate and drove slowly up the pretty lane. Amy shed a tear or two as it drove away. Agnes was made of sterner stuff, although she did feel a little sad at the old man's departure.

'Come on, Amy, there's plenty to do in there,' she said briskly and marched up the path to Wilma and Polly. 'Tonight we will go out and have a celebration dinner. You have been such a help in every way, Amy, especially with Polly and Wilma and all the other things. And may I thank you for letting me stay with you? It would have been so lonely in a hotel.'

'Oh, that would be so nice, Agnes, but I'm going to miss you so much when you leave. It's been wonderful having you as a guest and a friend.'

Agnes smiled to herself. She had a secret.

She was going to propose something to Amy at dinner tonight. A proposal that, when she had first thought of it, had surprised even herself.

Agnes had always thought of herself as a loner. Even when she had been a wife and fond of her husband, it had always been a relief to her when he had to go to America for a conference or visit. She had seldom gone with him, even though he encouraged her to do so.

The suggestion she was going to put to Amy at their celebration dinner that night was not prompted simply by thoughts of companionship. Help with the animal sanctuary she dreamed of bringing back to Kitten Cottage was essential, and she needed help from someone who loved and understood animals. She found Amy easy to manipulate and her undoubted admiration would be useful. Whether she would think of selling her flat and joining Agnes permanently she had as yet no idea. The worry about her brother might be a problem; if he did contest the will and win the case, Amy would have little money. Agnes was determined to do her best to thwart him. Amy would be a much happier person if she possessed the considerable money from the sale of her flat. But at first this sharing of life at Kitten Cottage would have to be on an experimental basis. Agnes had no wish to be saddled with Amy Horrocks for ever if it all went disastrously wrong.

Agnes, with Amy's help, shut and locked all the doors and windows of the house and the gates to the four kennels that had been renovated and repainted. The kennels were fairly large with a water bowl in each one. Beside them was a small room with a sink and an area for dog food, feeding bowls and a number of collars and leads hanging on the wall.

The cattery, also planned by Major Hayward's wife Alice, Agnes presumed, was nearer the house. Again there was only room for four occupants. These two heated buildings stood in about half an acre of scrubby grass with a narrow path of paving stones to each. The half-acre was surrounded by a high, stout wire fence, making the whole thing look rather like a tennis court. A large garden shed stood opposite the kennels facing the house; it contained an ancient lawn mower and garden tools.

It looked as if Mrs Hayward had intended to keep her little animal sanctuary very small, something she could handle by herself or perhaps with help from her husband. When they had first come to the cottage he and she had been fit and healthy and would have been able to take on the task of feeding and grooming and perhaps finding homes for the creatures they gave a home to and nobody claimed.

Major Hayward had told Agnes that his wife had been meticulous in trying to trace where each cat or dog had come from, but even though she advertised the lost animals in the local paper and had a postcard with their description in the local village shop and the post office, very few had been claimed. People had either just dumped the unwanted cat or kitten and moved away and left it, or turned the dog loose. He had said some of the animals that Alice had taken in were in a sorry state, stressed, beaten, frightened and even dangerous. All were in need of love and patience.

Now the house was empty Agnes would have to leave Wilma alone for the night. She was determined to move into the house the next day, so the big mournful dog would only be on her own for just the one night.

She closed and latched the new gate and stood for a moment looking at her new property, her new home. She hoped Major Hayward would be happy in his new surroundings, hoped he would sleep tonight and not be missing Wilma and his own place too much. She had been to see the home he had gone to. His room was spacious and his own pieces of furniture and his own bed made it better for him, at least Agnes hoped it did. She had promised to visit him and intended to keep her promise. She liked the old gentleman and during her short acquaintance with him he had never mentioned any relatives of his own or of his wife's. As they had had no children maybe there was no one to call and see how he was adapting to being away from his own home, in somewhere strange to him.

Agnes turned round and smiled at Amy who was sitting in the Porsche waiting for her. As she started the engine her passenger looked at her almost shyly, a typical Amy look.

'Only one more night and you will be living here. I have so enjoyed having you as a guest, Agnes. I can't tell you how much I shall miss you.'

'Well, I'm glad you will miss your guest, Amy. I have really enjoyed it too, and it has been a wonderful help.'

Agnes started the car and made for the flats. Tomorrow she would be moving into her new home. Poor Amy. Agnes knew how she felt. She almost dreaded being left and had come to rely on Agnes to tell her troubles to. Although she could still visit her in the cottage to talk to her, it would not be the same. Well, at dinner tonight, she would put her proposal to Amy. She would have a chance to take it or to leave it, go on as she was, or make a change.

*   *   *

Agnes looked at the large menu both she and Amy had been handed. She had chosen a rather exclusive small restaurant near the flats. Agnes was very strict about drinking and driving and this place was in easy walking distance. After a glass or two of wine they could stroll back without worrying about being behind the wheel of the car. Luckily the evening was dry and pleasant.

'Do you like fillet steak, Amy?' she asked. 'With mushrooms and baby asparagus?'

Amy looked down at the menu again. She had been studying the list carefully and Agnes was pretty sure she had been trying to work out the least expensive items. She looked at Agnes, her eyes wide, lips pursed.

'That's terribly dear, Agnes. I love fillet steak, of course, but look at the price of it!'

'Never mind that. I am celebrating my totally new way of life. Soon I will be cleaning out catteries and doggeries and goodness knows what – that is, if I make a success of the place in a small way!'

The steak was ordered, one medium and one rare, with a bottle of red wine. The whole meal including the sweet of lemon meringue pie was perfect.

Then the coffee arrived.

'Thank you, Agnes. That was the most perfect meal I have ever had. No, I mean it, truly. It's so wonderful, your new house and the animals! What a lovely way to spend your time, looking after things, animals. Some of them have been cruelly treated, dumped, left to starve. I should love it, I know.'

Agnes felt the time had arrived to put forward her idea. She poured more coffee then silently stirred hers round and round. She looked up at Amy who was looking at her, obviously wondering what the momentary silence meant. Agnes was still unsure whether the idea she was about to put to her companion was a good one or was she taking a chance? Amy had proved a good friend. She had put up with her, helped her begin to move into Kitten Cottage as well as making friends with Major Hayward and taking over Wilma and Polly. It had all been a great help. Agnes realized she couldn't have handled it all if Amy had not been so wonderfully helpful.

Amy's shyness and reticence had almost disappeared, at least with Agnes. But she seemed to have no other friends, and during the whole time she had been such a help to her, Agnes knew she remained haunted by the spectre of her brother and what he might do about their mother's will. She had however, during their busiest time, said little to Agnes about this problem, though Agnes knew she had received several letters from Australia. These might have been from her brother, his wife or even their lawyer.

They had been so busy, moving furniture, painting and repairing outbuildings. Now things were slightly more settled, Agnes determined to plunge herself more into Amy's worries in return for all she had done for her and she hoped would continue to do. This dinner was intended to mark the beginning of another kind of life for Agnes and perhaps also for Amy. It all depended on whether Amy was capable of taking a chance or was too timid to do so.

'Amy, how would you like to join me in the sanctuary and look after the animals that are brought to us?'

Amy looked up incredulously from dropping a few sugar crystals into her coffee. She clasped her hands together and fixed her eyes on Agnes.

'Do you mean it, Agnes, really mean it – for me to be part of the sanctuary, look after dogs, cats or anything that anyone wants us to take in and look after?'

Agnes nodded, well pleased with Amy's expression of delight. But the whole offer was not made yet. She wondered how Amy would react to the next part and hesitated before she went on with her idea.

'Yes. But more than that. We could try it out for an experimental period and then perhaps you could sell your flat as I have mine. Selling prices are way up at the moment, so if you have a mortgage –'

Amy broke in quickly, her face and manner stronger.

'No, my flat's fully paid for. Mother left . . .' She paused, looking suddenly guilty.

'Well, that's all the better! You can put the money into something. A building society perhaps, and it would bring you a nice income. But maybe you like your flat too much to want to give it up permanently?'

Amy's reply left no room for doubt about that.

'I hate it, Agnes! I've only liked it there since I had you as a friend. It's been so much better, more comfortable. I cannot seem to make friends with the other people in the flats, though they seem to get on with each other. I've never been a very sociable person, Agnes – you know that – even when I was training. There doesn't seem to be anything to do. I'm not much of a reader or television watcher. I don't like walking, or didn't until I could take Polly.'

Agnes felt great sympathy for her.

'Well, I can't run the animal sanctuary on my own, Amy, and I would rather have someone I know as a helper. Come and share Kitten Cottage. It's my cottage now and there's plenty of room there. You can easily find a tenant for your flat. We can come to some arrangement about expenses. We can share the food bills and telephone. Think about it!'

Chapter Seven

It took two months, which in Agnes's opinion was an extraordinarily short time, to get settled into Kitten Cottage. This was due in part to Amy's enthusiasm for the idea of joining Agnes and her desire to become part of the animal sanctuary.

Amy decided to let her flat for a year, and a tenant was quickly found. As she was leaving most of her belongings, furniture and curtains behind, there was no problem with organizing removal men or storage. This made the whole move so much easier and now they were ready to receive any creature in trouble. Agnes placed notices in the local shop, making clear that the little sanctuary was just a continuation of what Mrs Alice Hayward had started some time ago.

Agnes took one of the notices to the home where Major Hayward was now lodged. He was so moved by the fact that his wife's name and idea were being carried on that he became very gruff and put the notice carefully away in his desk, obviously trying very hard to cover his feelings.

'Nobody's brought anything to us yet, Major Hayward, but when they do, Amy or I will come and tell you about it. Perhaps nobody will.'

'We didn't get many, mostly lost cats or dogs. One cat had a litter of kittens in our little cattery. Alice was thrilled and managed to find homes for all of them.'

He smiled at the memory.

When Agnes arrived back at Kitten Cottage it was nice to have Amy there to welcome her with tea and home-made fairy cakes. Sometimes Amy's wish to please became a little overpowering, but Agnes was quick to acknowledge to herself that the situation she had put herself in could have proved pretty isolated if she had chosen to live alone, and Amy always retired to her own little sitting room and her own television in the evening. She was getting to know when Agnes wanted her own company and acted accordingly.

This particular afternoon, however, there were not only fairy cakes and tea but another letter from Robert, Amy's brother. His letters lately had been more and more threatening. This one which Amy handed to Agnes to read had arrived in the morning and was not so much threatening as triumphant. Robert intimated that both the lawyers, his own and their mother's Mr Robinson, seemed to agree that the matter of the will and their mother's state of mind should be gone into carefully. This he was intending to do.

'He will take all my money away from me, I know he will. Anyway, I suppose it was only really all intended for him, to be left to him, so that's that!'

Agnes shook her head, almost angrily. She hated the feeble attitude Amy was taking. Had she been in such a position, she would have fought every inch of the way. However, she had no time to put forward her argument and tell Amy to try to be more positive because there was a peal of the bell at the front gate. Agnes had had a bell put there so that anyone bringing in an animal could ring at the locked front gate and then Amy or she could go out to them.

So far no one had brought anything so at the ring of the bell they looked at each other in delighted anticipation, got up from the tea table and made their way down the gravel path to the gate.

Two small boys stood there, one holding a cardboard carton with 'Horace' painted in big black letters on the side. They opened the torn lid as the two women approached.

'I'm Tim, he's Billy.' The taller one motioned towards his blue-eyed companion.

'What have you got there?'

Agnes peered into the box. It was a very thin and

miserable-looking hedgehog. The two boys looked at her expectantly, one pair of blue eyes and one pair of brown.

'You'd better come in. Where did you find it?'

They gave her their rather muddled explanation. On their way to school that morning they had seen him 'sitting' in the middle of the road. Afraid he would get run over, they had carried him over to the grass verge – well, a good way into the field even – and hoped he would be all right. But he wasn't. When they came back from school there he was, 'sitting' just where he had been before, only this time they noticed one foot was bleeding and it looked as if he had been run over or bitten by a dog or something. The boys asked if they would take him in.

'Of course we will,' said Amy.

'He's probably hungry and needs a meal. Bread and milk, do you think? I've heard they . . .'

Agnes shook her head and turned to the two lads.

'You can leave him here. I'm going to take him to the vet but first we will give him a little dog food – they like that, I know.'

She nodded at Amy and soon the sound of the electric tin opener could be heard coming from the kitchen.

'I told you they'd help. It says so on their paper!' The blue-eyed boy was looking much more cheerful.

This was the first animal that had come, or been brought, to the sanctuary and though it was not quite what she had expected, Agnes was pleased to have it and determined to give it the best of care and attention. She took the hedgehog carefully out of the box and offered it a little food. The creature sniffed around then found it and ate about half.

'Come back and see how he is tomorrow, will you, Tim and Billy?'

Agnes carried the cardboard box containing 'Horace' out to the car. She went to the same vet who had looked after Polly when she had been nearly strangled by a vandal.

He did not recognize Agnes at first until she mentioned

Polly. He examined the little creature carefully. It did not attempt to curl up.

'Well, it's lost its foot, that's for sure! These chaps don't stand much chance in the traffic. They are not quick movers, but he's got a more severe disability than that. He's blind and probably very old.'

The vet held Horace up so that Agnes could see the white-filmed eyes and shrugged his shoulders.

'Do you want me to put him down, Mrs Turner?'

Agnes put Horace back in the cardboard box.

'No. He was brought to us for help by two children. They won't think it's much help if we just kill him.'

The vet shrugged his shoulders again and smiled.

'Up to you, Mrs Turner. He's dehydrated and thin. They can drink milk or water, whatever people say. No, there's no charge.'

Agnes explained where she lived and what she was trying to do. The vet immediately recognized her address and remembered the previous owners.

'Oh, wasn't that Major Hayward and Mrs Alice Hayward? I treated several strays for her. Very nice people.'

Back at Kitten Cottage, Horace was installed in one of the cat places, given plenty of straw and grass to lie on. The vet had sprinkled some antibiotic powder on the wounded foot. Amy was quite excited when Horace drank nearly a saucerful of milk then started to bumble around his little cat kennel. More food went down as well. Horace began to brighten up a bit.

'Horace, our first inmate! Perhaps word will get about now and people will bring more animals to us. Maybe even a cat or a dog or something else a bit more usual. Anyway, Amy, now Horace is settling in we can give our mind to Robert – and believe me, there is no sanctuary here for your dear brother. No sanctuary at all!'

Without telling Amy, Agnes had been devoting a lot of thought to her brother and what to do about him. Now that she came to explain her ideas, she was not surprised to find that Amy at first did not or could not agree with them.

'Oh, I couldn't do that, Agnes, I really couldn't! I mean,

he is saying things about me influencing my mother to leave me her money. Why should I do anything to help him?' She shook her head positively.

Agnes had to be patient and put her point again to Amy after she had listened to all her protestations and refusals, as Amy put it, 'to do such a thing'.

The 'thing' that Agnes suggested was that Amy should send the money to pay for her brother's fare from Australia and also pay for a small bed and breakfast or pub for him so that he could communicate easily with Mr Robinson, Mrs Horrocks' lawyer. If Amy made it possible for him to contest the will, that would show that she had no fear as to what her brother would uncover. Indeed, she could then be seen to have nothing whatever to hide and to have been only too helpful, by paying for the whole procedure!

After a time, despite some reluctance to part with her money, Amy admitted that she could see the point Agnes was making.

'You mean people wouldn't think I had anything to hide if I paid for him to come here and try to say Mother changed her will because I persuaded her? Well, I didn't, did I, Agnes, but I did give the drugs, didn't I, suppose they . . .?'

'Suppose they what, Amy? It's nothing to do with that – it's just got to do with the will. Why did she change it, and was she out of her mind when she did it?'

Amy agreed, fairly miserably, and eventually wrote to her brother asking him to let her know when he wished to come to England and offering to pay for the whole journey and then for him to stay in a small bed and breakfast place she and Agnes had noticed several times in their journeys to Brighton to buy things for the sanctuary. It looked suitable and was probably inexpensive.

Robert Horrocks' eventual reply to this proposal was non-committal, almost implying it was the least he felt his sister could do. He would let her know the date he considered coming and how much it would cost.

Amy was furious at the tone of the letter and Agnes had to persuade her to go ahead with the idea. She felt it was just what one would expect from a man who would make such accusations.

Agnes managed it though and they waited for Robert's next letter to arrive.

What came first, though, was a letter from Mr Robinson, telling Amy that her brother had suggested coming to see him at a later date to learn a little more about Mrs Horrocks' last will.

'Of course he has every right to ask any questions he wishes and to contest the will if he wishes to try to do so. I feel I must inform you however that your mother's will, which you are aware I drew up, will not in my opinion be contestable.'

The lawyer's letter did a lot to comfort Amy but, as Agnes well knew, she remained petrified that the last action she had taken towards her mother would be discovered. Amy would always remember and regret what she had done despite what Agnes had told her a hundred times: that she could not undo what she had done and bring her mother back to life, and she must just forget it. Her poor mother would probably thank her if she could.

After all, Agnes had been in very similar situations in her life and had made herself banish regret or shame or remorse. What she had done she had done for the best. She tried to make Amy feel the same, but it was an uphill task and Agnes wished the sanctuary would fill up a little and take Amy's mind off her problems.

Agnes's wish was partially granted that very afternoon when there was a peal on the gate bell. Amy was in town shopping.

The two dogs barked and as Agnes walked down the gravel path to the gate she was surprised to see a shiny black BMW parked outside and a chauffeur standing at the gate, holding a large expensive-looking cat basket from which was coming a furious sound between a meow and a growl.

The man motioned towards the back seat of the car, opening the door at the same time. This revealed a straight-backed elderly lady.

'Get into the car for a moment, I want to talk to you about Tippy's stay with you. I understand Mrs Hayward is no longer with us?'

Agnes could only nod her agreement and wait for more information.

'I am Mrs Symington Smythe. Tippy has stayed here three times before, only for two nights. This is what I want on this visit, two days and nights.'

'Couldn't she stay at home for two nights, Mrs Smythe, have someone come in to feed her?'

'If that is what I wanted, that is what I would have arranged. Tippy has come to you. She is to stay in her kennel or whatever you call it until the day after tomorrow when I call for her.'

She paused and glanced towards the cat basket, then turned to Agnes.

'Mrs Turner, isn't it? I have heard about you from Major Hayward.'

They arranged fees for Tippy's stay. Mrs Symington Smythe drove off without saying goodbye to Tippy.

Agnes carried the cat through to the house, closed the door and window of the sitting room and opened the door of the cat basket. She was curious to see the cat. Tippy hissed.

'Come on then.' She spoke softly.

Agnes tried to coax the reluctant animal out. No luck. Agnes felt sorry for the black smooth-haired creature, skulking at the back of the cat basket, her green eyes glaring, white teeth showing as she gave a few more growls and hisses.

Agnes left the cat basket open, put down a saucer of milk, fetched from the kitchen with careful precautions getting through the sitting-room door. Then she went and sat on the settee some way from the cat. After about ten minutes Tippy emerged, peering left and right with wide frightened eyes. Then she approached the milk. Agnes did not move. She noticed however that the cat's back legs seemed weak. Tippy drank the milk and Agnes moved her foot and the cat backed into the cat basket, as far as she could go.

Agnes put her hand into the basket and the cat lashed out at her. Agnes drew her hand back but not before she had received a scratch on her wrist. The blood oozed a little but the scratch was fortunately not deep. She put a tissue from her pocket over the small wound.

'Tippy, what is it, what's been done to you to make you behave like this?'

After two days Agnes was to find out. For those two days she and Amy coaxed the cat. She would come out, use the tray and eat a little but when they came near her Tippy would retreat back into her basket, growling and hissing. Mostly she used the basket as a lavatory.

'We can't send her back like this! What's the matter with her, Agnes? She seems sort of weak, doesn't she?'

Amy was very worried too about the cat.

'No, we can't, and we are not going to, Amy. This cat has been cruelly treated in some way, I'm not quite sure how – but I'll find out, don't worry!'

The day Tippy was to go home, the car arrived at the gate. The gate bell pealed. Agnes went out. There was only the driver. He was standing by the gate.

Mrs Symington Smythe had not come. Agnes approached the gate. She looked worried.

'Hello, miss, I've called for the cat.'

He touched his cap, looking at her expectantly.

Agnes shook her head and took time to reply. Then she made her voice and expression distressed, almost tearful.

'I'm afraid Tippy died yesterday. I found her in the kennel. She must have died in the night. She was quite cold. I could not let Mrs Smythe know as she did not leave her address or telephone number otherwise I would, of course, have contacted her.'

The man's reaction was surprising.

'Best thing that could have happened to that poor little soul. She was never allowed out of that basket. She tortured that creature. Just let it out to do its business in a tray then back in. She didn't always give it the tray but made it wait, do it in the basket. Then she would slap it.'

Agnes could hardly believe her ears.

'But why, why did she do that to her?'

The man shrugged and took off his cap to wipe his forehead. It was a warm muggy day.

'Her husband died and he thought the world of that cat. She hated it but she hated her husband more. They were at each other's throats all of the time, so the old bitch took it out on the animal. It's a damn sight better dead!'

'I'm afraid Tippy's buried. I thought it better – this weather, you know! Will you take the cat carrier back with you? I would rather you didn't. She might do that kind of thing again, to another cat.'

'No, I don't think so, it was just his cat. She may telephone you. Meanwhile I'll leave it with you. You never know how she will react, she's off her head anyway.'

Agnes could have cried when she tried to imagine what Tippy had been through. She had to ask more questions.

'How long has this been going on, this cruelty?'

The man shrugged. 'Two years the man has been dead, or a bit more perhaps. He was a nice old chap. He'd turn in his grave if he knew what that poor little soul had been through.'

He got into the car and slammed the door shut, then opened the window and asked, 'Shall I tell her you expect a donation?'

He smiled as he asked this. Agnes shook her head. She was aware she felt slightly sick.

He closed the window and the car drove off. Agnes went back to tell the horrible tale to Amy.

To her delight as she entered the sitting room she found Amy kneeling in front of the cat basket with Tippy half in and half out, letting Amy stroke her head.

The noise of the door opening frightened the cat and she retreated backward into the privacy of the basket.

'What did you say about Tippy? What did Mrs Smythe say when you said she was dead – I mean, pretended she was dead?'

Agnes explained that Mrs Symington Smythe was not there and did not come to call for the cat. Then she told the rest of the story, making Amy break down in tears.

Not an unusual state for Amy, but this time Agnes didn't blame her.

'Don't worry. We will do our best to undo what the bitch has done. Tippy can live in the house with us. We will have to keep her in for a couple of weeks or even more, and somehow I'll find a way to deal with Mrs Symington Smythe. The man told me where she lives. That helps.'

'*Deal* with her? You won't have anything more to do with her, will you, Agnes?'

Agnes did not reply for some minutes, then she looked directly at Amy. Her eyes narrowed.

'You never know what might come up, Amy. Let's wait and see. Anyway, we have got your brother to cope with as well, haven't we?'

Agnes knew Amy was only waiting for Robert Horrocks to let her know the cost of his visit.

Once he was here in this country then Agnes felt she would be able to see the man's vulnerable points and make use of them.

Meanwhile, Agnes had an idea. She would go to the address the chauffeur had given her, just to look at the house the beastly woman lived in where Tippy had been so outrageously treated! What good that would do she wasn't sure, just to see the house, the village – then what? She had as always no idea, but that didn't stop her telling Amy she was going to see a friend, getting into her car and making for Mrs Smythe's village.

Just an afternoon's drive, she told herself. Just a 'recce'.

At the moment, nothing else.

Chapter Eight

Tenby, the village where Mrs Smythe lived, was a pretty little place. Agnes slowly drove round the narrow lanes and after a while she found the house.

It was large, modern and quite impressive.

A wide gravelled drive swept round the central front lawn. The BMW was parked near the front door, shining and clean as usual, just as it had been when it had been drawn up at Kitten Cottage.

Agnes motored down the lane at the side of the house. The garden at the rear of the house was large and beautifully kept. A man was working away, edging the lawn. He did not even look up as Agnes passed in her car.

A big party could be held in that garden, a really big party, for some charity or other.

Agnes smiled to herself, got out her mobile phone and asked for the number of the local post office.

'Could you tell me please the name of the local paper? I mean the paper most people read in Tenby?'

The woman in the post office was most helpful and even gave the addresses of three newspapers. Agnes wrote them all down and thanked her quite profusely.

She couldn't wait to get the notices written and posted off to the various papers.

Amy must help!

She must come and put notices up in the village shop and the hairdresser's. Agnes had noticed a little salon in the main street. She did not think it would be wise to do it herself in case someone described her to Mrs Smythe and she recognized the description.

Nobody had seen Amy at all, so she would not be recognized.

When Agnes got home, she broke the news to Amy, very much with her tongue in her cheek.

Amy was incredulous.

'Mrs Symington Smythe, giving a huge wine and cheese party in aid of the Cats Protection Society? When, where?'

Agnes put her hand over Amy's. Her face had grown hard and stern.

'It's not enough punishment for what she has done to Tippy. She made that poor creature suffer all the time. It's all I can think of at the moment. I want you to help.'

'Of course, of course. Anything! Tippy is just a bit more adventurous. She came right out today, this morning. She used the tray, then walked about the room before she went back into the basket!'

'Oh, that is good news! Amy, Tippy will always live with us. No more finding another home for her, her suffering days are over.'

Suddenly Agnes burst out laughing. She was not given to laughing as a rule. Amy looked at her questioningly, eyebrows raised.

'Imagine when dear bloody Mrs Smythe reads the notices in the village that she is giving a wine and cheese party in aid of the Cats Protection. From what I've seen of her, and that's not much, she'll be too proud to back out of it now. It's been announced all over the village and all her posh friends will make her go through with it – and at least the Cats Protection will benefit. She deserves worse!'

Agnes suddenly felt flat. She would have liked to have done more.

Amy went back to Tippy who had half emerged from her cat prison.

Agnes went outside to collect Wilma who greeted her

with her usual slow tail wag. Polly had rocketed down the stairs to greet her.

Agnes walked though the gate into the large enclosure where Polly could tear around, do what she liked, and Wilma could walk her stately way beside Agnes, occasionally looking up at her with liquid brown eyes.

She paused at Horace's little closed-off cat cage.

He was blindly looking around as usual. He had stopped bumping into things now because his territory was small and safe. He had eaten his dish of dog food and drunk about half his water.

His injured foot had healed but he dragged what was left of the limb behind him, making the best of it.

Agnes stood and watched him for a long time, her mind considering a new track. Was this life she was watching better than a quick death on a busy road? Was the creature happy or happier? Who could tell?

Agnes strolled away, smiling at the antics of the two dogs, but her mind turned to the man Robert Horrocks, who was coming from miles, continents away. What for, what was he bumbling away from his cage for? Money, his sister's money? Her mind flashed back to herself as a staff nurse, gawky, uncertain, fearful, waiting for the dreaded Night Superintendent to come round the children's ward and find fault with her, tell her off and take away a little more of her self-confidence.

What changed her, what built her up? She knew only too well. Money. That old patient, whose cat she had rescued, had left poor Nurse Carmichael a lot of money – and Carmichael was no more.

If she sold her flat, Amy would have enough money to share, to give her brother the self-esteem he perhaps lacked. Agnes was surprised at her own thoughts. They didn't even know when he was coming yet or what kind of man he really was.

Agnes called the two dogs and went over to the little hedgehog. He turned his milky blind gaze up and seemed to look straight into her eyes. Could he sense she was looking at him?

'Horace, I must go to see Major Hayward, have a talk with him about you and Tippy and Wilma and how I deal with things.'

The next morning Amy got the expected letter from Robert. He estimated the cost of the trip at far higher than Amy had imagined but she had, she said rather bitterly to Agnes, expected this from him. Agnes would not be drawn into giving an opinion for the simple reason that she had not gone into the cost of the air trip, or what Amy had agreed to pay at the bed and breakfast place.

'Well, now you have to decide on the date he comes and how you are going to handle the whole thing, Amy.'

Amy nodded rather miserably, obviously hoping Agnes would advise her.

'You will probably have to go with him to see Mr Robinson.'

Amy nodded and traced a mark on the kitchen table with her finger, something Agnes had learned she always did when she was preparing herself to ask a favour.

'You couldn't . . . you wouldn't like to come with us, Agnes? I am sure you are much cleverer at talking to lawyers than I am, and probably Robert is.'

Agnes shook her head very positively at this.

'I wouldn't dream of getting involved, Amy. It is absolutely not my business.'

'But supposing he brings up the matter of my . . . her death? He might guess. I might say something to give myself away!'

Agnes's reply was brisk and to the point.

'Don't be ridiculous, Amy! You have your mother's death certificate signed by your doctor. Stop dreaming up fantasies as to what might happen and concentrate on what will happen.'

'Yes, you're right, Agnes. I'll try to stop imagining and write to him to tell him when to come. He says he could fix it up for a fortnight today, doesn't he?'

Agnes nodded, trying to make her manner as preoccupied and distant as she could.

'Well then, Amy, you've got a lot to do. Contact your mother's lawyer to make an appointment then write to Robert and fix up his accommodation. Also, you are helping me to look after Horace, Wilma and Polly and any other animal which may come along. Maybe we will get something a bit more conventional, like a dog or cat!'

She smiled as she said this.

'I don't mean another Tippy, but perhaps a cat who just needs homing, not one necessarily who has been mistreated.'

At that moment the door was pushed gently open and Tippy's frightened wide green eyes peered round the door. She then backed out.

'Oh Agnes, that's as far as she's been. How wonderful. I'm so pleased – it's worth anything, anything in the world to see her do that!'

'There you are, Amy. Now do your letter writing and once you've done it, forget all about Robert until he arrives. Then you can tackle that problem!'

Agnes did not feel as confident and on track as she usually did, however. She felt a great need to talk to someone, to someone who had no axe to grind, no bias.

She suddenly decided she would go out to see Major Hayward to talk to him, to tell him everything, except of course Amy's deadly secret. That could not be told! But the rest, she would ask him why she was changing, what was making her feel as she did. Different, gentle.

Agnes would tell him about Mrs Smythe and the wine and cheese party which as yet she did not know she was giving. That would make him laugh.

Chapter Nine

Mrs Symington Smythe gave a very successful wine and cheese party in her charming garden. The entrance fee was well justified and the Cats Protection Society benefited from the generous effort to the sum of £700. A wonderful effort it was!

Agnes read the small piece in the local paper with great delight. She wondered how Mrs Smythe had reacted.

But her effort to get back at the cruel woman for her treatment of Tippy had taken second place to the cat herself, who to Agnes's and Amy's equal delight was gaining in confidence and gradually, it appeared, forgetting the horrific time she had gone through for two years.

Maybe her trick had been more constructive than doing something to really hurt the woman. At least the Cats Protection had benefited! The little scheme had been a great success, and both she and Amy were pleased that in some small way at least Mrs Smythe had received a rather peculiar come-uppance.

The two small boys who had brought in Horace the hedgehog had been back to see him. Agnes had made much of them. Their concern was well rewarded with lemonade and cakes.

Agnes had made a small area by placing four pieces of wood in a square on the grass. Horace could bumble about in that. He could walk well and find his way around the square of grass, dandelions and pebbles. The boys were pleased.

Agnes did her best to explain that the hedgehog was old and blind and maybe wouldn't last all that long.

'He's like my great-grandad,' the youngest boy volunteered. 'He's not very long for this world.'

'But,' said his companion, serious brown eyes looking at Agnes, 'he's not getting any more hurt, is he? Though perhaps he'd rather be with the other hedgehogs in heaven or wherever. What do you think?'

At that moment Amy brought out a saucer of dog food and put it in the enclosure. Horace smelled it at once and then he clambered on to the side of the saucer and gobbled, making a snorting noise as he did so.

'That's good. He enjoys that, like my Grandpa likes his beer! I reckon it's worth it, Mrs Turner. I'm glad we brought him here.'

On that happier note, they left.

It made Agnes realize how little she knew about children and their thoughts on death or life.

It made her feel that if the sanctuary ever filled up, she would talk to as many children as she could. Not to teach them anything, but to learn from them, especially about their feelings, and the treatment of animals and looking after them.

Amy had at last telephoned her brother and made the arrangements as to when he was coming and booked the room for him. She was nervous and would hardly talk about his arrival.

Agnes was curious as to why his wife was hardly ever mentioned.

'Have you met his wife, or did your mother, Amy? What is she like? She runs a shop, doesn't she?'

Her friend clammed up at once, mouth firmly shut.

'Oh, she's supposed to be ill. I don't know. Mother disliked her. We never met her. Mum thought Robert married beneath him. She sounded common when she spoke on the telephone.'

That was it! Agnes did not want to get involved with any of the 'will' business, so did not pursue the matter any further. She couldn't help feeling, though, that Amy had been indoctrinated against the woman by her mother who at the time had been so besotted by her love for her son, no woman would have been good enough for him. It had probably been sheer jealousy that had bred the hatred of her son's Australian wife.

One thing Agnes did insist on, though, was that Robert Horrocks should be their guest for dinner the night after settling in for his short stay at the little hotel Amy had booked for him.

'It is the least I can do, Amy. It would be childish not to meet him as your friend. Don't you agree with me?'

Amy did agree and said she felt it was very nice of Agnes to suggest it.

'That will be the day we see Mr Robinson. I will know if he's now, if –'

Agnes interrupted her rather impatiently.

'Amy, you must know, your mother was quite all right when she made her will and you didn't even know she'd made it, let alone made it in your favour. Remember the story you told me about the gold pen Mr Robinson left behind? Even then your mother did not tell you why she had her lawyer to see her.'

Amy nodded in agreement. But in her usual rather pessimistic and downcast manner, she shrugged her shoulders as if she had already lost her inheritance. Anyway in two weeks Robert would be here and the two of them would have to fight it out between them.

Money could be as much a curse as a blessing, Agnes thought.

She needed a rest from Amy and decided to take Wilma and go to see Major Hayward. She always cheered him up and he loved to see Wilma. She liked to see him too. He was easy to talk to and gave good advice.

Agnes parked her car outside the residential home where Major Hayward now lived or – as he would say – where he now spent his time.

Agnes knew only too well how much he missed his home, and her visits, she hoped, cheered him up a little. She had been careful to get permission from the Matron of the home beforehand to bring Wilma to see him. It was only allowed if the weather was fine and the dog and her old master were able to meet outside in the garden, so a rainy day meant no Wilma.

Today luckily was fine and sunny so there were no problems as Agnes approached the large shady tree where Major Hayward was sitting in his wheelchair. The moment he saw Wilma, his face lit up and the moment Wilma saw him, she began to pull on her short lead towards his wheelchair. The reunion between the two was always a joy to Agnes.

'She looks so well – and younger, doesn't she?'

He rubbed the dog's head as she put it in his lap, her large tail wagging furiously.

'You groom her a lot, Agnes. That's the secret, isn't it? Her coat shines now. Alice used to groom her. She had a special grooming glove that I bought her.'

Agnes told him about Horace, about Tippy and about how much the horrible Mrs Symington Smythe had made for the Cats Protection.

He loved that.

'You haven't had a really ordinary inmate yet. Goodness knows what you will get next, Agnes!'

Then Agnes listened to what he called 'his news' of the home. Usually it was about who had died, or who had been taken ill. There was little cheerful news.

The home itself was an expensive one and, to Agnes's eyes, well equipped. The Matron was a nice woman. The nurses were mostly cheerful youngsters and the Major had a television and radio in his room and a daily paper provided.

According to him the food was quite good. Not what he was used to, but not bad.

'Too many carrots, they come with everything, Agnes. One day they will turn up in the rice pudding!'

Agnes stayed about an hour, as she usually did. He put his arm round his dog and gave her a hug. Wilma licked his hand.

'I expect she's thirsty, Agnes, sitting in the sun.'

'I've got water for her in the car, Major.'

He patted Wilma's head in farewell and looked into her amiable brown eyes.

'You've fallen right on your feet, Wilma. I wish we were all so lucky!'

He looked up apologetically.

'Complaining old codger, aren't I, Agnes? I should be thankful to be in such a nice place.'

'Shall I go and ask one of the nurses to take you indoors now, Major?'

He shook his head, still watching the dog.

'No. I'll sit a bit longer out here. Thank you for coming, Agnes. I so look forward to your visits. I just can't tell you how much!'

Agnes pressed his hand in 'Goodbye' and smiled.

'I think it's just the person on the other end of the lead you really want to see, Major,' she said.

He shook his head and was still smiling and looking more cheerful as Agnes led Wilma round to the front of the home to where her car was parked.

She hated leaving.

As she backed the car to turn and go down the drive she looked at the board at the front of the steps to the entrance. Gold letters on a green background: *Sunset Lodge Residential Home.*

Agnes shivered.

Would she one day be in a Sunset Lodge or some such? After all she had no one, not one relative in all the world who would look after her, and very few friends.

Agnes did not make friends easily.

She looked at Wilma sitting on her special blanket beside her in the passenger seat.

Wilma looked back at her and said nothing at all in reply.

Agnes drove through the gates, not looking at the second notice by the entrance. She was no stranger to depression. She dismissed the thought from her mind determinedly.

'Just soldier on, that's the way, Wilma. Day at a time as you get older.'

Wilma settled herself more comfortably in her seat and – was it possible? – nodded agreement.

Chapter Ten

As the time drew nearer for her brother's arrival, Amy got more and more nervous.

The day Robert Horrocks was due to land in England, Agnes packed her off to the airport with some relief, seeing her off in the car that Amy had bought when she moved into Kitten Cottage.

She drove slowly and when drivers behind her, irritated by the pace at which the car was going, hooted, she panicked. Agnes had driven with her once or twice – and that was only at Amy's request because she had not driven for some time. The experience had certainly put Agnes off going out with her again and she had rather shame-facedly discouraged Amy from taking Polly and Wilma out for walks further afield in her car.

'Oh, I do wish you were coming with me, Agnes! I won't know what to say to him after all this time.'

Agnes had been firm, however, and not given in. She shook her head determinedly as she had already done three or four times before when Amy had brought the subject up, almost tearfully.

'Amy, this is all to do with your family. Your brother, your mother, your mother's lawyer. You must handle it yourself. Personally, I don't think anything will come of it, so don't worry!'

She watched Amy's car driving away on what Amy felt to be the fatal day. Personally Agnes felt that Robert had come on a useless and rather stupid journey, but wills did this to people. Money, money, money! It wasn't love that made the world go round. It was that motivator in chief – money!

Robert had not suggested bringing his wife Barbara.

Agnes had listened to some of Amy's bursts of information about her brother and their youth together.

Apparently Amy's parents had both made much of their son. When the children played tennis Amy had to let him win. Always, always, always. If they played snap, Amy must not call first if two similar cards appeared. If by some mischance she did, Robert would throw a tantrum, stamp his small feet, clench his fists and hit anyone near him. The scene would normally end with the little boy being hugged by either his mother or his father and Amy being sent to bed in disgrace.

In other words Robert was completely spoilt.

Agnes had to admit when she heard some of these stories that she could well understand Amy's coldness about the relationship. Later the boy had been sent to a public school that had been expensive and probably reduced their finances to an uncomfortable level.

Amy had been sent to a state school and then on to a nursing course which set her on a career which she loved. Even that was frustrated after her father's death and she had given it up, just because her mother did not like living alone, having been for years spoiled, cosseted and waited on by her long-suffering husband.

Agnes took Polly and Wilma into the enclosure where they could run without their leads on. She closed the wire door carefully behind her and, while the dogs frolicked about, she paid her usual visit to Horace.

It was rather pleasant to be alone for a while. She looked across at her round house with a great deal of affection. As an animal sanctuary, so far it hadn't been quite what she had expected, but things would probably improve and she might even have to employ a kennel maid or boy. She took the dogs back to the house and shut the door. Amy had started off early so now Agnes felt she could indulge herself by sitting down with a cup of coffee and watching *Kilroy*.

She did give a thought or two to Amy and she wondered how they would fare at the lawyer's the next day.

Maybe Amy would remain with her, maybe not. A lot, she felt, would depend on the outcome of this meeting.

Robert would probably be jet-lagged. Well, that would give Amy an advantage. An unfair one, really, Agnes thought as she poured the coffee from the machine and added a dash of cream.

Then Amy and Robert had to go and see their mother's doctor, this being Robert's idea. Agnes sighed. What a lot of upset and unpleasantness, and whose fault was it all? Just circumstances getting out of control. A silly old woman changing her mind.

Robert was coming to dinner the following evening. Agnes had insisted, and had offered to cook the meal herself so that no matter what the outcome of their visit to the lawyer, doctor or whoever else, Amy and her brother could come.

She did realize that it was not only kindness but curiosity that had made her plan this. She wanted to know more about Robert Horrocks and why his obsession with getting his mother's money was driving him to such lengths.

Was he poor, so in need of money?

Of course, everyone wanted money but there was, according to Amy's descriptions of his telephone calls and letters, almost an air of desperation about Robert rather than the natural greed which seemed to possess most people.

Agnes finished her coffee and walked through to the kitchen with the empty cup and saucer. Just as she placed them on the draining board the bell at the gate gave a shrill peal. Agnes was pleased. Here might be another resident for the sanctuary, a cat or a dog with no great problems except perhaps the need to be found a new home.

She shut the two dogs in the sitting room and went out

of her front door and started up the gravel path towards the gate.

She could hardly believe what confronted her!

Amy felt her feet were swelling. The new shoes she had put on seemed to be getting a bit tighter. She wished she had worn her more comfortable ones, but she had wanted to look smart to meet her brother, who she suspected always thought of her as a dowdy old maid. The heels of these new shoes were slightly higher than she usually wore. She hoped they would make her look a little taller, smarter. She sighed.

Whatever she wore her brother had always managed to make her feel badly dressed, old-fashioned, dowdy. He never said as much but the way he looked at her was enough.

Robert was always so dapper, so smartly suited, straight-backed.

'Rather military-looking,' his mother used to say when describing him to a friend or an acquaintance who had never met Robert, never seen him. 'Rather military-looking.' It was said proudly.

Amy was growing panicky. The stream of passengers from the Australian flight was getting a good deal thinner and there was still no sign of Robert. She was panicking not so much because something might have happened to him or that he might have missed his plane. What she was much more worried about was what she would do about the appointments she had arranged. The appointment with her mother's lawyer, Mr Robinson, her mother's doctor and the bed and breakfast booking.

Then suddenly Robert appeared, slightly mixed up with a smaller crowd of travellers. Her brother was clearly helping an elderly lady with her suitcase. Obviously it had cornered awkwardly and the little trolley wheels had not been able to cope. Robert seemed to have dealt with the problem and was handing back the handle of the suitcase to the white-haired lady, who was all smiles and thanking him profusely for being, as it were, her 'knight in shining armour'.

As he turned away from the woman and looked around him, Amy had a chance before he saw her to take in her brother's appearance. It was a shock to her. Robert was three years younger than she was and she had not seen him for nearly ten years. The change in him was incredible. His hair had been greying but abundant and wavy; it had now receded and he was bald across the centre of his head. He looked shorter – due, as Amy realized when he recognized her and made his way towards her, to the fact that he walked with his back slightly bent forward. He had always held himself so straight, upright. No longer. His waistline was thicker and he peered around him short-sightedly although he was wearing glasses, something which he had certainly never allowed himself to do before, except when he was driving the car.

He smiled rather coldly as he advanced towards her and Amy noticed he was carrying only a medium-sized hold-all. He held out his hand to shake hers. No brotherly kiss, but then Amy's family were not given to kissing or embraces of any kind and indeed Amy could not remember her father ever putting his arm round her shoulders.

'Hello. We were an hour late. I'm sorry if I have kept you waiting, Amy.'

He sounded as if he were speaking to a complete stranger.

Amy shook her head and made some fatuous remark. She felt curiously disorientated, as if she didn't know the man standing beside her. She tried to pull her mind back to the present. Accept the change in her brother.

'My car is in the short stay car park. It's not far.'

He nodded and shifted his suitcase to the other hand.

They walked in silence to the airport's outer doors. The silence continued all the way to the car park. Eventually Amy felt she must say something.

'How is Barbara, Robert? You said in one of your last letters to Mother that she was not very well.'

Robert looked at her, not turning his head but glancing at her sideways, a peculiar look on his face.

'She's got MS. She's not likely to improve. I told Mother that, and she said I should not have married her. Perhaps that's why she . . .' He stopped.

He had sent photographs when he was first wed. They showed Barbara to be a small, pretty woman. In both photographs she had been seated, one in the kitchen at the table, the other at the counter of her beauty shop. Both pictures for some reason had made their mother furious. She had thrown them away.

'Messing about with creams and potions. Aren't there enough moisturizers and wrinkle creams already? They will never make a future at that!'

Sometimes Amy now wondered whether Barbara had been the cause of her mother's change of heart about her beloved and worshipped son, if this had made her decide to disinherit him.

Amy unlocked the car, took Robert's holdall and put it on the back seat. It was heavier than she had imagined. Before she started the car she turned to Robert. She felt suddenly full of sympathy for him and Barbara. She knew quite a lot about multiple sclerosis and could not but feel sorry for anyone suffering from it.

'I'm so sorry, Robert. It must be awful for her. You never know when and where the disease will hit next. Mother never told me.'

Robert snapped on his safety belt and Amy started the engine. For a moment Robert was silent.

'It's pretty awful for anyone having to look after her too.'

His voice sounded bitter and almost tearful. Amy drew away from the kerb. His reply seemed cold, but emotional.

'I'm sure it must be, Robert. I can imagine.'

'I suppose you can a bit – being a nurse, I mean.'

Amy nodded and they relapsed into silence again.

'Where are we going, Amy? Are you putting me up?'

Amy shook her head. Robert asked no more questions. At last they arrived at The Laurels. The sign in the window, *Bed and Breakfast*, was noticed at once by Robert. The house was pleasant, covered with Virginia creeper. The door was opened to them before Amy had a chance to knock. Mrs Beavan, the proprietor, welcomed them warmly and showed them up to Robert's room. She asked if they would like any refreshments, a cup of coffee, tea, or something stronger.

They refused but Amy followed her brother into the comfortable bedroom. Robert put down his suitcase and looked enquiringly at his sister.

'What now, Amy? Tell me all the arrangements.'

Amy had written down all the arrangements which she had made into a neat list. She handed it to Robert.

'Oh, lawyer, Mr Robinson first, tomorrow morning at eleven o'clock. Then the doctor after lunch, at three o'clock.'

'What about the funeral arrangements? I would like to see the undertaker.'

Robert did not look at her.

Amy felt herself going pale. Whatever did he want to see the undertaker for? What could he tell him, did he suspect anything? Amy realized how stupid she was being. Whatever could he know about how their mother had died? Amy felt her heart hammering away. She tried to calm herself.

'Shall we have a drink? I feel I need one.'

Amy crossed over to the telephone and ordered the drinks Robert suggested, then she sat down again.

Her heart was slowing down and she was feeling calmer.

'I hope all this works out, Robert, amicably for both of us. It must do, it just must do.'

Robert did not answer. He sipped the whisky they had ordered, then looked across at his sister and just shrugged his shoulders. Amy left her drink on the table and got up.

How could it all work out well? she thought. How could it possibly?

'I'll call for you tomorrow morning at ten o'clock. That will give us enough time to drive to the lawyer's – it better be ten, because sometimes parking isn't easy, even at that time in the morning.'

Her brother nodded. He looked slightly crushed.

'Thanks for arranging all this, Amy. It's really big of you, considering what I've come for. I do appreciate it, you've taken a lot of trouble.'

It was Amy's turn to shrug her shoulders. She bade Robert goodbye and went downstairs to her car.

But when she reached the car she couldn't leave. The thought of Robert sitting there alone thinking about tomorrow, as she would be when she got home, made her go back and knock on the door of his room. He was still sitting as she had left him, gazing into space.

'Let's go and get a meal somewhere, Robert.'

He looked up, surprised, and got to his feet.

'That would be nice, Amy,' he said.

Chapter Eleven

Meanwhile back at Kitten Cottage Agnes was dealing with what she guessed was a new applicant for a place in the sanctuary. This one was a small white belligerent-looking and emaciated billy goat. Parts of its sparse white coat were coated with mud. Two horns, large for the creature's size, grew at what Agnes guessed was a good position for butting up and then back. Even on introduction the animal lowered its head and assumed a slightly threatening stance, rocking backward on to its hind legs.

The two girls with the goat were clad in immaculate school uniforms but without hats. Clean white blouses buttoned to the neck, school ties knotted close to the collar, navy blazers, the left breast pocket carrying what was obviously the school crest, and knee-length well-cut skirts. The older girl, who looked about thirteen, wore neat black tights and black shoes. The younger shorter girl had white socks and similar shoes. Both girls had long golden hair, brushed severely back and secured in a pony tail, the hair shining with health and cleanliness. Convent school, Agnes thought. Well brought up, good family. Why the goat?

The older girl held the end of the rope that was tied to the goat's collar. As it strained at the tether, the tattered collar lifted and showed the red raw bleeding area underneath. The animal was pulling towards the grass. When it managed to reach the edge it began to chomp hungrily, ignoring the soreness of the collar scraping its neck.

'Poor thing, how did it get like that?'

Agnes's voice was full of pity. As always, any animal in trouble or in pain moved her, even though she knew little or nothing about goats. She was longing to take off the bloodstained collar and put something soothing on the wound. She moved towards it, but the older girl stopped her.

'Better not let him loose, he butts a bit, Mrs Turner. Could we put him in there?'

She motioned towards the next paddock.

The younger girl took over then. She produced a longer piece of rope and tethered the billy to a post inside the wire enclosure. He looked back longingly at the lawn, but when he saw the paddock was grass, he started on that.

'He'd better have some water, Mrs Turner.'

After a long drink from Agnes's bucket and three of Amy's fairy cakes which he ate, papers and all, they left him to go into the cottage so that the girls could tell Agnes the history of the billy goat and why he had arrived at her gate.

Agnes felt slightly surprised at herself, realizing that she seemed to have taken on the new member of her sanctuary without knowing a thing about him, who he belonged to or who the two girls were. She sat them down at the kitchen table and set out glasses of orange juice and a plate of chocolate biscuits while the girls made a fuss of Polly and Wilma. Tippy watched with some suspicion: she regarded all newcomers as enemies.

The goat's story was told by Susan, the older girl, with frequent interruptions from Chloë, her younger sister. Susan was thirteen, Chloë was ten, going on eleven, as she put it. Agnes's guess was right. They were both day girls at the local convent Notre Dame, about two miles away.

Their father and mother had bought a house in a little village not far away from the sanctuary.

'Well, a mile or two. We had to bring Clancy on the bus. He butted the conductor when he tried to put us all off the bus, he said it wasn't suitable for goats and that he wasn't allowed to carry livestock.'

'Chloë said what about dogs then, she argued with him, so we got here.'

Susan went on with the tale. They had moved in about two months ago and started school at the convent, only a cycle ride from their house. Their name was Wilson.

'Horrible dump, lot of old penguins. Look at the clothes they make us wear, look at the skirts.'

Chloë threw a ball for Polly, who dashed after it, sliding across the kitchen floor, loving a game.

'Never mind that, you both look very nice. Why did you call the goat Clancy, or was that already his name?'

Susan shook her head, her golden pony tail swinging to and fro as she moved her head.

'No, he didn't have a name. We didn't know if he was a girl goat or a boy goat, but Daddy said he was a billy. He's been done, you know, he's been doctored.'

Susan looked embarrassed.

Not so Chloë. She was obviously growing up to be a girl who called a spade a spade.

'She means he's had his balls cut off, you know.'

'Chloë, why do you have to be so awful?'

Chloë shrugged and sat down at the table again. Susan gave her a reproachful look and went on.

'We live in Tenby. I don't suppose you know it?'

'I know where Tenby is, I even know someone there.'

Apparently one day, while cycling to school, they had seen Clancy on the other side of an iron fence. He was tethered to a metal stake by a short rope. He was straining his sore neck to try and reach the grass outside the circle he had already eaten. No water or food anywhere near him. Chloë had gone ballistic and refused to carry on to school. She had stormed up to the house that she presumed was responsible for the half-starved creature.

An elderly woman was dead-heading flowers in the garden. She turned and looked at Chloë and the reluctantly following Susan. Chloë faced the grey-haired, beautifully dressed woman.

'Who owns that goat, that poor starving creature? Its neck is red raw and it's got no water and no food.'

Chloë was red-faced with anger.

Susan had tried to break in. 'My sister's very fond of animals, she's . . .'

But Chloë had been unstoppable. Agnes was full of admiration for the youngster. It was exactly what she herself would have done in the same circumstances.

Anyway, it had all ended up by the woman's husband joining the fray and suggesting that, if they were so worried about the animal, he would give it to them.

'"Take it away, take it away. It was my son's but he's at university now. The gardener is supposed to be in charge of it. He always forgets it and if I say anything to him, he says he's not a bloody goatherd." That's what he said.' Chloë had quoted the speech, interrupting Susan.

'So we took him, Clancy. Daddy went ballistic when we took him home. He's mad about his garden, so we put him in the shed and brought him to you today.'

'How did you know about me and the –'

Chloë interrupted again, though her older sister seemed ready to reply to the question as well.

'Mummy took us to a garden party run for the Cats Protection. I think it was Miss Smythe something or other, she gave your name to Mummy. Mummy's mad on cats so we went there and a lady knew about you. She said your name was Alice, Alice Turner or something Turner. You'll look after Clancy, won't you, Mrs Turner?'

One cat, two dogs, a blind hedgehog and a goat!

Agnes saw the two girls off, promising that she would keep Clancy and they could come and see him when they wanted to – but she warned them, 'not when you are supposed to be in school.'

They promised and just as they reached the gate, Chloë surprised Agnes by giving her a kiss on the cheek. She looked towards Clancy.

'You're okay, Mrs Turner, Clancy will be all right now.'

Agnes went indoors to telephone the vet. What she

knew about goats was minimal. She wondered what Amy would say when she got back. If she'd had a bad time with Robert it would at least be a diversion. She went and looked at Clancy. He looked at her. She put a hand out and daringly scratched his head.

Clancy lowered his head but not to butt her. She leaned forward and released the collar. It stuck on one part of his neck but Clancy shook his head determinedly and the collar flew off. He took a moment or two to realize he was free, then began to walk about uncertainly. He went over to the hay Agnes had spread on the grass beside the shed. He lay down and began to eat the hay.

Agnes felt the usual warm satisfied feeling that she always felt when making a neglected or hurt animal feel comfortable, relieved of pain. She closed the wire door. For the moment the little goat would rest and satisfy his hunger and thirst. Maybe with the collar removed, the sore bleeding neck might begin to heal, but even if it didn't, it must feel better. Agnes decided to give the creature time to eat, then get the vet to come and see him, give her some advice as to his shelter and feeding. She had not expected a goat but a sanctuary was what she had started and she would take in what needed her to look after it. What next, she wondered?

Her thoughts reverted to Amy. How was she getting on? Clancy had put the various appointments Amy had made out of her head. Today, after she had met her brother, they were going to talk things over. After that, the next day, they were going to visit Mr Robinson the lawyer. Also the doctor who had signed the death certificate, or had that been the locum doctor? Agnes could not remember Amy's rather rambling and anxious remarks about the various appointments she had made for her brother and herself. Anyway Amy would be back this evening and Agnes was not looking forward to hearing all the minute details of the day's arguments, especially as the whole story was bound to be punctuated by tears and sniffings! Perhaps the advent of Clancy would cheer her up a little. Amy really loved the animals, even blind Horace.

Mr Singer arrived in the late afternoon. He was the vet whom Agnes had consulted when Polly had been nearly choked to death by a beastly vandal swinging her round on her lead. He had also examined Horace for her and Agnes felt he looked on her as 'one of those barmy women who are animal mad'.

He was always charming, though, and he looked around with appreciation. 'What a delightful cottage. I've a terrible memory but didn't the last owner have a wolfhound?'

Agnes nodded and at that moment Wilma and Polly came out to greet him, Polly with her usual gusto and Wilma more slowly and sedately, as befitted her age and rather arthritic back legs.

'Yes, that's the dog, I think, but it was some years ago.'

Agnes explained how she had become the new owner of the cottage and explained too the reason for her continuing the little sanctuary that Mrs Alice Hayward had started and built the enclosures for.

He gave her advice on feeding the goat and where it should sleep. Yes, goats liked to sleep lying down on straw and the shed would do perfectly. He recommended a cream for the sore neck.

'Poor old chap, he's been damn nearly starved to death, go easy on the goat mix. I'll come back in a week to have another look at him.'

Clancy took to the examination and an injection with surprising calmness.

'Will he butt me? He seems surprisingly good with you, Mr Singer!'

The vet smiled reassuringly.

'May do,' he said. 'But he won't have much weight behind it, so you'll probably be all right.'

He went out to his car and came back with a small bag of goat mix.

'Not too much, just three handfuls, then feed him about twice a day.'

When he had gone Agnes felt a little more confident though she had forgotten to ask him if goats and dogs mix. Still, she'd have to see, try Polly first. She could avoid trouble more easily than Wilma. She had offered Mr Singer tea and he had refused – too busy, he had said.

'But I'd love to see inside your little round house when I come next week, if I may.'

Agnes was pleased. She liked the tweedy little man who obviously loved his work and the animals.

It was ten to ten when Agnes at last heard Amy's car draw into the space in front of the garage. Agnes had taken a torch and gone to the enclosure to have a look at Clancy at about nine o'clock. The goat was in the shed so she opened the door very quietly in case the creature would take it into his head to dash out and disappear into the night.

She need not have worried. Clancy was stretched out on the bed of straw she had prepared for him earlier – sleeping. He did wake, raised his head and looked at the light, then gave a comfortable wriggle and closed his eyes again. He looked totally relaxed. Agnes felt, as she always did when she had made an animal happier or more comfortable, a warm glow of satisfaction that nothing else in the world had ever been able to give her.

Amy came in a few seconds after she had parked the car. She looked worn out, white and wan. She sat down and did not speak. Agnes had the television on and when she pressed the remote control and the screen became blank Amy said, 'Oh, I'm very sorry, Agnes, were you looking at something? I didn't mean to interrupt if you were . . .'

Amy always, or it seemed like always, offered an apology before she said anything. This usually irritated Agnes but this evening she shook her head and put the remote control on the table beside her.

'I've not had a very good day, Agnes. It was so sad and sort of nostalgic to talk to Robert.'

Agnes went into the kitchen and mixed two brandies and ginger ale. Amy had followed her into the kitchen. She sat down at the kitchen table. Agnes put the drink in front of her and sat down on the hard chair opposite.

'Let's have a drink, you look tired and I've had quite a day too. So tell me all about it.'

Amy put her elbows on the table, pushed the drink in front of her gently to and fro, but did not pick it up. Her eyes filled with tears.

Apparently the plane had been late arriving and Robert had been helping an old lady with her trolley or case on wheels or whatever it was. What had upset Amy when she had at last caught a glimpse of him was how different he looked. She had not seen Robert for ten years and the change in him was dreadful, according to his sister.

'He looks so much smaller, Agnes. He is round-shouldered. He never had been and I suppose that is what made him look shorter. His hair was greying a bit when we last saw him, but it was still thick and curly. Now it's almost white and he's balding. He's got a white moustache and a rather straggly beard. His clothes too, Agnes . . . awful. He looks like a tramp!'

Amy stopped her long description of her brother and at last took a sip of the drink in front of her. She looked up at Agnes and drank a little more.

'Thank you, Agnes.'

'Well, what happened then, Amy?'

Amy outlined the rest of the day. There had only been time to drive to the bed and breakfast. The rather nice landlady had brought them a drink, then they had gone out for a meal. They had talked and talked, never touching on the present confrontation but mostly about his life in Australia, the progressing illness and disability of his wife Barbara and their house, which he had geared to her disability with loving care.

'He seemed so different, Agnes, not bombastic any more

like he used to be, but he still, in spite of all he said, wants to see the doctor who signed Mother's death certificate and the lawyer Mr Robinson and . . .'

Amy stopped for a moment and took a larger sip of her brandy. She seemed reluctant to go on, then she mentioned Robert's wish to see the undertaker.

'The undertaker, Agnes, why do you think?'

Agnes shook her head, as puzzled as Amy.

'That sounds as if he still intends to go on with contesting the will, doesn't it, though why he wants to see the undertaker I simply cannot imagine. Whatever can they tell him about your mother's death?'

'I don't know, I don't know. But I feel he still suspects me of something, in spite of how very different he seems to be. Anyway, I feel I couldn't just leave him alone there, that's why I took him out for a meal. I felt I had to, I don't really know quite why, Agnes. He seemed so alone.'

Agnes shrugged her shoulders but did not say aloud what she was thinking, which was that Amy was still feeling guilty about killing her mother and that, knowing her, she probably would all her life.

'Well, tomorrow, the lawyer and the doctor.'

Amy finished off her drink and almost got up. Agnes stopped her and told her all about Clancy, the girls and the vet.

'Come and see him. He's a poor little chap, but I have made him as comfortable as I can. Come on.'

Amy's eyes lit up when she saw the little goat.

'Oh Agnes, poor little thing. What happened to his poor neck? Was it a rope or something? And he's so thin.'

Clancy raised his head and gave a small comfortable bleat then snuggled his head back into the straw. Amy seemed so different, so cheered up as they walked back to the house together.

'Agnes, I'm so happy here. Soon there will be more animals and I love those we've got now. The trouble is, do you really want me here permanently, sharing with you? Perhaps I should, you know, go back to my flat?'

91

Agnes smiled at her, her eyes sincere.

'I don't think I want to live alone, Amy. Not any more. Let's see how it goes, shall we?'

Amy's face relaxed. Thoughts of her brother seemed to be pushed into the background for the moment.

'Yes, Agnes, let's see how it goes.'

In bed that night Agnes started to wonder whether she really did want to live with Amy for ever. The sanctuary was uppermost in her thoughts, and the fact that it might grow bigger as people got to know about it.

A kennel maid or untrained helper with the assorted animals she seemed prone to collect might not be as trustworthy or as animal-minded as Amy. Indeed it was astonishing how the already resident 'house guests' Polly, Wilma and Tippy the cat had taken to Amy at once and Amy to them. But would she mind sharing with another woman on a permanent basis?

Suddenly she thought of Clancy. Would he take to Amy or would he, as the two girls had hinted, take a run at her and butt her into the mud? This made Agnes smile to herself. Well, she had to deal with Clancy herself for the next two days at least whilst Amy was coping with Robert.

She was just about to drift off to sleep when she suddenly remembered she had asked Amy to bring her brother to dinner the following evening. This woke her up with a vengeance. Tomorrow would be a hectic day. She would have Clancy to cope with as well as the others. Dogs to feed, Tippy's tray to clean. She was not allowed out yet. Also shopping for the meal, a visit to the animal food shop to get some more goat food for Clancy. Quite a day! And, also no Amy there to help her. Tomorrow she would be tackling Robert and the lawyer, Robert and the doctor, and for goodness sake, Robert and the undertaker. Agnes decided she had better get several bottles of wine to ease the stress which she felt would be considerable when they both arrived back at Kitten Cottage for the meal. She felt tired as she cuddled down to sleep at last and moved her feet over to make room for Polly.

Chapter Twelve

The next morning Amy could not leave without going to see Clancy. The animal did not back away from her but came towards her, head lowered.

'Look out, he is probably going to butt you.'

Agnes was quite worried. The ground was muddy and Amy was all dressed up for her meeting with her brother and the lawyer, not to speak of the others. The little goat did not raise his head.

'He won't butt me. Come on, Clancy, come out of there!'

The goat looked at Agnes, lowered his head further, and Agnes retreated behind the shed's open door. Clancy came out of the shed. Amy stroked his head, stroked the slanting-back horns, looked at the sores on his neck.

'His neck seems better, Agnes. I wish I hadn't got to leave you with all there is to do, but it's only today and tomorrow and then he'll be gone – Robert, I mean, not Clancy. It's a lovely name for him.'

She went out of the gate, shutting it behind her, and looked back at Clancy who was watching her leave. As the car drove off Agnes watched it disappear up the lane. The thoughts that had been half forming in her mind began to reassert themselves. Amy here permanently, sharing in the running of the house, the sanctuary . . . Was Amy the kind of person she wished to live with, perhaps for the rest of her life?

They were both, or had been, nurses. That at least they had in common, but arranging the shared finances of the house, the sanctuary, expenses, that could be a chore. Better to let Amy live in her own domain? Just come in and help?

Amy Horrocks. She remembered her first meeting with her, Agnes smiled at the thought. Amy had implied that she had been Matron of a hospital. Only later had the truth emerged that it wasn't a hospital but a residential home where she had been Matron. Agnes had been a little suspicious at the time. Amy had seemed hardly Matron material. However, that didn't matter any more. Agnes knew Amy admired her and would fall in willingly with any arrangements Agnes suggested.

Still there was Robert. Today's visit to the doctor and lawyer might go in his favour, then Amy would be devastated. No, Agnes thought, that would hardly be likely. She looked forward to meeting Robert. Roast leg of lamb, roast potatoes, French beans and cauliflower. Then perhaps cheat a little with a Tesco dessert, ice-cream of some sort and, most important, plenty to drink.

She shut up the dogs, put Tippy in a separate room, padlocked the wire enclosure door and set out for the shops. Clancy she left to run as he wished in the enclosure. She noted thankfully that his neck was indeed less inflamed and that he was cropping the grass with appetite.

'In what way do you feel I can help you, Mr . . .?'

Mr Robinson glanced down at the notes on his desk, placed the tips of his fingers together and looked up again, after obviously freshening his memory regarding the name of the man sitting opposite him on the other side of his desk. He had greeted Amy as they had been ushered into his office by his receptionist, recognizing her. She had driven her mother to his office a couple of times, though she had never stayed for their meetings. Mrs Horrocks liked complete privacy and was always secretive about her visits. Not that Amy had felt much curiosity as to what the

94

consultation was about. She would sit outside, quite happy to wait.

Now she glanced sidewards at her brother seated in the chair a couple of feet from her. He was nervous and had to clear his throat twice before he could put the question to the lawyer.

'I was only wondering, Mr Robinson, if my mother was at all confused when she altered – or I presume altered – her will. She had always told me that she would leave her house to me. It came as a great surprise, the fact that she had left me, well, so little. Hardly anything at all.'

Mr Robinson pressed his fingertips together more firmly and also cleared his throat before he replied.

'I am afraid, Mr Horrocks, I cannot make or give any opinion on such a matter. People do wish to change their wills, particularly in later life, and it is our responsibility to do what they ask, not ask why they are doing it.'

He looked, Amy thought, slightly affronted, although it was difficult to assess him as his bland expression revealed very little.

Robert was looking extremely tense. Amy noticed that his cheeks were a little flushed and the hand he gesticulated with shook a little. She felt sorry for him, but as Mr Robinson turned to her, almost as if he did not want to hear what Robert had to say, his face did show displeasure.

'Miss Horrocks, were you there when I called to see your mother to redo her will? I can't remember seeing you. You would know your mother's state of mind, I'm sure.'

Amy's turn now to apologize but she had, she felt, to tell the truth. She looked first at Robert before she began. She had to say why the day Mr Robinson had come to see her mother had remained clearly in her mind. She spoke half to the lawyer and half to her brother.

'Mr Robinson, I was out when you came that day and certainly my mother never told me why she had asked you to call on her. Usually if she wished to see you, I would drive her to your office.'

Robert broke in then, hotly and with anger.

'If you weren't even there, how did you know she had had Mr Robinson to see her? You must have known, Amy, and at least wondered why.'

Amy shook her head. She felt miserable, but for her mother's sake she had to tell the truth. She knew the lawyer had been to the house but had not had the faintest idea why. She gave her attention to the lawyer and told him about seeing the gold Parker pen down the side of the cushion. How she had drawn her mother's attention to the expensive-looking object. Then and only then had she learned that Mr Robinson had been there. Mrs Horrocks had immediately recognized it as Mr Robinson's pen and told her she must take it back to him.

The lawyer's face brightened at once.

'I remember that now, I was most upset when I got back to my office and found it was not in my case. It was eighteen carat gold and a present from my wife. I did not realize it was you who had returned it, Miss Horrocks. Thank you. I am sorry I have not had a chance to thank you before. I would have been in sore trouble.' He smiled quite benignly, then turned to Robert.

'Mr Horrocks, I do understand your feeling of surprise at the way your mother's estate was left, but as I have said, people do change their minds and their intentions. I can only say that when I had that final meeting with Mrs Horrocks she was of sound mind. I knew your mother for some years, indeed many years, and I can assure you this was so. We had quite a convivial chat, as I recall.'

He got to his feet; the meeting was over.

Amy looked at her brother. At that moment she felt very sorry for him. She thanked the lawyer, who shook her and Robert's hand then bent down and shuffled a few papers on his desk, to make it even more clear it was goodbye.

Brother and sister left the room in silence. Once outside Amy put her hand on her brother's arm. He withdrew his arm quickly.

'Let's go and have some lunch. The appointment with

96

Mother's doctor is not till three, Robert, we have time to spare.'

He shook his head, his face gloomy and withdrawn.

'I don't feel like any lunch, Amy. I feel more like a large drink, if you don't mind.'

They walked along the street, came to Amy's car which was parked in a side street, almost beside a quiet-looking, rather old-fashioned pub.

'Will this do, Robert?'

He did not answer her, but walked straight through the door and up to the bar.

'Beer and a chaser, please – and you, Amy, what will you have, a gin and tonic?'

Amy shook her head. She could almost feel the tension in her brother, the frustration and hate, directed, she was sure, against her.

'No, I'm driving. I'll just have a tomato juice.'

She walked across the rather dark bar to one of the well-polished tables and sat down. Robert paid for the drinks and came over to her and placed the glasses on the table. He sat down heavily in the chair opposite Amy.

'I'm sorry, Robert, it's turned out like this.'

He waved his hand dismissively and grimaced.

'Not your fault, Amy. Mine, I suppose. I should have sucked up to her more, but I thought it was all a foregone conclusion. More fool me, but I was always the favourite, wasn't I? You didn't have much of a time of it when you were young, did you? It's just Barbara that's my worry. You've no idea what it's like, no idea.'

'Well, tell me, Robert. Don't keep it all to yourself. You never told Mother the truth, did you? About Barbara, I mean. You just said she was doing very well in her shop and everything.'

He nodded, took a deep drink of the beer in front of him, then swallowed the whisky at a gulp.

'She was against my marrying Barbara. When I told her she had multiple sclerosis, but that I loved her anyway and would look after her, she told me I was a fool. Barbara was pretty well then, just beginning the agony, the misery.'

He put his hands over his face for a moment.

'Well, tell about now, how is she now?'

'I want another drink. I'm beginning to feel I can do nothing for her now. Nursing homes are expensive, very expensive. I was relying on Mother's money to see us through. I should have realized something might . . .'

Seeing Amy's expression of sympathy, he added, 'It's not your fault, Amy, don't blame yourself.'

'But tell me, tell me, Robert!'

Robert went to the bar and came back with more drinks and sat down, his expression grave. He looked as if he could easily burst into tears.

'All right, Amy, I'll tell you how things are with Barbara and me at the moment.'

He sipped his drink and began. He obviously wanted to spill it all out but for some reason could not. He looked fixedly at the traffic passing by. Tears were near and he was ashamed.

'I can't, Amy, I can't talk about her. How she is now, what she can or can't do, I can't!'

Robert downed his drinks, got up and turned again towards the bar. Amy felt anxious about his appointment with the doctor. These beers and chasers would hardly set him up for a rational talk, or prepare him to ask rational questions. What these questions would be Amy hadn't the faintest idea. All she was certain of was the alcohol wouldn't help him.

'Don't have any more to drink, Robert. I noticed as we came in here a sandwich bar just up the street where I parked the car. Let's go there and have some sandwiches and a cup of coffee.'

Robert turned his back on the bar and looked at his sister. He gave a half smile and shrugged his shoulders.

'You're probably right, I've probably had enough ale.'

They left the public house and strolled slowly up the street and into the sandwich bar. Inside the café, the rows of coloured Formica table-tops gleamed with cleanliness. One or two people sat at the tables, eating and reading newspapers. A girl with bright red hair was reading a paperback. She looked up as Robert and Amy came in. The sun set her hair alight, red and shining. Her eyes focused again on her book and she started to eat one of the sandwiches on her plate, ignoring the newcomers. Robert did not look in her direction.

'You go and sit down. I'll get some sandwiches and some coffee. I can manage, you sit down.'

She made her way to the counter.

Amy returned with two plates of sandwiches and two cups of steaming coffee. She put a plate and cup of coffee in front of Robert, unloaded the tray and put her plate and cup and saucer before her own place opposite her brother. He looked at his sandwiches, lifted the corner of one and looked inside it.

'Smoked salmon, my favourite. You are pushing the boat out a bit, Amy, but now you have the money, I suppose you can afford it.'

Seeing the hurt look on Amy's face, he looked ashamed.

'I'm sorry, I really didn't mean that. You didn't even know you were going to get the bloody money.'

Amy forgave him the remark at once, glad that Mr Robinson had convinced him of the truth of what she had said. As if to make up even more for his hurtful remark, Robert started on the sandwiches, his eyes fixed on the food rather than his sister. Amy began to eat as well and for a few minutes there was a strained silence between them.

Then Robert looked up at his sister and spoke, his voice thick.

'You say you're running a sanctuary, well, helping to run one. Funnily enough so am I, but at the moment I don't know how the hell mine is going to continue running, my sanctuary for one.'

He stood up and looked at his watch, pushed his now

empty plate and cup and saucer away from him. Amy would have liked to ask him what he meant. Was he referring to a sanctuary for his sick wife, the money, what? But there wasn't time.

'Yes, we'd better get moving, Robert. We've a little way to drive. Do you feel better for the food?'

She felt the drinks were affecting him.

He looked at her vacantly, pushing the chair back under the Formica-topped table, smoothing his scant hair back into place. He looked suddenly very tired, very depressed.

The journey to the doctor's was not very long and took less time than Amy had anticipated. They arrived early. The receptionist was pleasant and said the doctor would not be back for about a quarter of an hour. Would they like to sit down and wait? They sat awkwardly on two plastic chairs. Amy was longing to ask her brother what he wanted to ask the doctor that she herself could not tell him, but she resisted and did not speak.

The certificate was signed, cause of death . . . here Amy drew in her breath sharply. Dr Harris, their normal doctor who looked after most of the residents, she remembered had been away. The locum had not been best pleased about being called out to a patient he obviously felt he could do nothing for. Today Amy guessed they would see Dr Harris.

She leaned forward and picked up a magazine from the large number scattered higgledy-piggledy on the table near them. She thumbed through it. There was a full-page picture of a woman's face advertising an anti-wrinkle cream. A picture of the cream in a glass and plastic pot, the lid off and a finger dipping into the mixture. She turned to Robert and showed him the picture. Anything to break the silence, the sense of strain that had come back as the doctor's waiting room had closed around them. There were no other patients in the room. Probably the next surgery started later on in the afternoon, even the receptionist had disappeared. Robert glanced at the glossy picture Amy was showing him. His face remained expressionless.

'That is the kind of thing Barbara makes, isn't it?'

Her brother's reaction was violent. He leapt to his feet, turned his back on Amy and strode up and down the room.

'No, Amy, it's the kind of thing Barbara used to do when she was able to do anything at all, anything. Don't talk about it, please!'

Amy wanted to apologize, to say she had no idea that his wife was so incapacitated. She realized she had hurt him, but just as she was about to say all this, the reception-ist suddenly appeared at the door.

'Dr Harris is ready to see you now, Mr Horrocks, Miss Horrocks.'

Amy, relieved to be interrupted, put the magazine back on the table. She had only time to say, 'Robert, I'm so sorry. I had no idea how . . .' before they were ushered into the consulting room.

Dr Harris stood up and offered his hand to Robert and nodded a brief greeting towards Amy, not looking as if he remembered seeing her before, but that perhaps was just his manner.

Amy remembered him though and felt the same dislike for him that she had when he was treating her mother and saying 'Nothing can be done for her.' What he should have said was 'Nothing can be done for you, Miss Horrocks, to relieve you of this terrible burden.' She tried to push this thought out of her mind as she equally briefly returned his greeting and sat down.

'Well, Mr Horrocks, what can I do for you? I believe this visit is in some way connected with the death of your mother, Mrs Horrocks, is that so?'

Robert seemed to summon up courage to say what he intended to say. He sat up straighter in the chair, cleared his throat and nodded.

'Yes, indeed, Dr Harris. I was a little shocked to hear of what seemed to be my mother's sudden death. I knew

101

from my sister's letters that she was very disturbed, mentally I mean, but I didn't get the impression she was in danger of death. As I say I was quite shocked to hear . . .'

Dr Harris lifted his hand as if to stop the flow of Robert's words. He looked slightly put out, impatient.

'Mr Horrocks, your mother was seriously ill as far as her mind was concerned. The condition of the patient's general health in these kind of cases is always cause for concern. Her heart, blood pressure, were all unstable, changeable as her dementia worsened. It is inevitable.'

Robert was silenced. He was about to break the silence with further questions – Amy could not imagine what they would be – when Dr Harris spoke again, severely and with the obvious intention of finishing the conversation, which he felt Amy was well aware to be a criticism of his practice and his medical acumen.

'Mr Horrocks, I myself was not present at your late mother's death, but my locum, a most reliable and able doctor, was and I am sure you have seen a copy of Mrs Horrocks' death certificate. You can be assured it is in order and correct. That is my final comment and I cannot imagine why you questioned it.'

Dr Harris leant back in his chair and put his fingers together in the manner of Mr Robinson. Amy, as she noticed this, felt a hysterical desire to laugh, but relief at Dr Harris's remarks about her mother's death, with no hint of suspicion that it was hurried by the administration of any drug, was like a rock being lifted from her shoulders, a huge rock.

Dr Harris had however not quite finished. Still keeping his fingertips neatly together, he looked at Robert reproachfully and his voice changed.

'I feel I must add, Mr Horrocks, that you have done your sister no service by questioning this matter. The last few weeks of your mother's life were not easy for Miss Horrocks. She handled the disturbances your mother caused with patience and care, not that Mrs Horrocks could help herself in any way of course. Even medication is not much help in this condition.'

He got to his feet. Amy felt vindicated to some extent about what she had done. Dr Harris put out his hand and shook hands with her. He did not offer his hand to Robert. Robert looked like a dog who has been told off by its master. Amy felt very sorry for him. She had killed her mother but Robert seemed to be getting the stick. Life was not fair. Suddenly she thought of Clancy with his sore neck, his starved little body. No life was ever fair, never.

The receptionist gave them a cheery smile as they passed through her office, but Robert was too preoccupied to notice the girl. As they reached the door, he pushed it open and let Amy out before him.

'He didn't say when she became . . . you know, Amy, out of her mind, incapable of reasonable thinking. He didn't say that, did he?'

Amy gave a deep sigh. She wished Robert was back in Australia, out of her sight. She tried to be pleasant.

'Tonight we are having dinner with Agnes. You will like her, I am sure, Robert. You can talk to her about Mother. She never knew her, of course, but I have told her all about my time with her.'

Robert got into the car, pulling forward his seat-belt.

'I don't know that I want to talk to anyone about it, Amy, especially a stranger. I seem to be getting nowhere anyway.'

Amy nearly burst into tears. She started the car. She felt he was behaving badly, yet she was conscious too that the real sinner was herself, not about the money alone, but about prematurely ending her mother's life.

Chapter Thirteen

At Kitten Cottage Agnes was preparing the evening meal for Amy and her brother. She was looking forward to meeting him. According to Amy, the change in him was remarkable. From, as Amy described him, rather a domineering, self-assured man, always dapper in his appearance and youthful-looking, he had turned into a dismal middle-aged man.

Agnes hoped the meal would cheer him up. She did not like or enjoy cooking. She preferred to be cooked for and at first had considered taking them out to eat at an hotel. However, she had decided a meal at home would probably be more comfortable for talking, particularly if the appointments with the lawyer and the doctor had been completely unproductive from Robert's point of view as Agnes was certain they would be. Neither lawyers nor doctors were likely to reverse a decision they had already made.

Having got everything as ready as possible Agnes called the two dogs and went with them into the wire enclosure. Clancy looked up as she clanged the door of the enclosure behind her. He was standing just outside the open door of the shed. Having looked, he ignored Agnes and the two dogs and went on eating from the little trough of goat pellets Agnes had put out for him that morning. Polly chased about after the ball thrown for her. Wilma sat down near Agnes, gazing as if to say, like an old person, 'They must run about. These young ones can't sit still for a moment.'

Agnes squatted down beside Horace's little enclosure. Each morning she or Amy moved him to a fresh piece of grass. He moved around each new place, bumping into the wood of his fenced-in area, walking with difficulty because he had lost the injured foot. Agnes watched him. Was it fair, was his life worthwhile? The reason Agnes had not had him put down at the vet's was really because she was thinking of the two boys who had brought him to her. It had been a good responsible gesture. It would have been a strange response to their faith in the sanctuary, as she had suggested to the vet, if on their next visit she was to tell them, 'He's dead, we had to put him to sleep. That's all there was for him.'

What it would have done to their childish faith in adults goodness knows. There was enough devious behaviour and deceit amongst the adults around the young already. But what of Horace, was he then just being used to make it appear that she was caring and trustworthy? Agnes sighed. What of Amy's mother? What was her quality of life when Amy 'put her down', 'put her to sleep'? Agnes got up. Was it a question of degree? Horace could amble about, eat all his food with enjoyment and did not appear to be in pain, whereas Mrs Horrocks had been screaming mad, violent at times according to her daughter, incontinent, no dignity left. Of course Amy had been right in what she had done, quite right. Agnes felt it was in a way her job to make Amy recognize that she had nothing to feel guilty about, nothing at all.

Agnes looked down at Horace who was just demolishing his dog food, making a snuffling noise as he did so, as he always did.

'Perhaps you're getting more joy out of life than Amy's mother, Horace!'

She called the dogs, walked round closer to Clancy. His neck sore was still there but no longer bleeding. He and Wilma put their noses together. Clancy, uninterested, resumed his morning meal. Agnes went indoors, looked at the time, and lit the oven so it would soon be ready to put the joint in and went into the dining room to lay the table. Outside the evening was warm. Agnes decided to let Clancy and Horace stay out a little longer and enjoy the late sun.

She wasn't quite sure when Amy and Robert would be arriving. Her mind was still on the problem of Horace and Mrs Horrocks – a philosophical mood. She got up and mixed herself a brandy and ginger ale. She was thinking of Robert's wife and wondering how she fitted into the picture of Horace and Mrs Horrocks. Was she so bad? Was that why Robert was fighting to prove the will invalid and the money really his?

She got up half-way through her drink and placed the lamb in the oven. It wouldn't take long, it was quite a small leg. She sat down again and went on sipping her drink. The thought of, what was her name . . . Barbara Horrocks would not go away.

Agnes got up again and went upstairs into Amy's room.

They both had medicine cabinets in their bedrooms – nurse-like – but not locked. Agnes opened Amy's cupboard. Aspirin, Rennies, camomile lotion, liquid paraffin, nitrazepam. Agnes was a little surprised at that. A box, new-looking, contained a bottle of Optrex and an eye bath. Hidden behind this was something she had half expected. A brown old–fashioned glass bottle, the label half taken off, but the name still readable: *Mrs A. Coleman*. Agnes took out the bottle and looked at it. It was still half-full of the yellow capsules Agnes knew so well. Nembutal. She put it in her pocket and pushed the Optrex carton a shade back.

Carefully she closed the door. The other half of those yellow capsules had been useful, very useful. Perhaps the remainder, the other half, could be equally useful. One could never tell! Perhaps one to two could end Horace's life, if she came to the conclusion that he was not happy with what was left to him.

But she knew she was not thinking of Horace. She was

thinking of Barbara Horrocks, a long long way away in Australia. Was her quality of life good enough? She would wait, talk to Amy's brother and find out more.

At that moment she heard Amy's car draw into the drive, the wheels crunched on the gravel. Agnes turned up the oven a little and put in the potatoes. She did not go into the hall to greet her guests. She knew Amy would be shy in introducing her brother after her comments about him the night before. After a few seconds they came into the room. Both Amy and Robert looked tired and depressed.

'Agnes, may I introduce my brother Robert?'

Amy was her usual formal nervous self.

Agnes came forward and took Robert's hand, not a usual gesture for her. She motioned towards the settee and Robert sat down as if he was glad to take the weight off his legs. Amy sat down beside him.

'You could do with a drink, Robert. Amy?'

After the drinks were served the atmosphere did relax a little. Agnes asked both of them outright how their day had been. It was a second or two before either answered. Then Robert spoke. His tone was bitter and he kept his eyes on his sister, almost ignoring Agnes.

'Well, I suppose you know all about the situation, Mrs Turner. I came here to contest my mother's will, but the way everyone – well, up to now – is answering my questions, it would seem I have little or practically no hope. Tomorrow I hope Amy will take me to see a Mrs Allen, Lily Allen, who worked at the residential home, as my sister is pleased to call it, when my mother died there and a year or so before.'

The roasting lamb in the kitchen was sending out delicious smells. Agnes excused herself and went and basted the little joint. Things had not gone so well, she thought. The wish to see this Lily Allen had obviously come as a surprise to Amy.

Was she alarmed, Agnes wondered? Could the helper, or auxiliary nurse or whatever she was called, perhaps shed more light – and perhaps for Amy a more disquietening light – on Mrs Horrocks' death? How, Agnes wondered, had Robert found out about her? Perhaps Amy had mentioned Mrs Allen in her telephone calls to Australia? She walked back into the sitting room where the brother and sister sat in complete silence.

'Just time for the other half of your drinks before the meal is ready.'

The vegetables were cooking and all seemed well in the kitchen but Agnes felt if the atmosphere persisted between the two of them it wasn't going to be a particularly pleasant evening.

Agnes left them and went into the kitchen to get on with cooking. Now and again, she went to the kitchen door to listen to see if Amy and Robert were talking. Surely they must have a lot to say to each other about today's visits, or about Barbara. Perhaps they had done the talking already, because not a sound came from the room in which they were both sitting. She returned to the stove. Well, Amy had told her nothing more about her brother except her astonishment in his appearance.

At last she took the food into the dining room and called them to say the meal was ready. The two filed into the dining room and sat down, still silent. Agnes had to do something to make things seem a little more normal.

'Robert, would you like to carve for me? I'm not very good at carving. It's only a small joint but perhaps . . .'

Robert carved beautifully and during dinner thanked Agnes for having him to her house. Agnes had a slight glimpse of the other Robert then. Amy loosened up a little too.

Conversation revived a little.

Amy was to drive him back to his boarding house. Agnes asked what the programme was for tomorrow. She asked the question as tactfully as she could. She already knew – because Amy had told her – that he wanted to see the undertaker, and apparently now also the crematorium to which his mother was taken. In a way, if Robert had been fond of his mother, Agnes could understand this sort of pilgrimage.

'When are you due to fly back to Australia, Robert?'

He shrugged his shoulders.

'I cannot leave Barbara for long, but I would like another couple of days at least. It's a long and tiring journey.'

Amy spoke up, rather sharply, frowning.

'I only booked you in the bed and breakfast for two nights, Robert! She may not be able to put you up.'

Again he shrugged as if he felt it didn't matter much. Agnes felt rather sorry for him. By the sound of it, he wasn't going to get anywhere with contesting his mother's will. Amy seemed pretty cold towards him.

'Amy, your brother could stay here for a few nights and fix the flight up for Friday. He can sleep in the spare room. It's quite comfortable . . . if you would like to, Robert?'

She turned to him. He hesitated before he answered.

'Thank you, I would like to.' Then he said, 'I'd like to go and see our house, Amy. We could do that, before I go back.'

Agnes felt that Amy agreed with a certain reluctance, but at least she agreed, and when the two of them got into Amy's car Robert looked more relaxed and less miserable than when he had arrived at Kitten Cottage earlier that evening.

Agnes waved them off.

'See you tomorrow evening then, Robert. You both may have to have a cold meal though.'

Robert nodded and smiled as they drove off.

Agnes went back into the house. There was the washing up to do, which she hated, and then the animals to cope with, which she loved. She decided to do the washing up first.

Why had she burdened herself with Amy's brother, she wondered? Mainly because she felt rather sorry for him. During his short stay maybe she could get him to talk to her a little about his wife and her illness and his life at home. According to Amy, while they were keeping their various appointments, waiting for the lawyer and the doctor and eating various meals together between the appointments, Robert had never mentioned the health of his wife Barbara. Amy had said that his reply, whenever she asked about his life at home, was always the same, non-committal and evasive, and that he would turn his head away, sometimes looking as if he was trying to hide something, didn't want to tell. She thought her brother was unstable, depressive.

Agnes felt Robert had something to be depressed about, something he did not want to talk about or maybe something he could not put into words. She hoped he would feel more able to talk to someone he did not know as well as he knew his sister Amy.

How often this had been the case with Agnes herself, when her troubles had nearly crushed her. She had longed to tell someone, anyone who was not in any way connected with her problem. But she, in a way like Robert, had possessed the gift, or was it a curse, of keeping her own counsel. Carrying secrets with you sometimes until they almost ate you away.

Well, if Robert wanted to confide in anyone she would try to make it possible for him to confide in her. It should be easy if he stayed a couple of days. Maybe she could help him. Maybe not but the chance of doing something excited her a little. Delving into other people's problems, learning things about them they had kept secret for years, usually for a good reason, always interested Agnes. Knowing something about a person, something which no one else knew, gave her a feeling of power. Usually she had no cause to use this knowledge, this confession, but once or twice in her life it had been extraordinarily useful.

Chapter Fourteen

Amy and Robert stood outside their old home. The house looked bigger than Amy remembered it. The garden had been altered, the drive made slightly wider and covered with new shining gravel. The front door had been painted blue instead of the pale green that their mother had always favoured.

'Can we go in, do you think, say we used to live here and would like to see the inside again?'

Robert had his hand on the latch of the gate.

Amy shook her head with more determination than usual. The place was abhorrent to her, bringing back as it did what had happened there. The memories of her running the home, giving up her beloved job at the hospital to slave away, trying to keep it financially viable, the patients, everything about it had been a disaster.

Robert's description of his old home was quite different.

'Do you remember Mum and Dad taking us to that pantomime, what was it . . .? I know, *Jack and the Beanstalk*, and Dad walked out because of the music. How he hated pop!'

Amy could not remember the incident at all.

'Dad thought I could be anything. A footballer, a rugby player, a brilliant cricketer, but Mum opted for a lawyer, a doctor or an accountant.'

'Well, you were clever, Robert. You had a good brain.'

Robert shook his head and laughed but the laughter was not real. It was ironic and sarcastic.

'Brains? I had no brains, Amy. They doted on me so much they thought I could do anything I set my mind to.

I knew better. I knew my own capabilities. Academically I was a mess, I just pretended.'

The next visit was to the crematorium. Robert was quieter here. He walked in, his footsteps echoing on the polished wood floor. He stood for a moment looking at the draped curtains gleaming, their colour accentuated by the sunlight on them. Amy tried not to look at them.

'That's where she went, was it, through those curtains? Well, it wouldn't have made any difference if I was here or I wasn't here, would it?'

He shook his head and turned abruptly and walked out of the chapel.

'There were lots of flowers, Robert, and quite a lot of people came, I told you that on the telephone.'

'I know, I know, but it didn't stop her altering her will, did it? You can't imagine what that money would have meant to me, Amy, but it wasn't to be.'

After a brief visit to the undertaker's office they drove back to the boarding house to collect his things. Amy paid the bill and sat on the bed and watched as her brother packed his few possessions into his case. She felt ill at ease.

'Did you need the money for Barbara, Robert?'

She asked the question almost timidly. He pressed down the lid of the case and ran the zip around it before he answered her question.

'What do you think, Amy, what do you think?'

He picked up the case and as the proprietor let them out, he thanked her pleasantly.

As they drove away Robert glanced sideways at his sister then said rather reluctantly, 'Thank you, Amy. Considering why I came here, to contest Mother's will, I must say you have been very kind and generous in helping me. I would not have been surprised if you had taken offence and not offered to help me either financially or in any other way. You've been very decent.'

Amy shook her head and managed a smile. A wintry one.

'I'm glad to do it for you, Robert. If you felt in any way

I had influenced our mother, made her change her mind, done you out of what you considered to be your rightful inheritance, I thought you should have the chance to prove it. Or maybe I should have the chance to prove I had nothing whatever to do with it.'

Her brother shifted uneasily in his seat and did not add anything further. Eventually, so quietly that Amy could hardly hear his words, he said, 'Well, we'll see this nurse or helper or whatever she was, Mrs Allen, wasn't it? I wonder what she made of Mother's mental state.'

Amy remembered where Lily Allen lived because she had given her a lift home once or twice. She also remembered that she had worked for her only part time, four days a week. Mrs Allen had two young children whom she managed to park with her mother-in-law four days a week. Whether she had been at the home the day her mother had died Amy simply could not remember.

In any case it would have made little difference as Amy had sat down with her mother when she breathed her last and waited for her to die.

Amy had telephoned Mrs Allen to say they would be calling. When they drew up at the small terraced house the door opened while they were getting out of the car. Lily Allen was most welcoming and smiling.

'Miss Horrocks, how nice to see you again. Do come in, I have made some coffee for us.'

They followed her through the narrow hall.

She led the way through into the sitting room where two young children were playing with toys over by the window. They looked about eight and ten years old.

'Half-term, so I've got them both at home, not knowing what to do with themselves.'

She shoved the two children outside into the back garden. They ran out followed by a rough black and white dog who looked very ready to join the children's play.

'Do sit down.'

Robert did not look at Amy.

Mrs Allen disappeared into the kitchen and came back

with a tray of three cups of steaming coffee, all before Amy had a chance to introduce her brother Robert. Mrs Allen put the tray down.

'This is my brother Robert, Mrs Allen, from Australia. He has come on a sort of little pilgrimage as he unfortunately could not get to our mother's funeral.'

Mrs Allen got up to shake hands with Robert.

'Oh, that must be very sad for you, not to be able to get here, but Australia is such a long way away. It is good that you could come now to pay your respects. I hope it has not been too painful?'

Robert murmured something and drank his coffee. Mrs Allen went on, obviously trying to be helpful.

'I knew your dear mother quite well. She was a lovely lady, always polite and thankful for what you did for her.'

Robert at last asked a question which made Amy tremble a little. How would Lily Allen answer him? She need not have worried. Lily's answer was non-committal.

'When did my mother become strange, irrational, out of her mind? Was it long before her death?'

'Oh, no, Mr Horrocks, thankfully she died soon after her poor mind went. She started to wander off, get out of bed, and created a great worry for Miss Horrocks, and indeed for all of us. I was not there the day she died. I think it was my day off, wasn't it?'

Amy broke in, looking towards her former employee.

'Lily was very good to Mother, Robert. Mother was very fond of her. Lily came to the funeral.'

Robert was silent for a moment or two, then he suddenly got up. Amy saw from the expression on his face that he felt nothing more could be learned. She hoped he was at last convinced that she had done nothing to influence their mother to change her will. The overdose that she had administered she knew had not even entered his mind. Robert thanked Mrs Allen for all she had done for Mrs Horrocks. His manner was formal but sincere.

114

'I'm sure you all did everything you could.'

They left the house and got into Amy's car. She looked at him; he looked grave but satisfied.

'Okay, shall we go back to Kitten Cottage now?' she asked.

He nodded and Amy started the car. Perhaps she had dreaded the interview with Lily more than those with the doctor or lawyer. Anyway it was all settled now, over, and soon Robert would go home. Australia was so far away. She wondered as she drove, once he had left, would she ever see him again? She was sadly certain that she would not want to cross the world to meet him again, or his wife. She felt no desire to meet her. She supposed in a way it was a shame. Brother and sister should have some bond between them, but even when they were children they had never been close, seldom played together. Never confided childish secrets.

Amy had always realized that their parents set great store by their son, rather than their daughter. She had resented the fact then and had never succeeded in banishing the feeling of hurt and resentment.

They were almost back at Kitten Cottage before Robert spoke.

'It was strange seeing the house again with new owners, no longer our home, just strangers. I was unhappy there, but it gave one a pang to see it.'

'Unhappy there, Robert, with Mother and Dad thinking so much of you, expecting so much of you, their darling?'

Robert laughed rather ruefully and rubbed his eyes.

'That was it, Amy, you put it so well. Expecting so much of me, an expectation I was never able to fulfil. They kept on expecting something wonderful of me. I don't know. I got tired of their expectations and opted out. Now I've got what I deserve, I suppose, nothing.'

He said no more during the rest of the drive back to Kitten Cottage and Agnes Turner.

*   *   *

115

Agnes knew she was in for a busy day and was relieved to see Amy's car drive away. She needed some time to herself.

Soon after they had gone a man arrived with a new sign for the gate. The new name was printed across what was pretending to be a piece of wood but was actually made of plastic. The words *The Sanctuary* stood out well from the light tan background. Agnes had decided that it would be a more appropriate name, but she hoped the change would not muddle the postman, delivery men or perhaps people who thought, or had been told, that Kitten Cottage was the place to bring injured or homeless animals.

They must get used to the new name.

The workman, someone she had met in the village or hamlet about two miles down the road, was going to be a boon or a blessing. As well as fixing the new sign he had also put a new padlock on the wire enclosure gate and taken off the shed door which was badly warped and would not shut properly. He shaved the bottom of it and rehung the door. Clancy, after a half-hearted attempt to run at him, head down, had stopped and then looked away as the man, John Hudson by name, spoke to him, not particularly harshly, but firmly.

'Now, mate, none of that. You haven't got the weight for it and your horns grow the wrong way. So just cool it.'

Clancy resumed his chewing with a watchful eye on this new individual talking to him and decided against acting goatish.

'You are not Dr Doolittle by any chance?' Agnes said, smiling.

The man shook his head, smiling also.

'No, miss, but I like animals. I reckon they are on the whole more reliable and truthful than most humans. Present company excepted, of course.'

He lifted the shed door into place and screwed the hinges on. The tool made a sharp screeching noise which sent Clancy off across the enclosure, running and jumping.

When the job was finished Agnes made a cup of coffee

116

for them both and they sat at the kitchen table. While drinking the coffee she told him about her ideas for the sanctuary. It was very relaxing to talk to someone, a complete stranger, about her very small plans for the future.

'I just want to look after any animal that is brought to my gate who needs caring for or has suffered cruelty or neglect.'

John Hudson drained his coffee and got up.

'Well, miss, any odd jobs you want done, count on me. I reckon animals have a rough deal. They could do with some champions.'

A peal on the doorbell, or rather the gate bell, interrupted them. Agnes was pleased to see it was the two boys who had brought Horace to the cottage.

They had called several times to see how the little hedgehog was getting on, the last time was only a couple of days ago, and Agnes, though pleased, was surprised to see them again so soon. Both of them looked rather sheepish. The small one was carrying a box, a cardboard box. 'Billy blue eyes' opened the tattered box.

'It's another Horace. We found him on the road again, about where the other one was. He's another boy, though. They won't start anything funny and make babies.'

Agnes tried to hide her smile and peered into the box. The blue-eyed cherub-like Billy pushed back his curls with his free hand and nearly dropped the box.

'Watch it, cack hand. Here, give it to me.'

Tim took the box and opened it more fully. The little animal moved around, leaving a trail of blood which appeared to be coming from its nose or mouth. But it moved without apparent difficulty.

'It's its mouth what's hurt, miss. You don't mind, do you, we're leaving tomorrow morning early, you know, moving on.'

'Moving on?'

Agnes looked for explanation towards the taller boy, whose shaven head was now covered with a fuzz which looked as if it would eventually be red.

'Yes, we're travellers see. People want us off the green, had enough of us. You know how they are!'

'Well, I don't really know. What will you do about school and where will you move to now?'

Billy shrugged. Agnes took the box from them.

'Come in. Would you like some orange juice, a piece of cake?'

In the kitchen, after placing the box just inside the garden enclosure, Agnes put large glasses of real orange juice in front of both of them and a plate of Amy's fairy cakes. There were eight on the plate. The boys ate three each but with a trace of good manners left two on the plate.

'Do finish them up.'

Almost before Agnes had got the words out Amy's cakes were gone.

'So I won't be seeing you any more then. I'm sorry.'

The bigger boy's cheeks flushed as Agnes said this.

'There aren't many people who would say that, miss, I can tell you.'

The younger one, wolfing down the last piece of his cake, grinned. He took the last swig of his orange juice.

'Oh, you may see us again, miss, if we manage to get the bikes and don't get pushed too far away. We'll come and see you and Horace and Harry – that's what we've called the other one – if you take him in, miss?'

Agnes nodded.

'Yes, I'll look after him and I will always be pleased to see you both if you want to come. If you get bikes? Will you get them for presents? They are expensive.'

Agnes was aware that Tim gave Billy a swift kick on the leg beneath the kitchen table.

'Oh, they'll be second-hand ones and we won't get them till we move on, I expect . . . well, maybe we will. You can't tell with Dad, but he's okay.'

Agnes had a nasty feeling that the bikes in question might perhaps in some way be related to the move and their dad might . . .

No, she dismissed the idea, she didn't want to think ill of these two boys.

After they had gone she went out with some warm water and swabs to have a look at the new recruit. Harry, as the boys had called him, was livelier than poor little Horace who had been half starved. This one was fatter. Once the blood had been washed off his nose she found a small cut. Agnes put him in one of the straw-carpeted cages to recover from the shock of being boxed and handled. She decided tomorrow she would introduce him to Horace in the morning, to see if they fought or got on together.

She had no idea how male hedgehogs behaved. Maybe they would fight. If so she would have to keep them separately until Harry, if he recovered, could be taken to a safe place as far from a road as possible and let loose.

The dogs to walk, John Hudson to pay – and she must arrange with him to do some other odd jobs that wanted doing. Tippy's tray, the three of them to feed. Agnes made herself some sandwiches after all this, then started to prepare the cold meal for Amy and her brother when they returned in the evening.

After going to see their mother's house, the undertaker and the crematorium, Amy and her brother would be depressed, might even have quarrelled. Agnes was not sorry she had asked Robert to stay for a couple of days. However Amy had acted towards him, she felt he would be affected by her behaviour. Agnes was still wondering whether to ask Amy if she would like to take up her abode with her permanently and a lot depended on whether her brother had done anything to upset her. If she felt so guilty about having the money or resentful about her brother's attitude, she might decide to pack up and leave, go somewhere well away from her, and not tell Robert where she had gone. Agnes felt she could make no decisions yet about any coming or going.

Agnes realized that the small piece of lamb left from last night's dinner when carved into pieces for three would not be enough, so she decided to drive out and purchase some

119

more cold meats from the local store. Quite a drive! She was soon back and cutting up cooked new potatoes to make a potato salad to go with the lettuce, tomatoes, spring onions and cut-up avocado. She laid the table and sat down to look at the news.

She felt tired and was not looking forward to walking the dogs or putting the hedgehogs and Clancy in for the night. She decided to wait a bit and give the job to Amy if she arrived back with Robert early enough to take the dogs out after they had eaten their meal.

At about twenty to six Agnes heard Amy's car draw up. She hastily mixed the drinks she knew they liked and felt would probably be badly needed. She was right. Both came into the sitting room, looking as miserable as Agnes had expected. She knew that they had been to look at their old home and also that they had been to see one of Amy's old employees, a nurse or auxiliary, someone who either had been present at Mrs Horrocks' death, which might frighten and upset Amy, or hadn't been present, which would disappoint Robert.

It appeared that the latter was the case, the woman hadn't been there. All the day's happenings spilled out from both Amy and Robert. Amy's brother had felt very nostalgic on seeing his old home. Amy confessed that she had not, but then, as Agnes suggested, Robert had spent his youth there, presumably a happy time. Amy, though, had taken a great deal of flak there, had to leave a post she loved to go and live there, cope with her mother in her good days and later in her bad and distressing days and nights.

After another drink while the soup gently heated, Agnes dished up and the three of them went through to the dining room. However miserable they had been during the day, they both appeared to enjoy the meal. Robert remarked that this was his favourite kind of meal, then looked slightly embarrassed and added quickly, 'Not that I didn't enjoy your lovely roast last night, Agnes, but cold meats and salad are great favourites with me.'

Agnes gave him points for sensitivity.

The meal finished, Robert offered to do the washing up, but Agnes suggested coffee first in the sitting room. Amy refused and went and put her coat on, saying she would walk the dogs, put Clancy to bed and see to the hedgehogs. Whether she wanted to give Robert and Agnes time to have a talk without her being there, Agnes was not sure. Anyway, if Robert wanted to talk about the will or his wife or Australia, she was prepared to listen, not to voice any opinion about any of the things that had happened since the death of Mrs Horrocks or poor Amy's dealing with the situation.

She realized she must be careful about answering any questions, should he ask them. About Mrs Horrocks' death, her state of mind, the changing of the will. She brought in two steaming cups of coffee and placed them on the table. Robert was gazing at the blank television screen, apparently lost in thought. He started as he heard the coffee cup put down and seemed to come back from whatever he had been thinking about. His eyes focused on Agnes then down to the coffee in front of him. He noticed the small glass beside the cup.

'Cherry brandy. I hope you like a liqueur, Robert, we don't have them often, only on special occasions.'

He smiled, picked up the glass and took a small sip, licked his lips.

'Thank you, Agnes, you have been so kind to me. I think that Amy has found a good friend, I really do. She has been very kind too.'

'I hope so. I am fond of your sister. She loves all animals, just as I do, and that makes a great bond between us as I am sure you can imagine.'

Robert nodded, sipped his coffee and seemed to slip back into his preoccupation. Agnes thought he might be thinking, worrying, about Barbara his wife.

Agnes sat quietly, not saying a word. She felt Robert might not want to talk to her, might feel it was disloyal to his sister to even mention anything about their present problems.

But, quite suddenly, Robert drained the little liqueur

121

glass, leaned back in his seat and looked directly at Agnes. It wasn't Amy he started to talk about, it was Barbara. His fists clenched, his eyes closed for a moment, then he burst out almost brokenly.

'It wasn't always such a mess. Barbara could do a little, though it grew less and less. I was quite successful. I had a job as a financial adviser, we weren't doing badly.'

Then as the disease progressed, he had to stay at home and nurse his wife, backed up with the thought that one day, although he didn't wish his mother dead, one day he would inherit his mother's money and be able to employ a nurse.

Agnes listened to him with complete sympathy. When she suggested that there might be a home where his wife could be looked after, he waved this aside. Apparently there were places Barbara could be admitted to but he had been to see two of them. He couldn't let her go there. The private homes were expensive but there again he had been counting on his mother's money so that if the worst came to the worst Barbara could go to one of these and have a room of her own, not simply be shut away in a geriatric ward.

The news that his mother had changed her will and he would get nothing, Barbara would get nothing, had come like a bomb falling on all his plans to make life a little better for her. 'Though God knows, in her present condition,' he added, 'life is not worth living, it's just a burden to her.'

Agnes fingered the brown bottle in her cardigan pocket. There were enough capsules to release anyone from a life that was not worth living. But she must know more.

At that moment Wilma made her stately way into the room followed by an excited Polly. They could hear Amy hanging up the collars and leads in the hall. She would be in the room in a few seconds. Agnes turned to Robert.

'Why have you not told your sister about your wife's condition? She seems to know little or nothing about Barbara. Why?'

Robert turned to her, his face contorted.

'And beg her for money, because I can't support an ill wife? I can't do that, Agnes, I cannot do that. I married Barbara and I love her with all her problems, with all my heart and soul. That sounds mawkish and dramatic, but that's how it is. There is a trained nurse, a friend, looking after Barbara while I am away. How she is going to manage, I can't dare to think, but she offered to do it and I am paying her what I can, which is not much.'

'Tell me exactly how Barbara is now, Robert. What her condition is. Please – I want to know. I may be able to help you.'

At that moment Amy walked into the room. She looked better for her walk and contact with her beloved animals.

'We must talk again, Robert, it has been most interesting and helpful, I am sure.'

Robert looked at her as if he didn't quite know or understand what she meant, but he nodded.

'Yes indeed, Agnes, it has been a relief to let it all out, but if you want to know more about how things are at home, I can't talk about it now.'

Amy came forward smiling.

'We've had a lovely walk, Agnes. Clancy's safely in the shed and the hedgehogs are put to bed.'

'I'll make some more coffee, Amy. You missed that and the liqueur. We will all have a repeat dose.'

Robert got up.

'Can I help?' he asked.

Agnes shook her head and went out to the kitchen, leaving the two of them together. But she was still determined to find out the exact details of Barbara's condition. Much more about it than she already had learned from Robert. What she had in mind was complete release for that imprisoned woman so far away. That was a terrible decision but one she was not afraid to take. She never had been.

Chapter Fifteen

The next day, Wednesday, Amy had a rather urgent appointment with her dentist. Robert had managed to defer his plane trip till Friday afternoon so he had two more days to stay with Amy and Agnes at what was now called The Sanctuary.

Agnes had half expected him to suggest he accompany his sister, if only for the drive. However, he said he would like to stay and help Agnes with the animals. As Agnes watched Amy drive away she could sense the relief in Amy. She waved as she drove off, a slight smile on her face. Agnes felt that after the change in her mother's will, the rift between brother and sister would never heal.

'Dog walks first, Robert!'

At the word 'walks', Polly pricked her ears, head on one side, then rushed off and came back with her lead. Wilma just raised her ears slightly and stood ready at the door, quite as aware as Polly of what the word 'walkie' meant.

'We can drive up to the Downs and give them a good run and ourselves a good walk – if you feel like it?'

Up on the Downs, the breeze ruffled the short mossy grass. Robert remarked on it as he walked, looking down at the ground.

'It's like walking on a cushion. We've nothing like this turf. Not in Australia – well, not as far as I know. It's such a huge place, there may be something similar somewhere.'

Agnes interrupted his thoughts as they walked, determined to try and get to know him better.

'Do you like Australia, Robert? Is it – did you find you were homesick, wanting to come back to this country – after you were married, I mean?'

Robert shook his head and kicked a round pebble which looked as if it had come straight off the beach, though the sea was a long way away. They had walked quite far and now they halted at a convenient bench seat. Both dogs came over and sat down at their feet, Wilma panting a little.

Agnes thought, as so much time elapsed before Robert spoke, that he had forgotten or perhaps chosen to ignore her question. She thought perhaps it had been too intimate, but she was wrong. When they were comfortably seated and Agnes had snapped on Polly's lead for safety's sake, Robert broke his silence.

'It was only – it was only such a small thing, Agnes. Such a small thing. She used to trip with one foot, going up steps. Nothing to worry about, we thought. We used to laugh about it even.'

Robert bent forward, elbows on his knees, hands covering his face. His wedding ring shone in the sunshine. He rubbed his eyes with his fingers.

Once started he seemed unable to stop. From the first small imperfection, the tripping on steps, he described the whole sad story of Barbara's decline. Agnes had some difficulty in hearing what he was saying until at last he leant back and took his hands down from his face. His eyes looked red and Agnes suspected that behind his hands he had been trying to suppress the tears. The story he told was enough, she thought, to provoke tears.

The little trip on the stairs became worse and once or twice she fell. Then her sight began to deteriorate, and a visit to the doctor dealt a blow to them both. She was on the downward slide to multiple sclerosis. It sounded such a list of one disaster after another that Agnes wondered how the two of them had been able to support it. At this

125

point Robert put his hand in his jacket pocket and took out a pack of cigarettes and a lighter. Agnes looked surprised.

'I didn't know you smoked, Robert – I hope you haven't felt you couldn't smoke in Kitten Cottage?'

He didn't answer, but lit the cigarette and drew on it deeply. The air was so still now that the smoke from his pursed lips came out straight and drifted away, keeping its shape. The little breeze had disappeared.

It was clear now to Agnes why Robert had been counting on his mother's money. Barbara's legs had become paralysed as had her right arm, and her speech was now slurred.

'She is helpless, Agnes. I wanted her to go into a good nursing home. She needs a great deal of nursing care, she's incontinent now.'

'It must be terrible, Robert. Too awful for you, but did your mother know all this?'

'Some of it, a little. But Barbara made me swear not to tell her I had a wife who could do nothing for herself. She needs constant care now. The friend who is looking after her told me she could manage a week. It has been wonderful. I know I shouldn't say it's good to be here away from Barbara, but the nights back home are sheer hell. To be able to go to bed and sleep without half listening for her to call me has been like heaven.'

Polly started frisking about on the end of her lead and Wilma stood up too and stretched.

'We'd better get back, Robert. Thank you for telling me all this. It may relieve you a little. It's good to talk, as they say!'

Robert crushed his cigarette out on the concrete beneath the seat. He smoothed Wilma's head. The dog's tail wagged slowly to and fro and they started to walk back to the car.

'I don't want you to think I want to be away from Barbara. I love her so much, Agnes. Not a moment of a day

126

goes by but I think of her, what she is doing, what she is having to put up with at this moment.'

He put Wilma's lead on as they were getting nearer the road now.

'People talk about remissions, times of partial recovery.' Robert's voice sounded bitter. 'But Barbara, as far as I can see, has never had any kind of remission, not one. Every change is worse, further downhill.'

They got to the car and Agnes put the two dogs in the back. She didn't start the car at once. The nurse in her made her ask the next question. If Robert did not feel like answering it, he certainly need not.

'Have you, or has Barbara, ever tried cannabis, Robert? There are such different medical opinions about the drug being able to give some relief to certain patients.'

Robert shook his head and lit another cigarette.

'No, never can get hold of any, it's very expensive. I did try. That's another thing about Mother's will. I felt if we got her money I really could buy some of it, just to see if it would help Barbara.'

Agnes started to drive towards home. Robert threw the unfinished cigarette out of the car window. He drew a long breath and let it out in a great sigh. He rubbed his forehead.

'Oh Agnes, what I could have done for her with that money. What I could have done for her, my poor darling. Not make her happy, but more comfortable.'

She did not reply – after all, what was there to say? She did wonder, though, how much of this story Robert had told Amy.

Back at the house Agnes made coffee for both of them. She wanted to lighten the mood a little. She told him the story of Tippy the black cat and how cruelly she had been treated by her owner, Mrs Symington Smythe, followed by the trick she had managed to play on the beastly Mrs Smythe in revenge.

'She had to give the garden party, of course, with half the village turning up at her garden gate.'

127

Robert was amused. He grinned widely and looked admiringly at Agnes.

'Not a good idea to cross you, I think, Agnes?'

'Well, Robert, come out and meet Harry and Horace.'

Agnes felt she had eased his misery a little, for a short time at least, but she still felt deeply sorry for him. With her nursing experience, she realized what it must be like to try and cope with such a helpless burden as poor Barbara must be. She also was very aware just what money could do to alter attitudes and smooth away problems. She had her own experience of that. Money had changed her whole life.

In the wire enclosure Robert walked about without speaking. He made no comment about Clancy, who got up as he approached and performed the curious little dance that had made the two girls who brought him to the sanctuary give him the name they felt suited him.

Robert paused long enough to stroke the little goat, rather making Agnes worry he might get butted. The goat seemed to like the attention Robert was giving him and showed no sign of belligerence. Agnes meanwhile lifted out the little enclosure for the two hedgehogs and got Horace out first, then Harry. She put them both in the little square of fresh grass.

At first Robert stayed where he was, gazing into space, the goat prancing around him. He was no longer attempting to pat the creature. He was not even looking at it. His eyes were fixed on the belt of trees a little way up the road. He seemed lost in his own thoughts, drifting far away.

Agnes did not call him. Perhaps he thought he had said too much to her, told her too much about Barbara's state, the humiliation she now had to suffer. Was he ashamed for her, ashamed of discussing a situation he could do nothing to improve?

Amy was, after all, his sister. Was he regretting the resentment he felt in the reversal of all his hopes?

Suddenly he turned and walked over to where Agnes was kneeling on the grass. He sat down beside her and watched as she put down a saucer of food for the two shambling little creatures. Agnes looked at him before she spoke.

Amy was right, she thought, he did look older than his years. But, with what he was having to cope with, who wouldn't age prematurely?

She leant forward and pushed Horace toward the food. He wandered a little from side to side before he found the saucer, then set to with enthusiasm on the cat food that Agnes had found was a favourite with both of them.

Robert looked up at her. Agnes knew before he spoke exactly what he was going to say or at least the substance of what he would say.

'Agnes, why did you – what is your motive in keeping this little thing alive? He can't see, he has lost a foot by the look of him. That stump may cause him pain. You don't know, I don't know and alas, he cannot tell us. He can only put up with it, stumble around and search for his food.'

She almost hesitated to talk about it. The comparison he was making with the helplessness of his own wife was obvious, yet such a comparison was difficult to mention or talk about. She hedged and told Robert how the vet had rather felt the same and indeed had offered to end the little thing's life there and then.

'Well, why ever didn't you take his advice, Agnes? What has he got to live for? He can't go back to his natural surroundings, he can't see, he can't walk properly. What do you want him for?'

Agnes gave her reasons. She had felt that the two gypsy boys would have been disappointed that all the sanctuary could do for the hedgehog they had in their eyes 'rescued' was to kill it.

Agnes could see Robert preparing to disagree and she was glad that the argument was temporarily stopped by the sound of Amy's car driving on to the path. They both got up and left the enclosure, followed by the dogs, to go and greet Amy and find out how she had fared during her visit to the dentist.

She greeted them with a rather lopsided smile. One side of her face looked a little swollen and an effort to reapply her lipstick had not been very successful. She locked her car door.

'Had to have a filling. It wasn't painful, but the injection was horrible. Worse than the filling.'

'Well, come in and sit down and have a drink. You look as though you could do with one. We have walked the dogs and coped with Horace and Harry. They are fine so we can all have a pre-lunch noggin.'

They walked into the house, Amy telling them she could not, should not have anything too hot or too cold. She was obviously feeling sorry for herself. Agnes felt herself giving Robert a sly smile.

'I will put no ice in your gin and tonic, Amy, I promise. You can manage that?'

Amy nodded and sank down on the sofa exhausted. Robert followed Agnes out to the kitchen. He got the ice from the refrigerator, held the tray under the tap. The loosened cubes dropped out with a thud on the sink.

'Don't worry, Robert, nurses always make a fuss!'

He seemed – perhaps because he had been able to talk more frankly to her than to his sister – less tense and silent. He put the ice tray on the draining board, and took something from his pocket. Agnes expected to see a packet of cigarettes emerge as she had said she did not mind him smoking in the house but no, it was his mobile telephone. He turned to Agnes.

'Do you mind if I ring Barbara – well, her nurse? It's a good time to get her. I feel I must know if anything has happened. MS is so unpredictable. In a way, Agnes, it seems to be able to hit you anywhere at any moment and I just felt somehow . . . I'll go outside, it won't take long. I won't be a moment.'

Agnes mumbled, 'Of course,' and continued making the gin and tonics. She dropped a piece of ice in Amy's drink and hastily took it out again, hoping the brief moment it had been in there would not make it too cool for the suffering Amy. She carried the drinks into the sitting room and placed them on the table in front of Amy, who was holding a tissue to her mouth.

'Does it hurt a lot, Amy? I'm so sorry.'

Amy nodded and dabbed her swollen lip and cheek.

'Yes, he wasn't very gentle, Agnes. He said he would ask the dental nurse to give me two painkillers, but she forgot to get them for me and I quite stupidly didn't ask her for them. I only remembered when I was half-way home. They were for tonight when I go to bed, but I wish I had them now.'

'Robert's making a call to Barbara on his mobile, he says it's a good time to do it just now. He won't be a minute. That's your drink, the one with no ice in it. That's Robert's.'

Agnes moved one glass to the other side of the coffee table.

Robert came in at that moment and sat down beside Amy. He still looked fairly relaxed.

'All's as well as it can be. No change according to . . . Well, there you are, no change is better than a change for the worse, I suppose. Thank you, Agnes.'

He picked up his drink and sipped it and nodded.

'Perfect. I always think at home they make their gin and tonics too strong. You can never stop them. It's done out of generosity, I imagine. Australians are like that.'

There was silence for a few minutes. Robert turned to tell Amy about their walk on the Downs, how much he had enjoyed it. How also he had met Clancy. He was silent about the little hedgehogs. Amy was in pain and Robert broke the silence again by saying that he expected the power of the local anaesthetic was wearing off. Amy only nodded rather miserably in reply to this remark. Then she said:

'I've got some paracetamol upstairs, Agnes. I think I'll take a couple, they may calm it down a bit.'

She got up and left the room, leaving her drink

untouched on the table. Robert had finished his, so had Agnes. She rose and picked up both their glasses.

'Let's have a crafty second, shall we, Robert? After all, we've given the dogs a great walk and seen to the animals. I think we deserve it, don't you?'

Robert nodded.

He did not speak, just traced the rose pattern on the arm of the settee, quite a long process, before he spoke again. He took a long breath. He seemed to find it very hard to say what he wanted to say.

'Agnes, I can never forget how kind you have been to me while I've been here. It is only a short time, but it seems longer. How I have been able to talk to you about my life out there, about Barbara. I threw away my inheritance, I suppose. Took it for granted. My fault, not Amy's as I've told you. How bored you must be with my stories! We, my sister and I, were never close and whose fault was that? Mine, I suspect now, always hogging the centre of the stage.'

Agnes turned to wave the remarks aside, though she suspected what Robert was saying was only too true.

Amy appeared from upstairs. She looked even more haunted.

'I had two paracetamol and feel a bit better now. My mouth isn't quite so painful. Sorry to make such a fuss.'

She sat down and reached for her drink. Robert relapsed into complete silence and Agnes went out to the kitchen to see if the casserole she had put in the oven before they walked the dogs was cooked.

She came back into the sitting room. As she did so, she noticed Amy pick up her glass to finish her drink. Her hand was trembling so much that the glass waved a little to and fro before she managed to get it to her lips. Agnes looked at her face more intently. Amy looked very pale. She replied to Agnes's enquiring look by just shrugging her shoulders and shaking her head. She looked as if she had seen a ghost.

'I'll leave it another ten minutes – the casserole, I mean.

Are you all right, Amy? You look a little bit shaken. Would you rather not have any lunch but go and lie down? You can have some later when you feel a bit better.'

'I – yes, Agnes, I don't feel much like lunch. If you don't mind, I will go and lie down. My mouth still hurts.'

As she reached the door she turned back to Agnes.

'Could you bring me up a glass of water, Agnes?'

'Of course I will. Now or later, do you mean?'

The request had puzzled Agnes. There was a hand basin and a glass in Amy's room.

'Later will do, it's just that . . . well, soon, if you . . .'

She left the sentence unfinished and almost ran up the stairs. Agnes waited until she heard the bedroom door shut with a little bang. She went back into the kitchen and took the casserole out of the oven and through to their small dining room.

The casserole, Robert remarked, smelled delicious.

They had a leisurely lunch, but not another word was said about Barbara. Whether the telephone call had reassured Robert or made him feel his usual despair, Agnes could not be sure. Amy did not appear for any lunch. Agnes was not particularly surprised. Probably she had fallen asleep, the paracetamol had soothed away the pain.

Then she remembered the glass of water Amy had asked for.

She had forgotten it.

After she and Robert had washed, dried and put away the lunch dishes, Agnes decided to go upstairs and take a peep into Amy's room and see if she was asleep, or wanting anything.

She took the glass of water with her.

The door of Amy's bedroom was shut. Agnes tapped very lightly. No answer. This worried her a tiny bit. Amy might be asleep, but what if she had suffered a sudden severe reaction to the local anaesthetic given by the dentist? As far as Agnes could remember, this kind of reaction happened almost at once. She gently opened the door.

To her surprise Amy was sitting on the side of her bed. By her side were scattered the contents of her medicine cupboard, which Agnes had seen when she took the bottle of Nembutal hidden behind the large bottle of Optrex. Amy turned tragic eyes to her, showing no surprise at Agnes's quiet entrance. She spoke before Agnes had a chance to ask her what was the matter – though, of course, she guessed Amy had discovered the disappearance of the brown bottle labelled *Mrs Coleman*.

'He's found those pills, he's taken them. He knows I killed Mother. I know he does. Why should he steal the evidence? He was only up here a minute, do you remember? He came up to the bathroom.'

Agnes did interrupt her then, trying to calm her.

'Amy, I don't even remember. When could he have had time to search? Come now, and how would he know where to look? When did he have time?'

Her friend would not be put off. She had been sitting, thinking it all out, working out when and how her brother could have started to suspect her.

'When we first came to dinner, he asked if he might go to the bathroom. You took him up and showed him where it was. Then, when you came down, you said you had forgotten to put out a towel for him. I went up and he was in the corridor outside the bathroom.'

Amy started as usual to let the tears fall, covering her face with her hands.

'That's when it was, that's when it was. I didn't think anything of it at the time, until now. The name and everything – the pharmacist even – it was still on the bottle. Agnes, what can I do?'

Agnes felt a growing contempt for this crying woman sitting on the bed. Having got rid of her troublesome mother, why had she kept the bottle? Why at least had she not removed the label from the bottle, as Agnes had already done? Why were people so stupid, so untidy, unfinished in what they did? No wonder they eventually got caught. She couldn't resist asking the question.

'But why, Amy, after all this time, having made use of the pills, did you keep the bottle? Was there another old lady in the home who was as bad as your mother and you could perhaps despatch?'

It was a cruel remark and Amy looked at her in horror. More tears started pouring down her face, her eyes opened wide.

'Oh, Agnes, how could you say such a thing? Of course I didn't keep them for that. I just thought – I don't know what I thought, I just kept them.'

Agnes tried to hide her impatience and irritation.

'Oh, I was only joking, Amy, for goodness sake. You did what you did and that's that, but I cannot believe Robert would take them. Why should he?'

Amy got up and with trembling hands began to put the things back in her little cupboard.

'If he suspects me of killing Mother, he might wonder why I had another patient's pills in my cupboard. It points that way, doesn't it?'

Agnes was aware her irritation was growing.

'Well, in the first place why and when would he be searching in your cupboard, for goodness sake?'

Amy had an answer for that straight away.

'You don't remember, he said he had a headache and had I any aspirin and I foolishly called it my drug cupboard, that's when . . .'

Agnes was not too quick in her refusal to accept this suggestion. After all, she had taken the selfsame bottle and she didn't altogether want to clear suspicion from everyone else. She still had it and was not yet sure what she wanted to do with it, but she had an inkling, a little idea at the back of her mind, lurking.

'Well, I think you are totally wrong, Amy. The little I have seen of your brother convinces me that he would never do anything so underhand, and anyway I don't think a thought, a suspicion that you had anything to do with your mother's death, has even entered his head.'

'Well, where are the pills then, the capsules, where is the bottle with Mrs Coleman's name on it, Agnes?'

Agnes shook her head positively, her voice firm.

'I don't know. Probably you put it somewhere else, not in your cupboard at all. Perhaps you moved it and put it somewhere else when you knew Robert was coming here, I don't know.'

Amy had finished putting the various medicines back in her cupboard, her mouth set in a sullen line, but at least she had stopped crying.

'Why don't you ask your brother, if you are so sure –'

Amy turned on her in even more horror.

'How could I!' she said.

Agnes thought, How could she indeed!

Chapter Sixteen

Next day was Robert's last whole day with them. Agnes was determined to make the end of his stay as pleasant as possible. It was not going to be easy because Amy was absolutely paranoid about the missing drugs. Agnes knew she had been up to her room half a dozen times emptying her cupboard, going through her room. The more Agnes tried to reassure her that Robert would certainly never take anything, the less she would listen. Robert was going to accuse her at any moment. Agnes got more and more bored with the whole thing. The thought of the brown bottle stripped of its incriminating label, lying snug and safe in the bottom of her handbag, did nothing to make her feel she should tell all and put poor Amy out of her misery. An idea was forming that perhaps there were better uses the little yellow capsules could be put to than given back to the obsessive Amy just to ease her anxieties.

Amy's facial swelling did not disappear. The tooth that had been attended to ached and the gum round it became red and swollen as well. It was obviously making her feel ill and a return to the dentist was necessary. So Robert's last day with them was going to be spoilt. Amy was not one to use the stiff upper lip method. When Agnes said so to Robert, they both laughed at the rather apt remark. 'Stiff upper lip' was exactly what poor Amy was suffering from at the moment, and was really nothing to laugh at.

In spite of Amy's rather feeble protests Agnes insisted that she should go back to the dentist. Agnes would drive her there.

'Do you want to come, Robert?' she asked.

Robert hesitated, then decided he would come. He wanted to buy a little present for Barbara, something he said sadly that she would be able to feel and perhaps see a little.

'Perhaps I could help you find something, then we could have a little light lunch somewhere if Amy can manage to take something.'

Amy shook her head. She looked quite pale and miserable.

'Well, we will see how you feel. You must have something to eat and anyway we would only need a snack because I am cooking a special meal for Robert's farewell dinner and I want us all to be hungry for it, so I hope the dentist can help you. I'm sure he will.'

Amy didn't look too thrilled and shook her head as she got into the car, a scarf round her mouth.

'Don't think I will feel like having anything to eat.'

Agnes tried not to sound as irritated as she felt.

'Oh, come on, Amy, you may feel better after you've seen the dentist. He'll probably give you some painkillers or antibiotics or something.'

When they arrived at the dentist, Robert opened the car door as if he intended to go in with her. Indeed he started to say in a sympathetic way, 'I'll come in with –' but she shook her head and clutched the scarf more firmly round her face.

'No, no, Robert. I'd rather go by myself, thank you.'

She didn't even look at her brother and walked away and up the steps to the dentist's front door, rang the bell and stood facing the door, not looking back at the car or at Robert or Agnes. Robert sighed.

'I'm afraid Amy will never forgive me for all this, and I suppose when I see Barbara again, I won't feel quick to forgive either, Agnes.'

'Perhaps you can come to some arrangement.'

Agnes made the remark purely for something to say.

Robert turned his head towards her, quickly curious.

'Some arrangement? You mean Amy doing a bit of sharing? You must be joking!

'No, no, I didn't mean –'

'Amy's not a sharer, Agnes. I even suppressed my dignity yesterday and suggested she perhaps could lend me a little to tide me over. Do you know what her answer was?'

Agnes shook her head, a little surprised that Amy had not told her about Robert's suggestion, or at least asked her advice.

'No, what did she say? What was her answer?'

'She said if she did lend me any money, how was I ever going to pay it back?'

Agnes could scarcely believe him. Surely Amy would never be so blunt, so horrible. Was Robert lying? He turned away and looked out of the car window. Was he avoiding looking at her?

'Well, we had better wait for her, she may not be long.'

They sat there, the car windows open. Neither spoke. Agnes was still digesting Amy's supposed reply to her brother's request for help. The dentist's surgery was in a pleasant leafy road. The birds sang and only an occasional car drove by. All sorts of thoughts trickled through Agnes's mind, particularly one.

Could Robert be a liar? Could Amy make such a reply?

It was so out of character, but then Agnes really knew nothing about Amy's attitude to money. Would the fact that she had had to watch her spending, her income so carefully when she had been trying to make the residential home pay its way, would that have made her so adamant about lending Robert some of her inheritance? Then another thought – did she know as much about Barbara's condition as Robert had told her? Had he told the truth about his wife?

'How would you pay me back?'

It was so unlike Amy.

Or was it?

Agnes could not even imagine her saying such a thing, but then did she really know Amy, could the relationship between the two be quite different to what she imagined? She glanced sideways at Robert. He was gazing ahead of him, his expression quite blank, twisting an unlit cigarette between his fingers.

The dentist's door opened and a white-coated receptionist spoke to Amy as she made to close the door behind her. Amy, her face still partially covered by her scarf, nodded to the girl and made her way rather tentatively down the steps. Robert got out of the car and opened the door for Amy.

'Feeling any less painful, Amy?' he asked.

Amy nodded and got into the front passenger seat next to Agnes which Robert had vacated for her. He closed the passenger door and got into the back of the car. Agnes waited until they had both clicked on their safety belts. Then she suggested:

'Amy, you didn't have anything to eat at breakfast so let's go and have a light snack that you can manage. Even a milky drink would be better than nothing. It's silly to starve yourself.'

Amy, rather to Agnes's surprise, agreed with her.

'Well, yes. I could do with something, I think, Agnes.'

Agnes looked at her watch and turned round to face Robert.

'We haven't got Barbara's present yet, Robert.'

They motored into the shopping centre. Agnes knew a little craft shop which sold cushions, unusual ornaments, lamps, all sorts.

'Would you like to stay in the car, Amy, or come in and have a look round? Perhaps you would like to get something for Barbara?'

Amy obviously had not had such a thought, but she undid her safety belt and agreed to come in with them, although without enthusiasm.

140

Agnes had bought several things in the shop before and the proprietor recognized her at once.

'Oh, Mrs Turner, how nice to see you again.'

Agnes turned to Robert before she explained what they were looking for. She asked him if he minded her describing the condition of the person they were hoping to find suitable gifts for.

'No, not at all, Agnes. It's no use buying something Barbara can't see very well or make any use of.'

Agnes explained then made her way to a corner of the shop which was piled with pretty herbal-smelling pillows. They were enclosed in zip-sided plastic covers. She began to pick them over.

'May I take the covers off for a moment? I would like to know what they smell like. I don't want one too sweet.'

Agnes brought one over to Robert who was wandering rather aimlessly round the shop, picking things up and putting them down again.

'What do you think, Robert? Would this be a nice smell to have under your nose? It's not too sweet and I didn't want anything too lavendery, if you know what I mean. Would this give Barbara pleasure, do you think?'

Robert put the little pillow against his face.

'It's nice – it'd send me straight to sleep.'

Agnes handed the pillow to the proprietor to wrap up.

'Now, Robert, what have you found for Barbara?'

Robert shook his head and followed Agnes rather dismally round the shop. Agnes picked something up. It was a string of transparent glass beads about the size of golf balls strung together like a necklace. As the little spheres turned round in the hand they twinkled in the light and one or two of them made a little bubbling bell sound, too soft to be annoying. Robert let the little toy slip through his hand. He smiled as he did so.

'She would love that. It might do her hand good, well, make it work a bit better perhaps. I'll have it.'

Amy had watched both transactions with a strange,

almost lost look on her face. She turned to Agnes. She looked almost tearful She had a small flat box in her hand. She held it out to her brother.

'Would this be any good to her, Robert? It's not pretty, though.'

Robert opened the box and took out the contents. A small white round object fixed to a square black base.

'It's a touch light, just sits on the bedside table and you only have to touch it with your finger and the light switches on. Touch it again, and the light goes off. It might be very useful to your wife, might it not?'

Robert gave Amy a quick kiss on her cheek. She shrank back a bit but did not turn her face away. She made no attempt to return the kiss.

'That would be wonderful, Amy. Barbara cannot turn a lamp on. This would make life so much easier for her. It can sit on the table beside her bed. It's neat, Amy!'

Out of the shop Amy, Robert and Agnes walked along the street to a small pretty public house. Inside was mostly polished wood, gleaming and dark. All three were pleased with their purchases, but Agnes could not forget what Amy had, according to Robert, said when he had suggested a loan. 'How would you pay me back?' Added to this she had noticed that the little 'touch light' that Amy had chosen for Barbara's present had cost a tiny amount compared with what she and Robert had purchased. As she sat drinking her tomato juice and nibbling a sandwich she felt rather guilty at such a thought. After all, it had been a very useful present if a cheap one! Was Amy just mean by nature, just naturally mean?

The lunchtime snack was taken in almost complete silence. Agnes was busy thinking about her future relationship with Amy. Her attitude to her brother had rather changed her opinion of her friend. But she was also preoccupied with the question, was Robert economical with the truth? Had Amy really refused him a loan or had he asked for more? Agnes felt that for some reason he had not been as frank with his sister as he had been to her about

142

Barbara's condition. Amy was silent probably because her tooth was still bothering her a little. She was never very talkative.

Robert went to the bar and ordered more drinks. He seemed the most cheerful and the most talkative of the three but soon he too lapsed into silence. They finished their little meal and Agnes was glad when at last they were walking down the street and back to the car.

'I'm delighted with the things we have got for Barbara.'

Robert sounded really pleased. This time he got into the front seat next to Agnes.

Agnes, looking for signs and symbols, wondered if the cheap present had been as obvious to Robert as it had been to her. Had this made him take the front seat as a little 'pay back'?

As she started the car, she tried to dismiss these imaginings from her mind. She was rather wishing she had not got involved with this pair's problems. She felt like the 'piggy in the middle'. Anyway, once tonight's dinner was over . . . She was making it quite an occasion because Robert would be leaving the next day. She was giving them guinea fowl, something she had not cooked before, that was on her mind too. However, tomorrow would see the end of it all. She looked forward to waving goodbye to Robert. Amy was driving him to the airport and that, Agnes felt thankfully, would be that.

The drive home was uneventful. Robert did ask Amy how her tooth was feeling in quite an amiable voice, to which she replied rather coldly:

'Better, thank you, Robert.'

Agnes wondered if, once home, she would start the search for the damned capsules or would she give up, feeling certain that Robert had got them and that she would never see them again, until he might perhaps produce them, show them to his lawyer and tell where he had found them and accuse her of doping their mother and making her act in an uncharacteristic manner. That is, change the will. Amy was in such a state, goodness knows what she was dreaming up. Her guilt was so uppermost in her mind.

They reached the turning into the lane where The Sanctuary was. One more corner and the dear little house would come into view. Agnes felt she would be glad to be home and with her beloved animals again. As they reached the final turning, they were all in for quite a shock. Parked directly outside was a large black BMW that Agnes thought she recognized as Mrs Symington Smythe's. Sure enough, the man who had brought her with the cat and later called for it, to be told by Agnes that the cat had died, got out of the car.

He smiled cheerily at Agnes and turned to get a large cat carrier, suitable for at least two cats, from the passenger seat of the car.

'I found this. It must have belonged to the gaffer. Mr Symington Smythe. I didn't know there was another one. I thought it might be useful to you?'

'Thank you. It might be indeed, but does Mrs Smythe know you have brought it to me?'

'Oh, didn't you know? She died suddenly. She had a heart attack shortly after the garden party. Lots of people came to her funeral, village people. I think it was because of the party – it made a good impression on people, and it was such a surprise. Everyone who knew her thought she hated cats. But I think it was that party that finished her off, you know.'

He got back into the car but before he did so he lowered his eyelid in a big wink.

Agnes felt he suspected the truth.

'Came as a great surprise to her, that garden party. She seemed to be in a state of shock afterwards.'

'Thank you anyway for the basket. Very thoughtful.'

Agnes was really grateful.

He lowered the window to say goodbye, but asked one question before he drove away.

'Did that cat, you know . . . her cat, really die?'

Agnes did not answer, just smiled at him. He put the

144

BMW into gear and drove away, the car's engine hardly making a sound, and he was gone.

Agnes stood with the basket in her hand. Well, that served the old woman right! Agnes felt a sense of quiet satisfaction at this unexpected outcome of her plan. Amy of course knew the story. Robert too. Agnes had told him about the poor badly treated cat and how she had revenged the beastly treatment, and they both knew that the cat was living happily in Kitten Cottage, now The Sanctuary. Robert was about to say something when a noise from the house interrupted him. It was the sound of a phone ringing. Robert put his hand up to his breast pocket. His face fell, anxiety written all over it.

'That's my mobile, I thought I had it in my pocket. I always do in case Marie, the nurse who is looking after Barbara, wants me. It must be something wrong, something wrong with Barbara. I should have put it back in my pocket.'

He rushed up the path to the front door of the house. Agnes hurried after him to unlock the door. She opened it. Robert rushed across the little hall to the table where the mobile lay ringing. Just as he reached it the mobile stopped. Robert looked as if he was going to burst into tears. He picked up the phone, went into the sitting room and through the french windows into the conservatory. He pressed the mobile and stood with his back to the sitting room and started to talk. Amy was going to follow her brother into the conservatory but Agnes put out her hand to stop her. Amy nodded and went upstairs to her room. Agnes hoped she was not going to start another futile search for the capsules.

Agnes still had the cat basket in her hand. She put it down and went to the door of the conservatory. She had no wish to listen but just to check that he was having no difficulty in getting back to whoever had rung. Agnes worried a little that someone, maybe the nurse friend who was looking after Robert's wife, had tried before while they had been out. Maybe it was the hospital. Maybe

Barbara had suddenly taken a turn for the worse. Perhaps rather unlikely with her disease, but decidedly not impossible. She took another look out of the door leading to the conservatory.

Robert had his back to her, one hand holding the mobile to his ear, the other hand gesticulating. Agnes guessed it must be about Barbara. As far as she remembered from what Robert had told her, his wife could not speak very well. Maybe Marie was talking to him.

Agnes made her way to the kitchen. She was slightly depressed about her dinner. She had hoped to make it a festive occasion. Guinea fowl, red wine, avocado with prawns to start, but Amy was at a low ebb with her sore tooth and mouth and goodness knows what the telephone call would do to Robert if it was bad news. He certainly wouldn't feel like a special meal, even if it was to celebrate his last night before returning home. Anyway, she decided she must get the dinner prepared and cooked. She hoped for the best.

Amy came into the kitchen. She looked better.

'Can I do the vegetables or shall I give the dogs a walk – which would be the most help to you?'

Polly heard the word 'walk' and starting tearing round the kitchen and out into the hall looking for her lead. Wilma, not able to hear as well as Polly, got the message even so and followed Polly out from the kitchen into the hall, tail wagging slowly. The dogs had answered Amy's question.

Agnes felt she would rather tackle the cooking. She had plenty of time. She wanted to do it all carefully, even if it was not going to be enjoyed as much as she had hoped. At least she would have done it as positively and perfectly as she could. It would be an expensive meal to spoil.

Bother everybody! she thought, then felt a little ashamed of herself. After all, Amy hadn't known she would get a tooth playing up and poor Robert, well, he had such a sea of troubles she could only do her best for him and, perhaps somewhat thankfully, say goodbye to him tomorrow.

Then The Sanctuary. The animals could take over again and she would have time to think whether she really wanted Amy to live with her or whether she should go back to her own flat. Perhaps it was time to tell her that she didn't think sharing a house was working out.

Agnes cut the avocado in half and levered the stone out. Maybe she would think differently when Robert was gone and Amy was better. Maybe she would come around to the idea that she would rather have Amy living permanently in the house with her, not be alone. She heard the door of the conservatory close. She looked into the sitting room. Robert was sitting in the middle of the sofa, his elbows on his knees, his face buried in his hands.

Agnes went back into the kitchen. She felt she must give him a little more time. Perhaps Barbara was dead. She half wished Amy had not gone off with the dogs. They would be up on the Downs by now, having a lovely run. Whenever Robert came round from whatever he had been told on the phone, she would have to handle it. Perhaps in a way, she thought, she was more able to cope than Amy. In spite of being brother and sister, they never seemed close.

Agnes went on with her preparations. She covered the prawns with mayonnaise, spooned them into the avocado and put them on little dishes, each avocado resting on a crisp lettuce leaf. She had just popped these into the refrigerator when she was conscious that Robert was standing looking at her from the kitchen door.

He looked very old, his face ashen. Agnes felt almost certain that he was going to tell her that Barbara was dead. She walked into the sitting room, her hand on Robert's arm. They both sat down on the sofa. Agnes did not know what to say, how to start, whether to ask what had happened. At last he began to speak. He looked directly at Agnes before he began to speak, and as if he imagined what she was thinking, he said:

'She's not dead, Agnes. Perhaps it would be better if she

was, for her sake. Now she's got more to put up with. I can't think how she will cope with it!'

Then he went on to tell Agnes what had happened. Apparently in the middle of the night Barbara had awakened her friend, complaining of difficulty in breathing, asking for a window to be opened wider. Marie had done her best to reassure her and after a while Barbara's breathing became easier. Marie thought some of the breathlessness was due to panic. She had said to Robert on the mobile that Barbara had never suffered from breathlessness before and it would frighten her if she was having even slight difficulty in taking in air.

They had got through the night.

However, by morning, Barbara was still struggling to breathe and Marie had rung the doctor. He had taken, through no fault of his own, over two hours to get there and by that time Barbara's problems were much worse. When the doctor had at last arrived he immediately rang for an ambulance and Barbara had been taken to hospital. Marie had gone with her. There they had been most helpful and Barbara had been given oxygen which relieved her almost at once. A consultant examined Barbara's chest and then checked her general condition. Marie was in the room all the time and all through the examination and she told Robert she had been worried about the grave expression on the consultant's face as he listened to the patient's chest.

He smiled at Barbara and put back her oxygen mask, then he motioned Marie to accompany him out of the room, presumably to talk to her privately. Once the door of the examination room had closed behind them, he pointed to the chair near the small desk and sat down himself behind it. He looked grave.

Marie had told Robert all these details, hoping that Amy and Agnes would be able to console him when he started to regret as bitterly as she knew he would the fact that he was away and should have been there by his beloved wife's side. After all, Amy was a nurse and so was Agnes.

Then the consultant had given his opinion.

'Mrs Horrocks is a very sick woman, as you already know, Miss Becker. The present symptoms are unusual but not unexpected. Multiple sclerosis is an unpredictable disease, apt to throw up any signs or symptoms at any time. Nothing can be done for Mrs Horrocks, except constant oxygen if she needs it – and I think she will, I'm afraid. It will relieve her.'

Robert could not go on for a moment. Again he covered his face with his hands, almost weeping.

'Then comes the awful part, Agnes, awful for Barbara and awful for Marie. I would never have left if I had anticipated anything like this happening.'

Agnes let him be silent for a moment to try and compose himself, control his feelings.

Amy had returned from walking the dogs. Agnes, so engrossed in Robert's story, had not even heard her come in. During Robert's silent moment, Amy quietly went over and sat down in the armchair near them.

Agnes looked at her and tried to convey by her expression that things were not at all well with Barbara and that Robert was in the middle of recounting what Marie had told him during the long conversation on the mobile. Amy nodded to show Agnes that she understood.

'I'm so sorry, Robert, that things are so bad.'

Amy's voice was very quiet and sympathetic.

Robert didn't seem to notice her sympathy.

'So bad, Amy? You don't know how bad. They sent her home, just with Marie and the oxygen, said they couldn't admit her because there was not a bed available. What they really meant was there was nothing they could do, so she would only waste a bed if they let her have one. There's nothing to be done.'

'Did they really say that, Robert, really and truly?'

Robert went on then with what Marie had said to him on the mobile almost word for word. He sounded very bitter now, as if he was blaming the doctors, the hospital, everyone, but most of all himself for leaving her with only Marie in charge, to take all the responsibility that should really have been his.

'She was ringing this morning, while we were out. Why didn't I remember to put the mobile in my pocket? I always do, I always do. Why didn't I this morning? Anyway, they're back home now with an oxygen cylinder, and it does help. But when it doesn't, what then?'

Agnes tried to reason with him, telling him he was going home tomorrow, what more could he do?

Amy said nothing. Suddenly she got up, stood almost in front of Robert, her cheeks quite pink.

'If you hadn't thought these awful lies about me, and come here to England to prove I had done something wrong, you would have been with Barbara when this awful thing happened to her. It's your own fault.'

Amy turned on her heel. Agnes had never heard her speak so loudly, so fiercely. It was as if she hated her brother. Perhaps she really did.

Amy made for the stairs. There was a moment's silence, then the bang of her bedroom door. Robert had not said a word to her in reply, he just watched her leave the room. When he heard the crash of the bedroom door he seemed to come to life and spoke.

'You see, she is guilty. She knows it too, that's why she's been so odd to me. She did make Mother change her will, I know she did. Mother would never have done it other- wise. She may have been mad at me for not sending her cards or coming to see her, or marrying Barbara, but she would never have turned on me completely. Amy made her do that and now my poor love has to suffer for it. I'll never forgive her, never.'

'I must get on with the dinner, Robert – if anyone's going to feel like eating any dinner at all.'

Agnes was quite shocked by Amy's outburst.

The emotional scene she had just gone through made Agnes almost pleased to retreat into the kitchen. Robert had left the sitting room and gone into the garden and into the wire enclosure where the dogs were.

Polly was tearing about after a favourite rubber ball. Wilma was stretched out on the grass. She loved her walk, but her added years made her tired afterwards. Robert was standing over by the trees, the smoke from his cigarette spiralling upwards. What he must be feeling, Agnes could well imagine. Hate does terrible things to you and at that moment Agnes guessed the hatred, blame and guilt he felt about himself made him wish to be alone.

Scraping the carrots, peeling the potatoes, getting the guinea fowl ready made her feel normal, better. As she did the chores a thought came into her head, a sudden inspiration. The little brown bottle in her handbag. Would it help, could it help?

She turned on the oven and walked over to the window. Amy had certainly failed the test, she thought. She certainly would not want to live with her permanently now. How to tell her? Well, she'd find a way somehow.

She watched Robert. He had started walking slowly up and down the small area of grass between Clancy and the little patch where the hedgehogs were housed today. He looked at none of the animals. Agnes could imagine how he felt, but nothing could be done for him. In hours he would be home, shouldering the problems that he had left and now even more problems on top of them. He suddenly turned and made for the house.

Agnes went hastily back to her chores, not wanting him to think that he was being watched or spied upon. He came into the kitchen and sat down at the kitchen table. He was still smoking.

'Agnes, you must feel all your kindness has brought you nothing but listening to accusations and quarrels. I am sorry about it all.'

At that moment, Amy came into the kitchen. She had of course been crying. She looked pale and ill.

'Yes, I'm sorry too, Agnes, and here you are cooking us a lovely meal to say goodbye to Robert. I feel we should thank you and try to forget what we have said to each other. Could we call a truce, Robert, and enjoy this last meal together?'

She did not look directly at Robert, neither did he look at his sister.

Agnes tried to lighten the heavy situation. She looked from one to the other.

'I think that's an excellent idea. I am taking a lot of trouble with this meal and I hope you can enjoy it. I don't want it all to be wasted.'

She felt she must add a little note of criticism.

'Well, you are both adults and in fact your horrid problems and arguments have nothing whatever to do with me. How you settle them is your business and your business only, that's all I have to say. A truce is a good adult idea.'

'I'll go and change, try and make myself look a bit more suitably dressed for dinner with two ladies. I look a mess at the moment.'

Robert left the kitchen and went up the stairs.

Amy was tearful again and came over and kissed Agnes on the cheek. Agnes tried not to turn her face away, but she was aware of feeling distinctly cold towards Amy. Although Amy had been kind to her in some ways, in another way she had used her and Agnes did not like being used, even as a go-between.

The dinner, cooking-wise, was undoubtedly a success and Agnes was pleased with her own efforts. The guinea fowl were delicious. Robert had a second helping, telling Agnes that he was stoking up for his trip back to Australia. He appeared cheerful and Agnes felt he was really making an effort. They talked about Barbara's presents and how he hoped she would enjoy them, but not a word about the worsening of her condition. Agnes promised him a good breakfast before he set off tomorrow.

'We will make it a brunch,' she said.

Amy did not contribute much in the way of eating the meal or in conversation. Agnes had to admit that she did not look at all well. She played with her food, apologizing to Agnes for her inability to eat much. Her face was still a little swollen on one side and she looked pale and ill. Whether this was due to the sudden flare-up between herself and her brother one could not be sure. As she served the fresh fruit salad Agnes felt again how glad she would be to see the back of both of them, particularly Amy. Perhaps because of Robert's obvious love for Barbara and his guilt at leaving her, she felt a little more sympathetic towards him.

They all three went out in the dusk to put the animals to bed. Robert had a long talk with Clancy rather to Agnes's amazement, but in Amy it did not even raise a smile. She hardly seemed to notice.

'Don't go butting anyone, Clancy, and blotting your copy book. Behave in a gentlemanly way as you always have to me and you will be all right.' Clancy did a little dance in reply as he always did when he liked someone, then returned to his shed and rolled on his bedding, before Robert shut the door on him and bade him goodnight. Agnes gave him full marks for his cheerful demeanour, knowing what he was going back to and maybe dreading that the complications and suffering might be even worse than Marie had let on.

Amy put Horace and Harry in their little straw and hay cage, but she was quite silent and did not say a word to either Robert or Agnes.

Once indoors Amy did break her silence by refusing the coffee and liqueurs Agnes suggested as the best way to round off their evening. She said she did not feel at all well and would rather go to bed. She looked even paler and more wan than she had at dinner. Agnes suggested it might be the antibiotics, which sometimes made you feel wretched. Amy agreed. She said goodnight to both her brother and Agnes and took herself upstairs. This time she did not bang the bedroom door but closed it very gently.

'She certainly does not look very well, Agnes,' Robert had to admit.

Agnes agreed and went to fetch the coffee and liqueurs.

On the whole the dinner had been a bit of an emotional disaster and Agnes wished she had not planned it, but it was over now. Whoever had been at fault, whoever was telling lies and cheating, it was only causing more and more unhappiness.

After they had finished their coffee, Robert insisted on helping Agnes wash up. She agreed. During that time she hoped she would be able to suggest something which might help Barbara out of all her misery. As she got up to go to the kitchen, she picked up her handbag. She had no motive, well, not at the moment.

Agnes washed and Robert dried the plates and dishes. She watched him and noted how expertly he dried and stacked the crockery, like a man who had had to do it for some time, used to the chore.

'Is Barbara able to eat very much, Robert?'

Agnes asked the question not just out of idle curiosity – she really wondered how Robert managed to feed his wife, when maybe her swallowing was difficult and she couldn't taste or enjoy much.

'Oh, she can still eat some things. Tomatoes if I peel them and cut them up small. Junket. I can make a junket now. It took me ages to get it to "junk" if you know what I mean. One of the nurses taught me.'

Agnes felt a twinge of pity, not only for the man beside her, but for the woman he was trying to keep alive.

'This breathing trouble frightens me a bit, Agnes. I mean, hasn't she got enough? Paralysis, incontinence, partial blindness and inability to speak clearly. This inability to get her breath will be too awful, it will frighten her as much as it will frighten me.'

'The oxygen will help a bit.'

Agnes turned away from the sink to face Robert.

'Suppose the oxygen runs out, Agnes, in the middle of

154

the night and she can't breathe? What happens then, what do I do then?'

'There is a little dial thing, or there used to be, at the top of the cylinder, tells you when it is running out, or getting low.'

'Good God, what have we come to, Agnes?'

Robert suddenly threw down the drying-up cloth on to the draining surface and with his fist hit the steel as if he had to take it out on something.

'I just don't know what to do. I don't know what to do for the best or the worst. Sorry.'

He picked up the cloth and resumed the drying up.

Agnes tried to turn the conversation a little away from thoughts that were obviously making Robert lose control of his emotions.

'It looks as if I will be driving you to the airport tomorrow, Robert. I don't think Amy will be fit enough, that tooth business has really taken it out of her – and now the antibiotics.'

'Well, that will please her, Agnes. The less she sees of her dear brother at the moment, the better as far as she is concerned, especially after my outbursts and hers.'

Agnes made no reply to this remark.

'But it's very nice of you to offer to take me. I could get a taxi, you know, and not put you to the trouble.'

'No, no. I don't mind taking you at all.'

They left the kitchen and went into the sitting room to watch the ten o'clock news. Then Agnes went upstairs to see if Amy needed anything before she settled down for the night. Amy was not asleep and said she needed nothing and had taken two more paracetamol in the hope that they would give her a good night's sleep. She looked pale and miserable, but said nothing more about her brother, either about his stealing the capsules or about his outburst while she had been downstairs, much to Agnes's relief. She mentioned that she would drive him to the airport tomorrow. Amy made a feeble protest.

'Oh no, Agnes. I think I'll be all right by then, surely?'

'Well, we will see. If you feel rotten I will drive him there, parking and everything is a bit of a hassle at Heathrow and if you don't feel well it makes it a good deal worse, so don't worry about it, Amy. Now try to get a good night's sleep. Goodnight, Amy.'

She closed the bedroom door quietly behind her and joined Robert downstairs. The news was over and he had switched off the television. He looked up as Agnes came into the sitting room.

'There is a play coming on. I don't know if you want to see it or not. It looks fairly run of the mill from the *Radio Times*.'

Agnes shook her head. She had made up her mind what to do with the bottle in her handbag.

'No, I don't want to see it, Robert, but I would like to talk to you. I don't know which way you will take what I am about to suggest. It's entirely up to you. I am only offering something that might be a help to Barbara and to you.'

As she said this, Agnes pulled the handbag beside her a little closer. The bottle right at the bottom under her purse made a little rattle as she did so. She wondered, with a half smile, was that a little sign? Were the drugs saying, 'Let us out to where we can do some good'? She leaned back and closed her eyes for a moment. She knew that Amy's brother was looking at her with some curiosity, his attention fixed.

'What are you going to suggest now, Agnes?'

There were two lights on in the sitting room. Neither was brilliant, so the lighting was subdued. A standard lamp on the other side of the room had a heavily printed shade with roses and green leaves. Nearer the settee was a small table lamp with an amber-coloured shade.

Robert was leaning toward the small lamp and reading the programmes listed on the page of the *Radio Times*. The screen in front of them was a blank dark square. Only the tiny red light below the screen indicated that the television was ready to spring into light and colour at

156

the touch of the remote control which was balanced on the arm of the settee. He put the magazine down beside the amber light.

'Is there anything you want to see, Agnes?'

Agnes shook her head, placed the remote control on top of the television and leaned back to indicate if she could that she was not prepared to go to bed or leave the room for the moment. She wanted to say something.

The air was heavy with silence. Robert had his eyes on the blank screen. He seemed to be waiting for Agnes to speak, to say what she wanted. To say what? What was he expecting?

'Robert, I want to ask you a question, a very personal question. Please don't feel you have to answer it, just tell me to mind my own business or anything you like, I won't be offended, you must believe that.'

Robert shrugged his shoulders and slid down the seat a little as if he wanted to rest his back and neck. His eyes turned towards her.

'Ask away, Agnes, I am sure I won't be offended. Is it something about Amy, the will, my mother?'

'No. It's not about . . . it's about your wife, Barbara. I can imagine what you go through looking after her. I have in my nursing years nursed two multiple sclerosis patients but I was only on the ward. When I had done my rota of duty, then I could leave and forget about them.'

Robert put his two hands, fingers interleaved, behind his head. He merely nodded, almost ruefully, as Agnes stopped speaking as if he had nothing whatever to add to what Agnes had said.

'Tell me, does Barbara wish sometimes that she could die and get out of it all? Do you wish she could?'

The man beside her did stir then. He sat up and leant forward, his head in his hands. There was little or no emotion as he answered Agnes, one hand smoothing back his thin white hair.

'Wish sometimes, Agnes? Wish sometimes? She is long-ing to die. I was afraid, afraid of how her death would be,

157

how it would happen, but I longed for her release too. Every morning, I – we have twin beds, every morning I get out of bed and go to her hoping . . .'

The time had come for Agnes to do what she wanted to do. She picked up the handbag from beside her on the settee and opened it. She would have to tell the story she had already dreamed up. It must be her responsibility. The bottle in her handbag was her bottle, acquired by her long ago when she was doing a small stint of private nursing. She had stolen them. None of it must be in any way related to Amy. Tomorrow he would be gone, she hoped with enough courage to use the pills she would give him and set Barbara, that poor caged, suffering animal, free.

Robert went on now he had started, blurting out his feelings. It was as if he could not stop himself.

'It makes me feel guilty when I even think of it, wishing my wife dead, but she so shares my wish . . . Quietly in her sleep, Agnes. Is that too much to ask?'

Agnes got up and poured another small brandy for dutch courage. She put one glass on the table in front of Robert and sipped her own. Unless this man goes soon, I shall turn into a dipsomaniac, she thought with a rare touch of humour.

Then she told her story. The pack of lies she had thought up. It sounded good and very authentic as she told it. It tripped off her tongue with ease and absolutely no feeling of guilt.

The man beside her on the settee, now sipping his brandy, never took his eyes off her as she spoke, as she told her story with never a hint that Amy ever had any capsules, and putting the blame on herself completely.

She told Robert she had been nursing a titled lady in a lovely country house, quite a way from the nearest town. Her patient had fallen at home, broken her hip and been taken to hospital. Her hip was pinned and eventually she was discharged and allowed home, with two nurses. The patient had improved and was walking a little. As she improved, the doctor had suggested that the day nurse would be sufficient because, with the aid of sleeping pills, the pain was relieved and she was beginning to sleep most of the night. Agnes had stayed on until the old lady was much better and then the worst had happened. The patient had a stroke and died almost at once. She never regained consciousness.

By this time Agnes was almost believing in the story herself. After the funeral she had left. As she was packing her things prior to her departure, she went to the drug cupboard. There were the capsules. Agnes told how she had put them in her handbag with the intention, she said, looking at Robert earnestly, of returning them to the chemist. At this she picked up her handbag again and drew out the bottle of Nembutal. To Robert she described them as pentobarbitone, quite correctly. She held it in front of Robert, explaining to him how there were enough pills to put his wife out of her misery. An overdose, she said, and explained how Barbara would just go to sleep and not wake up. She finished her story, handing the little bottle to her companion.

He took it in his hand, the capsules rolled. What questions would he ask, Agnes wondered? Would he hand the bottle back to her in horror, refusing even to contemplate such an act? But no. He turned the bottle to and fro in his hand, looking at its contents, then he turned to Agnes, his face perhaps a little paler.

'Are there enough pills here to do it, Agnes?'

Agnes had anticipated that question and she could assure him there were. Robert stroked the bottle with his thumb almost like a small caress.

'Just like – just like going to sleep, Agnes? They won't make her sick or let her wake up again?'

Agnes shook her head. She was very curious to know exactly what he was thinking. Although his question made it sound as if he was not horrified at the idea, not pushing the very thought aside, out of his mind, perhaps thinking to himself, I could not do this to her, ever.

The heavy silence in the room grew heavier. Robert

picked up his glass and drained the brandy, his other hand still holding the little bottle. Putting the glass down, he looked more fully at Agnes.

'Thank you, Agnes. What can I say, that I will use them, that I won't? I don't know, but it is wonderful to have the solution here in my hand. To know that if it gets worse – even if it doesn't but Barbara says she cannot stand any more – then I have got this. Thank you, thank you so very much.'

He slipped the bottle into his jacket pocket. Agnes got up and turned off the standard lamp and he switched off the small one beside him. The room was plunged into darkness, with just enough light from the hall to see their way out of the room. Agnes switched off the hall light and they made their way upstairs, Agnes following her guest. As he reached his bedroom door, he turned to Agnes. His expression was full of gratitude. He half smiled and put his hand out. Agnes took it in hers. His hand was very cold.

'Sleep well, Robert. Don't think too much about it, not yet anyway. There is time to think later.'

He nodded, went into the bedroom and closed the door softly behind him.

In bed, about an hour later, Agnes tried to put out of her mind what she had done. The ball was now in Robert's court. What he did when he got back to his home in Australia, what he felt he must do, was now nothing to do with her.

Before going to bed, Agnes had called in to see Amy, who woke up as she entered the room. Her face was still swollen, in fact looked a little more swollen than when she had retired to her bed. Agnes was quite worried about her.

'Have you taken your antibiotics, Amy?'

Amy shook her head. Agnes went downstairs and made a warm milky drink and took it upstairs to Amy.

She sat on the side of the bed and watched her take her pills, waited while she went to the bathroom, thinking that

Amy would not be fit enough to drive Robert to the airport tomorrow. She did not mention this to Amy as she saw her back into bed.

'Thanks, Agnes. You get on well with Robert, don't you? A good deal better than I do, I think.'

Agnes was diplomatic in her reply.

'Well, I've only known him for a few days, and you had a whole childhood with him.'

They bade each other goodnight.

Agnes did not get to sleep easily. She was not troubled by the thought of whether she had done right or wrong in giving the capsules to Robert. Rather more by the hope that she had not wasted them and he would end up not using them. She supposed that Amy would always think that her brother had taken the bottle from her cupboard, but what did that really matter?

It was nearly three o'clock before Agnes fell asleep. She couldn't stop thinking about Robert, about how he was feeling. Was all this keeping him awake as it was her?

If he loved Barbara so much perhaps he would hold back from administering a dose that would take her away from him. She had not touched on religious views with him. Did he expect to meet Barbara again in another world, free of pain and any suffering and humiliation? Or was his love so great that he would not even think of his own coming loneliness, but only of the release for his beloved wife? It was an enormous act to perform. It would take great bravery to do the deed, and it was something he must tackle on his own.

Once long ago she had . . . well, better not to think about that. The thought in her mind at that time, she remembered, was, Well, what is done is done and cannot be undone. But that had been different, that had been done to someone she had no love for, no feeling for, only to rid the world of an old selfish nuisance, who thought of nobody else but herself.

Chapter Seventeen

Agnes got up early. Her sleep had been so broken by the events going on around her that she felt as if she hadn't slept at all.

She glanced at the kitchen clock. Seven thirty. Still in her dressing gown she decided to make herself a cup of tea and take one up to Amy just in case the antibiotics had done the trick and made her feel better – even, perhaps, able to drive her brother to the airport.

The cordless kettle snapped off and she poured the water into the small flowered teapot.

She walked across the kitchen and drew up the blind.

The morning was sunny. At least, she thought, if I have to do the drive it will be pleasant – and the run would do the Porsche good!

As she turned back to the tea tray she heard someone coming down the stairs. Agnes expected to see Amy but it was Robert.

He was fully dressed and smiled, almost apologetically.

'I didn't know you were up, Agnes! You must have been very quiet. I didn't hear you.'

Agnes pointed to the tea tray, smiling.

She was determined to keep this last morning pleasant, as the weather looked outside the window.

'Tea, Robert? Pour yourself a cup. I've only just made it. I'll take a cup up to Amy and see how she's feeling. Better, I hope!'

Agnes poured out a cup for Amy and left the kitchen to go upstairs. She knocked softly on Amy's bedroom door.

A feeble 'Come in' answered her knock.

Amy was sitting on the side of her bed, still in her nightdress. The swelling at the side of her mouth was smaller, but still there. She looked wretched, pale and depressed. She took the cup of tea from Agnes with a subdued 'Thank you, Agnes.'

She sipped the tea and made a little face as the hot liquid passed her lips, but continued to drink it carefully.

'How do you feel? Have you taken your antibiotics this morning?'

Amy shook her head and reached down to her bedside table, took the blister pack and pressed a pill out, put it in her mouth and swallowed more tea.

'I don't think you are well enough to take Robert to the airport. I don't mind taking him a bit.'

Amy looked up at Agnes with a miserable face.

'I would pay for a taxi to take him, but I don't want to, I really don't want to have anything to do with him, especially because of the way he's been and him taking the pills from my room.'

Amy put her hand over her mouth as she spoke as if it still hurt her to talk much.

Agnes ignored the remark about the pills. She did not want to have to try to reassure Amy all over again. She had to admit Amy was getting boring.

'Well, you have a rest. I'll cope with the animals. We don't have to leave until eleven thirty. I will take Robert, there is no need for him to take a taxi.'

Downstairs in the kitchen Robert was pouring a little more boiling water on the tea. He had poured a cup for Agnes. As she came into the room, he looked up.

'How's Amy, will she be able to take me?'

Agnes shook her head, sat down at the kitchen table and drank her tea. Robert had finished his.

'I feel I'd like to take a walk, we've plenty of time, haven't we, Agnes? You said if we started about eleven

163

thirty, that would bring us to Heathrow in good time. I feel a walk would help me think.'

'I understand. While you are out I can cope with Clancy, give the dogs their walk when I get back. I do know how you feel. It's good to be alone and quiet for a bit, you've got a long long journey home, cooped up with other people.'

'Thanks, Agnes, for being so understanding. I'll take off then. I feel I need to be alone for a while.'

He left. Agnes watched him go down the front path, open the gate and close it carefully behind him. He turned to the left, stopped, looked both ways, lit a cigarette and set off. He soon disappeared from Agnes's sight. She turned away from the window, glad to be alone at last. She felt the house was almost her own again. Amy would probably not appear. Now Agnes felt she could cope with her very favourite people of all, the animals.

She was about to put on what she called her garden clothes, and was just going upstairs to her bedroom, when suddenly the gate bell pealed. It was still fairly early, only half-past eight. The postman? Why was he ringing the gate bell – she had a little mail box for letters and packages at the side of the gate. She pressed the gate release. Perhaps he had a packet which was too big to go in her post box.

Agnes opened the front door to be confronted by the postman. She knew him fairly well. Only a few days ago she had cleaned and Bandaided a bleeding finger he had caught in a gateway down the lane.

'Morning, Mrs Turner. Sorry to trouble you but I found this down the lane, brought it on my bike.'

Both his hands were supporting a small damp-looking cardboard box.

Agnes peered inside the box. One very thin wet black and white cat lay at the bottom of the box with several kittens which were trying to feed as the postman proffered the box.

'I thought you'd know what to do, Mrs Turner. The box

was put on the side of the road. I can't go to the cats' home because of my round.'

'Don't worry, I'll look after them, of course I will. Thank you for bringing them. I hope I can do something for them.'

'Thank you. Well, I must get on with my round, Mrs Turner.'

He departed looking much relieved.

Agnes carried the box through to the kitchen. She fetched a blanket, warm from the airing cupboard, and put it on the kitchen floor. She gently lifted out the mother cat and put her on the blanket. Then the kittens. The black and white cat was so thin and cold and inert that Agnes wondered if she would survive. She heated a little milk. The cat raised her head then sank back again. Agnes decided to try a little food, some of Tippy's cat food. She turned away for a moment to open the tin. When she turned back the cat was standing, wobbling slightly, but to Agnes's relief was polishing off the warm milk. The litter were not in as bad shape as the mother, so Agnes carried the blanket through to the sitting room and placed the mother nearer the radiator, went back and reunited her with her brood. The mother cat was stretching as the warmth got to her.

Agnes, still in her dressing gown, rushed upstairs and dressed. She was determined to give the cat a tiny bit of cat food. She was aware of the risk of giving too much at first but the kittens were clamouring for food, rather a different case. Agnes put newspaper all round the blanket and a tray with litter next to the family. The kittens were too young to know what it was for but perhaps the mother might use it. Then she went out to the other animals. In coping with the cat and kittens she had quite forgotten about Amy.

Having put Polly and her big friend in the enclosure and let Clancy and the hedgehogs out, she went upstairs to see how Amy was.

To her surprise her friend was up and dressed, but not looking all that well.

'I'll cope with the animals, Agnes. That's the least I can do with you driving Robert to the airport.'

'Well, if you feel well enough, Amy. But let me tell you, we have a new addition. Come and see! Well, not one addition, actually four!'

Amy's face lit up when she saw the family. Gently she stroked the mother. Immediately she began to purr. Agnes thought, as she had many times, how well animals seemed to react to Amy.

Agnes told her what the little cat had had to eat so far. Amy nodded. The kittens, probably because of the warmth, had dozed off and were lying almost on top of each other, one upside down, little white paws in the air. Agnes brought in a tiny amount of milk she had gone out and warmed. The cat immediately got up, not so wobbly this time, drank the milk and started to try to wash her face. This proved too much for her and she flopped down, still purring under Amy's stroking hand.

Amy's face, maybe because of the heat from the radiator, had grown pinker. Even so Agnes told her not to do too much and insisted that she would take the dogs for their walk after she had returned from seeing Robert off.

Amy agreed to this and did not even mention the vanished drugs. Indeed she didn't even mention Robert. Maybe she was delighted he was going home.

Hard to tell, Agnes thought.

But then there was a lot about Amy that Agnes found hard to tell. She couldn't forget what she had said to Robert, or what Robert said she had said, when he had asked her to lend him money.

'How could you ever pay me back!'

It was so heartless, so unfeeling. But had she really said it?

If she had not, why should Robert make the story up, or why had he felt the need to tell Agnes who, after all, was almost a stranger?

Was it wrong to feel no loyalty towards her? Would one

think more of him had he kept quiet about Amy's answer to his plea?

It was hard to make up one's mind. Agnes pushed it all out of her mind for the moment, but the doubts remained.

Brunch for all three of them was the next thing on the agenda.

Agnes decided to make omelettes. Easy and quick.

Amy could perhaps manage an omelette. She had not had much to eat since this tooth business started. Agnes went into the kitchen feeling like 'The Universal Provider'.

Amy, Robert, the new family of pussy cats, two hedgehogs, a black cat, two dogs and a goat!

Well, the days at least were not dull or boring.

Agnes took the eggs out of the refrigerator. As she did so she heard Amy speak to someone in the hall.

Robert was back from his walk. She could get on with the cooking.

'How long have we got before we start, Agnes?'

Robert walked into the kitchen, asking the question as he did so. He had more colour in his cheeks now and looked better, more relaxed.

'I enjoyed my walk. It's strange how when you are out walking on your own your thoughts seem to come easier.'

'I expect it all depends what you are thinking about. What are you trying to work out, Robert?'

It was then that Agnes realized she must be careful what she said. Probably when he was back in Australia with Barbara he would not be able to leave her long enough to take walks.

Well, it was up to him now, all up to him.

Before breaking the eggs, she went to the sitting room to take a quick look at the new family. The mother cat had used the tray, which proved she might have been somebody's pet, probably someone who wanted to get rid of her when she proved to be in kitten.

How could they! Leaving her in a box on the side of the road, in all probability in the rain. Ah well, Agnes thought, that is humans for you.

Back in the kitchen she broke the eggs into a basin. She heard Robert go upstairs, she thought, to bring down his small amount of luggage.

Amy was out in the enclosure with the animals.

Brunch would just fit in nicely before she and Robert took off in the Porsche for the airport. She hoped this, the last meal they would have together, would be at least amiable. She wondered too how Amy would react to what might be the last time she would see her brother.

There appeared to be so little affection or sympathy between them. She could not visualize Amy going to Australia to see her brother or to even go to his funeral, much less his wife's.

Amy returned but didn't come through to the kitchen. Neither did Agnes hear her go through to the sitting room. She listened.

Silence.

She took the pan off and went to the kitchen door.

Amy was sitting on the third step of the staircase holding her head, rather in the way Robert did, hands over her face.

'I don't want anything to eat, Agnes. I've done Harry and Horace, fed them as well, and Clancy is all right. I've left the dogs out there. They are running about. They are all right, Agnes. I couldn't do . . .'

She stopped and put one hand on the banister as if, although she was sitting down, she felt giddy.

'I feel so wobbly I think I must go and lie down again. I am a mess, aren't I? I wish to goodness I had never had this wretched tooth done. I felt quite all right before. Maybe it's the antibiotics.'

Agnes was adamant that when she got back from the airport she would call Amy's doctor and ask him to come

168

to see her. Amy protested feebly as she usually did about doing anything definite.

'I don't want to be any trouble to anyone, Agnes.'

She started to cry and turned and made her way unsteadily upstairs.

Agnes went back into the kitchen and turned on the stove and made two omelettes instead of three. She was slightly worried about Amy but there was little she could do, short of ordering a taxi, which Robert would feel he had to pay for, and she didn't want an argument about that or anything else. All Agnes wanted to do at the moment was to get rid of Robert and get rid also of the feeling of tense animosity that neither sibling could ever quite cover up, no matter how they tried – and they had tried. She gave them a few marks for their efforts.

Robert came into the kitchen and sat down at the table. He looked enquiringly at Agnes as she put the plate in front of him with the rack of toast and the coffee.

'Only two? Amy not up to eating again?'

Agnes explained that his sister had managed to cope with the animals and then felt dizzy so was upstairs again on her bed. She told Robert about her plans to call Amy's doctor when she got back from seeing him off at the airport. Robert nodded in agreement but shook his head even as he agreed.

'She hasn't eaten anything since the dentist, has she? She used to do this when she was in her teens.'

Agnes stopped eating and looked at him in surprise.

Robert continued eating his omelette with enjoyment.

'She was hospitalized with anorexia nervosa when she was about sixteen, sixteen and a half. She only weighed about four stone. I was younger and spoiled rotten. I didn't realize I was spoilt. I hated the notice Amy got when she was being sick, starving herself, getting thinner and thinner, getting noticed. I was vile to her. She was, is, such a nuisance.'

Agnes had stopped eating, his words had so surprised her.

'What did your father and mother do about her illness?'

Robert shrugged his shoulders, pushing his empty plate away.

'Then Amy decided to be a nurse. All her problems ended. I think that's what she really wanted – to be in charge, the head of affairs. Probably she never forgave my mother for making it impossible for her to continue as sister of her beloved ward where she ruled the roost. She would never ever forgive my mother, our mother for that. That's why I came over here. I was certain my mother would never cut me out of her will. I'm sure Amy saw to that. I don't know how, Agnes. But it's too late now. I've lost, or rather Barbara has. She's won, Amy's won.'

He finished his coffee and got up, put his plate and cup and saucer on the draining board.

'You have never told me before about Amy when she was younger.' Agnes was curious as to why he had divulged this now.

Again he shrugged.

'Agnes, you have been more than good to me and I felt you must be sick and tired of hearing about our family troubles. I just thought it had no bearing on anything. I could tell you so much more, but I'm not going to. I'm going to say goodbye to Clancy.'

Agnes felt he just wanted to end the conversation and let him walk out of the house and toward the wire enclosure which she had not yet locked. As she watched him, walking rather slowly, his sparse white hair ruffling in the breeze, she felt sorry for him, very sorry. Yet, with reservations.

She put the dishes in the sink and turned the tap on. As she did so she thought she heard a sound like the mobile phone from the garden. She looked out again but Robert was out of sight.

After washing up and putting away the dishes Agnes dealt with the new family of cats. Mother was much improved but Agnes could not leave them in the sitting room with Amy hors de combat. She took them out to the biggest cat kennel, lined it with hay and put the blanket on top. There was enough room to leave a saucer of milk and food for the mother and a tray of litter. The mother cat started on the food at once. Agnes closed the wire door.

She felt slightly harassed but the family would have to stay there till she got back from disposing of Robert. He came across from Clancy's shed at that moment. In the morning sun he looked pale, drawn and ill. He went straight out of the enclosure without speaking to Agnes and walked toward the house. Agnes locked the enclosure door.

'Time we were starting, Robert – well, almost.'

He made for the kitchen.

'I must say goodbye to Amy. It would look churlish not to. I'll make her a drink if I may, Agnes. She always liked it when she was feeling unwell.'

He opened the kitchen cupboard and took out a small jar of Bovril and put some milk on to heat. He unscrewed the bottle top.

'It's Bovril in hot milk. Perhaps she won't drink it but she used to. It's the salty flavour, I think, that makes it less bland.'

He waited till the milk was steaming then poured it into a mug and added a heaped teaspoon of Bovril. The liquid became light brown and spotted with Bovril. He looked at Agnes, smiling.

Agnes smiled back at him.

'Funnily enough, I have heard of that mixture before, even made it for a patient. It will do her good, if she will drink it.'

'I'll take it upstairs and try to talk her into drinking it and say all is forgiven.'

Agnes was not too sure how the last piece of the sentence would go down.

'I won't be long. We've got half an hour, haven't we, Agnes?'

Agnes nodded. She was rather pleasantly surprised by Robert's action. At least brother and sister would not part

171

without saying goodbye, particularly as they might never meet again. Maybe Amy would drink the milk and Bovril. She certainly needed something. Agnes wondered if this refusal of all food was a throwback to her youth.

'We've only got about half an hour, Robert, then we must start off. We don't want to be late.'

'No. I only want to say goodbye and try to . . . Well, I don't know what I want to do really.'

Agnes noticed that the hand holding the mug of milk laced with Bovril was trembling.

'Are you all right, Robert? You look a bit shaken.'

'Yes, I'm fine. I'll soon be home now, Agnes.'

He lowered his eyes and turned away from Agnes and mounted the stairs. The stairs in the little round house were twisted and he disappeared from her view, but not before Agnes had seen him pause for one moment, one hand on the banister as if to steady himself. Agnes grimaced.

What a pair she had got mixed up with!

Chapter Eighteen

Agnes looked at her watch and checked it with the clock on the dashboard of the Porsche. 11.33 was indicated on both watch and clock. Three minutes late. Agnes was always very punctual herself and expected the same from everyone else.

Robert was late, only three minutes, but it irritated Agnes. She did not start the car engine and two more minutes passed. Agnes was almost at the point of getting out of the car and going in search of him when she saw him closing the Sanctuary gate and hurrying round to the car. He yanked open the passenger door and got in hurriedly. Agnes had put his holdall in the boot earlier.

'I'm so sorry to keep you waiting. I thought I would do my best to make our goodbye as amicable as possible under the circumstances.'

'And did you manage it, Robert? How was she?'

Robert eased himself more comfortably in the car seat and straightened his tie before he replied.

'Oh, better, I think. Anyway she ate my – I mean, drank my milk and Bovril. She was dressed and sitting on the side of the bed when I left her. I think she'll be all right now, though her face is a bit swollen.'

Agnes started the car and drove smoothly out of the gravelled parking space and into the country lane. As they passed they heard Polly's excited bark. She was probably chasing round the enclosure, watched by a serious Wilma, who enjoyed being with Polly, but obviously regarded her as a young excitable teenager.

Agnes wished she hadn't to do this journey but comforted herself by admitting that the Porsche could do with a good long run. Since buying the cottage and coping with the animals and then with Amy and Robert, she had not had time to do much motoring.

She hated passengers talking while she was driving. As they approached town and the motorway and the traffic increased, she was glad that Robert was proving a very silent passenger. Agnes stole a glance at him while they were waiting in a slight jam. He looked completely wrapped in his own thoughts, far away. Maybe, Agnes thought, he was preparing himself for having to tell Barbara that there would never be any more money to make life more reasonable, more comfortable for her. He spoke suddenly, completely contradicting what Agnes had supposed he had been thinking.

'It was nice to hear Polly's bark. Almost like a goodbye, wasn't it? But of all of them I liked Clancy the best. He is such a personality.'

Agnes hardly knew what to say in answer to this rather sentimental remark, but she did believe it to be true. He had, like his sister, loved the animals, all of them.

'She was barking this morning when I was getting our brunch in the kitchen. I thought it was your mobile, it sounded just like it, Robert, her high little bark.'

Robert's reply was quick and adamant and negative.

'Oh, no it wasn't. I didn't have a call today.'

Agnes relapsed again into silence as did her companion. They drove on, more slowly now the traffic was building up. Agnes needed all her concentration. She enjoyed driving, preferred driving alone, but for some miles she might have been alone as far as talking went.

'Do come in with me for a bit, Agnes. I have a sort of fear of being by myself. I suppose it's because I'm not used to being alone. I dread the next twenty-odd hours.'

Agnes had no wish to stay with him at the airport. She had planned to let him go in on his own while she went straight back to The Sanctuary, the animals and the – she hoped – recovering Amy. After all, he had no luggage to cope with, only the holdall which he now took out of the Porsche. However, perhaps she should do as he asked. Trying to look pleasant, she followed him out of the short stay car park and through the glass doors, thinking as she did so of what he was going back to, nothing optimistic or helpful to tell Barbara. Only the fear of a new symptom, a new hazard in the illness he would have to learn to cope with.

Pity made her follow him across the great milling hall of the airport, stand beside him while he checked in, then go and sit down with him on one of the red upholstered plastic seats.

'I'll get you a coffee, Agnes, won't be a minute.' He was off before she could reply.

Agnes did not want coffee, did not want to be here. Next to her a small boy began to scream and stamp his feet, a real tantrum. His mother, or at least the adult woman with him, took little notice but went on reading her paperback. The child eventually shut up and threw himself on the seat face down, still kicking but at least he had stopped the screaming.

Robert returned with the coffee and sat down beside her.

The screaming child started again, then to make matters worse, he ran along to Robert and stood in front of him, stopped screeching and yelled some unintelligible word that sounded like 'Eaties.'

His mother got up and apologized to Robert.

'He wants food. He's just had his breakfast.'

She yanked the child off by the arm and dragged him back to his seat where the screaming started again, this time louder, if anything.

Robert grimaced and raised his eyes heavenwards.

'Let's move to a quieter place, Agnes.'

He was smiling a rather strange complacent smile. Agnes could not interpret it at all. She wanted to go, leave Robert to get on the plane and get Barbara back into his mind again. At the moment he seemed to be preoccupied with other thoughts. He made several remarks about the people round him, some quite funny. Agnes thought how weird it was. All because she had met Amy at the flats. Amy Horrocks, self-styled hospital Matron who turned out to be nothing of the kind – well, almost nothing of the kind. Here she was, in Heathrow airport, sitting beside Robert Horrocks, sipping rather inferior coffee and longing to see the back of him. It seemed like a conspiracy against her peace of mind, but she had to admit Amy could hardly have invented her bad tooth.

'I must get back, Robert, it's quite a drive. I hope all goes well with you when you get home.'

She picked up her bag to take out the car keys. Robert put a restraining hand on her arm gently.

'Just stay a moment longer, Agnes, please. I have something to tell you, something important.'

Agnes put the mug of coffee on the floor beside the red plastic seat. She determined to leave it there when she got up, which she intended to do almost at once. The 'something important' Robert was saying he had to tell her, she could not imagine would interest her in the least. She did not want to listen but his first remark stopped her in her tracks.

'It *was* my mobile you heard this morning, Agnes, not Polly's barking. I did have a call from Marie this morning.'

Agnes felt a slight interest, not so much in the telephone call, but why Robert had lied to her about it. What did it matter to her one way or the other?

Robert drank the whole of his coffee in one long gulp. Agnes felt he was playing for time. He crushed the plastic mug with one hand and thrust it under the seat, wiping his mouth with his hand. His eyes, looking at her, were narrowed, rather menacing-looking. Agnes waited.

'This morning Marie rang me. Barbara had another attack. Marie hadn't a back-up cylinder of oxygen – apparently they'd wanted a deposit for a second one. It's always money, isn't it?'

He suddenly choked, his eyes reddened. Agnes knew before he said it exactly what he was going to say.

'Barbara died in the night, with just Marie there, and I feel in the end it was Amy who killed her. According to Marie, it wasn't an easy death. I must go now, Agnes. Thank you for all you have done for me and indirectly for Barbara . . .'

Robert's voice gave way. Agnes could see now how hard he was trying to keep his emotions in check.

'I'm so sorry, Robert, but glad for Barbara. It was too much, what she was going through. I must go, you must go – and again, I'm so sorry.'

There was another call on the Tannoy, his flight. He stood up and turned to her.

'I was a little worried about the pills, Agnes. Would they allow them through?'

Agnes was under the impression that medication being used by the traveller was allowed and could be taken on board in hand luggage. She said so. Robert shrugged his shoulders, shook his head and picked up his holdall.

'Well, Agnes, no need to worry about those pills any more. You'll see when you get back what I've done with them.'

Agnes felt herself go cold. The beastly capsules, Amy and the milky drink he had taken up to her just before they left. Surely he couldn't have!

Amy, she must get back to her. Robert turned to go. His flight was being called again.

'Robert, you didn't . . .?'

There was no time to answer the question, the insistent call to the plane had stopped any reply.

He turned away. He looked smaller and older than ever. His mouth was clamped in a straight line. He did not meet Agnes's eyes again but turned, gripping his luggage tightly.

'Goodbye, Agnes. Look after the animals. You can trust

them to be truthful to you, they won't lie. Everyone else does, but never them.'

He was gone. Agnes stood for a moment watching him go then turned and walked to her exit. Once in the Porsche she sat for a moment, aware of the urgency in her mind, but quite unable to act on it.

She thought of Amy and the pills, Amy and the milky drink given to her by her brother. What would she find back at The Sanctuary? She started the car and began the drive home. She had to drive very slowly behind a large Rolls which was taking its time to get back into the main stream of traffic. Chauffeur-driven, with an elderly lady who must be warning her driver to take it very slowly. Agnes almost had to stop. As she did so Robert's departure flashed across her mind like a little piece of film.

As he walked away from her, his stoop evident, the sparse white hair ruffling slightly in the air-conditioning, head poked forward, he had not looked back. Agnes felt again a great sense of relief that he was gone. But what had he left behind in The Sanctuary? The pills, had he . . .?

The Rolls in front of her gathered a little speed, the grey-haired passenger leaned back, relaxed. Agnes speeded up a little more. The car in front took a turn to the right, she to the left. She concentrated on her driving, trying to keep anything else out of her head. What she would find on reaching home, well, she would find. There was nothing at the moment she could do. She realized though that really she was more worried about the cat and kittens than Amy or what Robert had done to her. At the moment, motoring along the road, rather tired after so much driving and the emotional chatter with Robert, Agnes felt that Amy was expendable. But the poor little mother cat and her three babies . . .

Almost at once, Agnes regretted her thoughts, tried to tell herself that it was wrong to think in such a way. A human life must be considered more valuable than an animal's. But Agnes in her heart knew she would never be able to think like that.

178

The journey home seemed to take for ever. At last Agnes turned into the lane – one more corner and there was The Sanctuary at last. What would she find there though? Her heart was starting to beat uncomfortably fast and her mouth felt dry. Surely Robert couldn't have . . . not his own sister . . .

Amy's car was still parked in its usual place in front of the garage. Agnes drew up behind it and turned off the engine of the Porsche. She took a deep breath. Whatever she was about to find, there was nothing she could do about it now.

She put her key in the lock and opened the front door. It was very quiet in the house – ominously quiet?

Agnes went into the kitchen. Before going up to Amy's bedroom she would go and see how the mother cat and her kittens were. The poor black and white cat would be hungry again by now. And Polly and Wilma – they had been left alone in the enclosure for so long, they must be wondering what had become of everyone. Yes, she had far too much to do for the animals before she could think about Amy.

As she approached the wire enclosure Polly came racing up, barking with excitement. Agnes opened the gate and went in, picking up Polly and giving her a hug. Wilma greeted her with her usual dignified approach, tail wagging to and fro. She looked well and her coat had improved with the constant grooming she got nowadays from Amy as well. Her muzzle though was growing greyer. She followed Agnes across the grass to where the two hedgehogs, confined in their little enclosure, were bumbling about as usual.

Agnes went back to the house and brought the cat food and milk from the kitchen. She filled a shallow saucer with food for Horace and Harry. Horace had to be gently guided towards the saucer and the little dish of milk. Harry made for the saucers at a rate of knots. He was almost ready to be taken somewhere safe and let free. Agnes wondered if he would find a wife and set up a new family – as far as possible, she thought, from any busy road or motorway. Hard enough to find!

The new arrivals, Agnes was anxious that they were beginning to recover. She opened the wide kennel door. The black and white cat was looking much better and tackled the food greedily, which made Agnes think she had probably not been fed while she was away. She put in a dish of milk. One of the kittens, eyes still closed, walked straight into the milk and out the other side. Agnes smiled again, stroked the mother cat and shut them in again. As she did so she thought how she must tell Major Hayward about the kittens and take Wilma to see him. It had been a long time. She stopped in the middle of the enclosure. What was she thinking? She had taken Wilma to see him about – she closed her eyes for a moment and thought. Eight days ago! She shook herself, she felt curiously disorientated.

Robert's visit, Amy's preoccupation with his visits to the lawyer and the doctor, his stay at the cottage, the bickering and hidden hatreds and disagreements had seemed to go on much longer than the actual few days.

Well, it was over now, one way or the other, but that did not solve the problem. Agnes changed Clancy's bedding, fed him and gave him fresh water. He seemed singularly unimpressed by her return. He did do his weird little dance and kicked his bedding about before bounding out on to the grass. All seemed well in spite of her late morning and early afternoon absence.

She stood for a moment, not looking forward to the next thing on the agenda. She gazed round and realized she would have to have help. More animals might come in. She hoped they would. She didn't mind living alone. This little round house made her feel secure and safe. She believed she could be happy alone and now the thought of asking Amy to share the cottage with her had certainly flown out of the window. Well, she had put it off long enough, but no longer. She must make some tea, take it up to Amy and see how she was. Agnes shut the enclosure

180

door. Only Polly followed her through, but Polly was family.

In the house Agnes went into the kitchen and laid the tray. Two cups and saucers, milk jug and teapot. She switched on the cordless kettle and stood waiting for the snap of the little green trigger. She put two teabags in the teapot, poured on the boiling water, feeling that she was doing everything in slow motion. She felt odd. She did not want to take the tray up to Amy, did not want to at all!

But at last, after waiting for what she told herself was time for the tea to infuse, she picked up the tray, went upstairs and tapped on the bedroom door, very lightly.

There was no reply. Agnes tried once more, then she balanced the tray on one hand and pushed the door. It opened. The blind was pulled down and the room was almost in darkness. Agnes, coming in from the brightness of the garden and the kitchen, could see very little. She blinked and waited a moment for her eyes to adjust before she could take in the scene in front of her.

The bed was unmade, the bedding ruffled and folded back, rumpled. A glass of water, by the look of it, had been overturned and the water spilled on to the rug beside the bed.

Not like tidy Amy at all!

Agnes felt anxious. She went into the bathroom.

No signs.

She came back into the bedroom. Amy's shoes and her slippers were under the bed. That was a good sign.

Had she gone out on her own?

But where? Why was her car still parked in the drive in its usual place? Amy was no walker.

Agnes took the tea tray back downstairs to the kitchen and poured herself a cup. She felt she needed it.

Where was Amy?

Surely she would not just walk out and leave everything? Well, not quite everything.

The wire enclosure door had been locked. Also the front door. Robert would hardly . . . Then she realized he had

181

followed her out of the animals' enclosure and banged the front door behind him. The catch would have automatically locked.

Should she call the police? How long had Amy been gone and where was she?

What had Robert said about the pills?

'You'll see when you get back what I've done with them.' What did he mean?

Agnes suddenly hated the lot of them. Robert and Amy, even Barbara in a way. They had all barged into her life, into her lovely little round house, the pleasant association with the animals. Robert at least was gone, and Barbara now. Was Amy gone too, despatched by her loving brother? She half hoped so.

Polly was dancing round her feet, wanting notice and some milk too.

Agnes decided involving the police was too drastic an act. After all, Amy had every right to go where she wanted to. She had been here in the house this morning. What could she say to the police? Nothing that would sound sensible or even worrying. She went and sat down in the sitting room, looking at the blank television screen, much as she and Robert had done the evening before. Polly jumped on to her lap. She often posed as a lap dog, curled up and tried to be small and appealing.

Agnes gave her a hug. As she did so Polly suddenly stiffened. The dog's ears pricked up and she looked towards the door. Agnes heard the sound too, the sound of a car drawing up at The Sanctuary's gate, then a pause with footsteps going round the gravel walk where the cars were parked in front of the garages.

A key turned in the front door as Agnes stood up. Polly had already jumped down off her lap. The sitting-room door opened. Amy stood framed in the doorway. Polly ran to greet her, barking a welcome.

Agnes certainly did not feel like giving her the same. Her voice was crisp and rather cold.

'Where have you been, Amy? I leave you ill in bed and come home to find you out!'

Amy came a little further into the room and sat down. She still looked pale and anything but well. She rubbed her forehead as if she had a headache, but bent and caressed Polly. Agnes moved towards the kitchen.

'I made you some tea when I got back, that was some time ago. When I took it up to your room you were not there and I was quite worried. You said you were giddy?'

'I felt poorly. I called a taxi and went to Dr Edwards. I thought it would save you the trouble of calling him and having him here when you got back, Agnes. The receptionist said I could see him at once.'

'Well, you shouldn't have. I'll go and make more tea.'

Agnes was aware that she was speaking coldly and that Amy had probably been trying to save her the bother of a visit from the doctor but at that moment she wished Amy just wasn't there. She wanted to be alone, alone in her new home with her animals. She went back into the kitchen and filled the kettle again, then went upstairs to her own bedroom to change her shoes.

As she crossed the room to her wardrobe she saw the brown bottle, still containing the Nembutal, standing on the little locker beside her bed. So that was what Robert had done with them! All that worrying about Amy had been for nothing! Agnes picked the bottle up, tipping it this way and that in her hand. The little familiar rattle of the capsules was in a way curiously comforting. She opened her own little cupboard, her medicine cupboard as she, nurse-like, called it and put the bottle inside behind a bottle of Joy perfume. She closed the door firmly and changed her shoes, then made her way downstairs.

As she did so she heard the familiar click of the kettle. It had boiled. She would make the tea.

'Did you know your brother had a telephone call from Marie?'

Amy looked up quickly from her teacup. She put the

digestive biscuit down, having tried to bite it but given up with a wince of pain. Her tooth obviously still hurt her. Agnes had visions of another visit to the dentist but this time, surely she could drive herself?

'No, I didn't know he had a call. What was it about? Did she say Barbara was worse or . . . what was it?'

'She is dead. Barbara is dead, Amy. Robert had the call during the morning. He didn't tell me until he was just leaving. I was quite shocked. He seemed calm, resigned. Perhaps he was relieved, but he must have wished he had been with her.'

Amy's reaction to the news of Barbara's death was rather surprising to Agnes. She had expected at least a show of the usual facile tears, but now there was an almost complacent look on Amy's face. But Agnes did notice that, as she poured herself a second cup of tea, the hand holding the teapot was shaking a little. Perhaps she was not quite as composed as she wanted to appear.

'He didn't tell me. I didn't know. I didn't even know he had a call, but it's a happy release for Barbara, isn't it, Agnes, and for him in a way.'

She sipped her tea. Her eyes peering over the cup were quite dry. Agnes could not read the expression in those eyes.

'Well, the funeral will cost Robert a lot, I expect, although I don't know if they are as expensive in Australia as they are here.'

Amy put her cup down and looked wide-eyed at her.

'Well, that's really my brother's problem, isn't it, not mine.'

There was a hardness in Amy's voice that Agnes had not heard before. She could hardly believe that timid little Amy could speak like that. Then she remembered what Robert had told her his sister had said when he had asked her to lend him some money to help with some medical comfort for Barbara when she was alive. That had been a direct refusal too. Agnes felt now that Robert had been telling the truth.

So she determined to say no more about Robert. She had little time for either of them and soon, very soon, she must break it to Amy that she would prefer it if they lived separately and that she did not want Amy to keep her bedroom in The Sanctuary. Whether she would ask her to go on helping with the animals, should they grow in numbers, she couldn't yet make up her mind. She decided she would not bring up either matter until Amy was better, had finished her course of antibiotics and was looking a bit less pale and wan than she did at the moment.

However, her resolve to get rid of Amy was going to be strengthened by an incident that happened a week later.

Chapter Nineteen

Five days went by before Agnes and Amy heard from Robert, then two letters arrived. One for Agnes and one for his sister.

Agnes's letter was really a thank you for all the hospitality and support she had given him during his stay in her house and for the time she had spent listening to his troubles and worries.

He touched only briefly on his wife's death, which he said had caused great grief to Marie who had long been her friend. Robert ended the letter sadly and with what seemed to Agnes to be great love for Barbara. He said that he missed her more than he could say. He no longer felt needed. He mentioned that her funeral was in two days' time and, for financial reasons, would be a very simple one. This, however, he felt was in accordance with Barbara's wishes. She had not wanted anything showy.

Robert, though, felt that he could do so little for his wife and it still rankled with him.

Amy took her letter upstairs to read and when she rejoined Agnes tending to the animals she did not refer to it at all. So Agnes did not mention hers either.

If Amy was ashamed about how she had behaved, she gave no sign of it. She still looked very pale and ill and was still on her antibiotics. Agnes believed she had two more days before the course would be finished.

Because of this she put off any suggestion of Amy returning to her flat. Not only had she hated the way she had behaved to her brother, or more perhaps the way she had ignored the suffering of his wife Barbara, but she felt Amy's behaviour was becoming too intimate, too sisterly.

Agnes, by nature, was a loner and even in her marriages had always managed to keep her own counsel. She was never one to tell all, to embrace emotionally any other human being. Amy's rather cloying dependence was beginning to irritate her more and more.

Two more days, and she was determined to give Amy her marching orders as nicely she could, but give them she must!

However, when the day arrived and she was all ready, had even rehearsed the speech, Amy's toothache started again and the puffy look at the side of her mouth reappeared so Agnes had to admit she could not be pretending.

The pain was certainly the real thing!

This time Amy seemed to be very worried about the problem and agreed with Agnes that she must visit the dentist again and insist that the tooth be taken out. It was towards the side of her mouth and would not be at all unsightly if it was removed.

Agnes suggested she telephone the dentist and insist on seeing him that day. Amy did this and the receptionist agreed. A three o'clock appointment was made. Agnes was relieved that the treatment would be speedy and she hoped it would cure the pain altogether and make it possible for her to talk to Amy about the new arrangement she was anxious to get on with. Amy's presence was beginning to irritate her more and more.

There was more irritation on the way. Amy expected Agnes to go with her to the dentist – for support, she said.

When she replied, rather tersely, that she felt Amy was perfectly capable of going to the dentist by herself Amy became tearful and almost entreated Agnes not to make her go alone.

'I love to be with you, Agnes. I need to be with you!

I know you are not as fond of me as I am of you. Ever since I met you at the flats. Straight away I was . . . When you were so kind to me and helped me, I really thought . . . I thought you felt the same as I do!'

To say Agnes was horrified by Amy's words was an understatement. She had met this kind of crush in nursing and had always managed to avoid it.

She left the room and went into the kitchen and stood thinking.

If Amy felt like this she would have to get her to leave immediately. She really couldn't stand this kind of adulation from another woman.

Or perhaps it was just loneliness, nothing more?

Amy always seemed to have had a rough deal, especially from her family.

Agnes remembered Amy saying, long ago when she was in the flat, that she never went out with the other nurses or partying. Agnes had thought she was like herself, not liking parties with lots of other girls.

But this declaration of fondness business had really frightened Agnes!

She jumped when the peal of the gate bell interrupted her thoughts. Another animal, she supposed. She made her way out of the kitchen and, as she was crossing the little hall, she caught a glimpse of herself in the mirror. She made a little grimace at herself.

Well, she may not have liked going out with the girls partying, but she had had two husbands and an exciting lover. She had never felt like Amy about any woman.

How beastly. She shivered.

Perhaps she had encouraged Amy too much, but she had not dreamed the friendship was anything but . . . anything but normal.

Ah well, all she had to do now was retract everything she had offered Amy. Not an easy task, but it was essential it was done.

In answer to the ring from the gate she opened the front door and looked down the path.

A car was parked just outside the gate and a man was standing by the car with his back to her. At first Agnes did not recognize him, then he turned and looked up the path. He must have almost given up but then heard the door open.

It was Mr Singer, the vet. The one she had taken Polly to when she had been nearly strangled by a beastly boy swinging her on her lead. Also Horace the hedgehog had visited him.

'Hello, Mrs . . . Mrs Turner, isn't it? I've been visiting an overweight Cavalier spaniel further down the road and felt I must visit Kitten Cottage. I see you have changed the name. A better one, I think.'

Agnes was genuinely pleased to see him. He had been so kind to Polly and the little hedgehog and also to Clancy when his neck was so sore.

She opened the gate to let him in.

He looked curiously around him and walked towards the wire enclosure. Agnes showed him round. He remembered Wilma who seemed to recognize him and came up to him, wagging her tail slowly, as she always did.

'I thought Major Hayward was going to have to have her put down. She's old and rather large to adopt.'

Agnes explained how she had taken on the dog when she had bought the round house and also told him that Major Hayward was in a residential home and where it was.

The vet thought the Major had died some time ago.

She then gave him further news of him and told how she took Wilma over to visit him and how delighted they were, Wilma and the Major, to see each other. She explained that the Major was pretty lonely and liked visitors, hoping the vet might drop in and see him if he had time.

'I used to come here to dinner when Alice Hayward was alive. She was a wonderful cook! I must go and see him. I really thought he had died.'

Agnes showed him the cat and kittens. The vet then

189

asked what the little wooden enclosure on the grass for. He went over, looked and laughed.

'Didn't you bring that little hedgehog in to me, Mrs Turner?'

Agnes nodded and told him the story of Horace and now Harry and the gypsy boys who had brought them.

'They come and see him so I'm glad I kept him.'

'Well, he seems to be prospering, blind or not.'

The vet remembered Clancy and commented that he seemed better, after feeling the little goat's sides and neck.

It was nice to have him looking at the animals, walking about, making comments.

The vet was not a very good-looking man, but solid. Slightly overweight, with glasses which seemed to live rather low down on his nose. He pushed them back with his forefinger. He was what Agnes would call a 'tweedy man'.

Probably his profession tended to influence his clothes.

As they walked out of the wire enclosure Agnes turned to close the door. When she turned back she saw the lace curtain of Amy's bedroom drop back into place.

Spying, Agnes thought with disgust.

What would she make of the visit of a man to see Agnes, her friend whom she professed to love so dearly?

It was largely her own fault. She should have guessed, been less approachable.

Agnes had nothing against lesbians. Nothing. It was just that she hated to be thought of as one herself, to be considered as one half of such a relationship, a horrible misjudgement.

Perhaps she was overreacting but she did want Amy gone out of her house as soon as possible. She would talk to her about moving this very night.

Agnes turned to Mr Singer.

He was looking at the house. He lit a cigarette and drew deeply on it, and nodded approvingly.

'You have made a lot of improvements, Mrs Turner. The

Major let it get a bit run down. He couldn't help it, poor old chap. He had just lost Alice and was in a wheelchair. He could hardly walk at all.'

Agnes felt reluctant to see him leave.

'Do come in and see what I have done inside. I have kept a lot of their furniture, had a lot re-covered and the whole place recarpeted.'

Over a cup of coffee the vet told her a lot about the round house and the thatcher who had recently rethatched the roof. He also explained the decoration on the apex of the thatch, so beautifully done.

A 'special signature', he called it.

'Johnny Matthews, old Matthews' son, did your roof about a year ago, I suppose. He learned to thatch when he was a boy. His father taught him. Have you met him, Mrs Turner? He's one of the few village craftsmen.'

Agnes shook her head.

Amy came into the kitchen where they were having coffee.

'I'm sorry, I didn't know you had a visitor, Agnes.'

Agnes introduced Amy who half smiled, nodded and made for the back door which led out into the garden.

'I'll go and feed Clancy, he's always hungry!'

Agnes watched Amy leave. Did she resent the fact that there was a stranger, or almost a stranger, talking over a cup of coffee, apparently enjoying Agnes's company? Not only a stranger, but a man.

Oh dear, the sooner Amy left, the better!

It flashed across her mind, as her companion finished his coffee and got up to go, that there would be a lot crying from Amy when she heard the news.

Agnes walked with the vet down to the front gate and to his car. She felt really pleased to have seen him.

'You should find another stray goat, a male of course! Goats don't like being alone, Mrs Turner.' He smiled.

Agnes watched him get into his car. She was sorry to see him go.

He wound the car window down.

'Would you come out for a drink one evening, Mrs Turner? It's been so pleasant meeting you again. Or perhaps dinner?'

'I'd like that, but do please call me Agnes.'

'Great. My name's Guy.'

He smiled again. His smile was boyish and rather shy. He drove away and Agnes stood by the gate watching the car disappear round the slight bend where the trees hid it from view.

She went back to the house feeling better for his visit, cheered.

She put the coffee cups on to the draining board.

The visit had made her feel a bit sorry for Amy who, at that moment, came down the stairs dressed up a little, Agnes imagined, for her visit to the dentist.

'I'll take you, Amy. If he does decide to take that tooth out, you won't feel like driving yourself home afterwards, so it's better if I take you.'

Amy's face lit up but she demurred at first.

'Oh, I can't ask you to do that for me, Agnes.'

But Agnes's rather brusque reply to this stopped her.

'Well, you didn't ask, Amy, I offered. So come along! Polly can come with us. She doesn't like to see the car going out without her.'

Amy agreed, still clucking a little about Agnes putting herself out, being so kind etc etc . . .

Agnes ignored her protestations. She was tired of them.

'We will leave Wilma in the house. If it rains I don't want her getting wet, it doesn't do her arthritis any good.'

Once in the car she kept the conversation firmly away from the future. Amy tried once or twice to consolidate her position, using the word 'we' frequently.

'We could perhaps get a companion for Clancy,' or 'I wonder if we will be able to get homes for the kittens once they are old enough to leave their mother, do you think we will?'

Agnes did not reply to many of the leading questions,

but when they arrived at the dentist, she turned to Amy and spoke with determination. She couldn't let this go on.

'Well, Amy, let's get your tooth settled before we start to talk more about what "*we*" are going to do!'

Surely that was pointed enough.

She snapped back her safety belt, unsmiling and rather grim-faced. She was pretty sure Amy understood for her face was miserable as she got out of the car. 'Clonk' went the locks as Agnes pressed the remote control, a sound rather appropriate to the ending of a relationship, Agnes thought as she followed Amy up the steps to the dentist's front door.

A white-coated girl let them in and led them through to a waiting room.

'I thought I had better come in with you, just to see whether he decides to take the tooth out. He may not. Dentists try to save teeth forever these days.'

Amy's thanks and 'Oh, what a bother for you, Agnes' poured out as Agnes expected. She sat down, picked up a copy of *Homes and Gardens* and retired behind it. She was conscious of Amy's nervousness as she also picked up a magazine and sat down. They were the only two people in the waiting room. Both sat in silence. The only sound was the ticking of a large black clock on the big mantelshelf on the other side of the room and the occasional faint rustle as a page of a magazine was turned over.

After about ten minutes the door opened and an elderly lady was ushered in by the receptionist who had opened the door to them. The old lady leant heavily on a stick as she limped across the room.

'He won't keep me waiting long, will he?' she asked.

The white-clad girl shook her head reassuringly. She did not close the door but turned enquiringly to Agnes then to Amy, not sure who was the patient.

'Miss Horrocks, Mr Shane is ready to see you now.'

Amy got up and cast a quick anxious look at Agnes.

The stick-carrying lady looked very pointedly at her

watch. She obviously thought she should be called, not this 'Miss Horrocks'.

The girl did not look in her direction but led Amy out of the room, closing the door very quietly behind her.

Agnes put the magazine back on the table and gazed out of the window.

She wanted to think, to plan Amy's departure. It had to be done. It was hard luck that she would appear to be going back on her idea but plans sometimes had to be changed.

She gazed out of the large window through the net curtains, thick and expensive. She could just see the traffic passing by.

It helped her to think. The amount of movement of the cars and vans passing by was somehow soothing to her.

'They never keep to their appointments, do they, never!'

The elderly lady's remark made Agnes jump. Lost in her thoughts, she had completely forgotten there was anyone else in the room.

She made some vague reply and continued to watch the passing traffic.

Robert filtered through her mind. The funeral, all the misery he must be going through, but there would be relief too. She hoped a little of the other feeling might be tempering his grief, that he might be glad there was no more suffering for Barbara.

Agnes wondered if Amy would write to him.

Funerals cost a good deal of money. Somehow she couldn't imagine Amy sending off a helpful cheque to him.

However, that was nothing to do with her. She had got herself too involved already. Now she had to break this steely cloying bond with Amy!

The waiting-room door opened and Amy walked in, a white cloth held to her mouth. The receptionist was with her, holding her arm.

'The tooth was extracted, Mrs . . . er, your friend's tooth was so loose, Mr Shane was able almost to lift it out.'

Amy nodded her head and pressed the cloth closer to her face.

'Miss Horrocks has an appointment tomorrow, just for Mr Shane to look at the . . . He has given her a short course of antibiotics as she's apparently been . . .'

She looked directly at Agnes then hesitated, stopped by Agnes's expression of sheer annoyance. Agnes spoke tartly.

'I'm not Miss Horrocks' mother. I think she can manage to take her pills without any supervision from me!'

'I'm sorry. I just thought you . . .'

The receptionist looked embarrassed and turned to Amy, giving her the whole message about tomorrow's appointment and the antibiotic course. Amy nodded, and then looked at Agnes.

'Sorry, Agnes. Of course I can manage the pills myself.' She turned back to the receptionist. 'I'll be here at three o'clock, as you said.'

Amy turned and crossed the hall to the front door. Agnes followed her, feeling slightly ashamed of her outburst. She certainly had not minced her words. Yet at least she had let Amy know how she felt. After all, she had only had a tooth out, easily apparently, and now was on antibiotics which she seemed to have been on for ever as far as Agnes was concerned.

In the car and on the drive home hardly a word was spoken between the two of them. Not surprising, as Amy kept the white cloth, which looked like a small surgery towel, over her mouth. When they eventually arrived home she went in, still without a word, and ran up to her room. As she made her way up the stairs, Agnes heard a little sound from behind the towel that sounded as if Amy was starting to cry.

Well, Agnes thought, that was hardly unusual.

The door of Amy's room closed.

Agnes decided to make her a drink. She couldn't just

leave her to cry and carry on by herself. The wretched socket might start to bleed and she would have to drive her back to the dentist.

Nurse she might have been, but she had never had any experience with dental patients. The thought of the socket bleeding put Agnes off the warm drink idea. She would just go up and see if Amy wanted anything, a hot water bottle perhaps. Anyway, she would ask.

She tapped gently on Amy's bedroom door. A muffled voice said, 'Come in.'

Agnes pushed open the door.

Amy had drawn the curtains and was lying on the bed, outside the coverlet. Her light coat was thrown over the end of the bed. She looked up as Agnes came into the room then buried her head in the pillow, hiding her face.

Agnes pulled one curtain half back so that she could see Amy more clearly.

The towel was still near her mouth, but not covering it completely.

'The socket's all right – it's not bleeding, is it, Amy?'

The reply she got was tearful but positive at least.

'No. It's not bleeding and I really don't think you would care if it was, Agnes, thank you.'

Agnes gave up and left the room.

As she went down she knew that Amy could not forgive her, never would forgive her. She wondered if there had been other women, nurses or patients at the hospital, on whom Amy had forced her affections, maybe only to be rejected. Her mother seemed to have used her, not loved her.

Agnes felt uncomfortable and longed to be alone again.

Directly Amy had recovered she would start. What a nuisance about this new course of antibiotics! Still, at least it was only a short one this time. Agnes couldn't wait to start making it obvious, if it wasn't already, that she wanted Amy out. Out of The Sanctuary and out of her life!

Chapter Twenty

'Wilma has undoubtedly fallen on her feet. If only Alice could see her! She's a bit greyer round the muzzle like me but her coat looks wonderful!'

Major Hayward caressed the dog's head.

Wilma, an old habit, put one paw up and rested it on her old master's knee. Her brown eyes, soulful and seemingly recognizing him, as she always did, made him smile and go on stroking her.

As usual the Major wanted to hear about any additions to the animal family. He liked to hear the smallest details and Agnes felt he must often think about all the animals and The Sanctuary.

Agnes told him all about the postman's delivery and the progress of Horace and Harry. Strange stuff to tell an old army man incarcerated in an old people's residential home! The Major, however, listened with interest and Agnes made whatever she had to tell as amusing as she could.

She suspected that all her tales reminded him of the things Alice, his beloved wife, had loved to do.

Rescue and help.

Agnes did not tell him about the change of name from Kitten Collage to The Sanctuary. She thought the change might be hurtful to the memory of his wife.

Today, as they sat in the garden under the beech tree where they usually sat, a little removed from the other residents, Agnes felt a bit preoccupied.

In the pocket of her cardigan she had the bottle.

The fatal brown bottle of the remaining Nembutal.

She was not quite sure why she had brought it with her.

Amy had spoken of the missing bottle now and again, so she still had its loss in her mind, still maybe suspected her brother of stealing it.

But Agnes could not be sure!

Amy might search, even perhaps in Agnes's bedroom. So for safety's sake she had brought it with her.

For the last two or three days the subject of Amy's moving out, finding somewhere else to live, had been avoided. Amy had done her share of the chores with the animals and seemed to love the work. The occupants of 'the little zoo' as the vet had called it were devoted to her, and Mrs Symington Smythe's black cat Tippy followed Amy everywhere, almost 'to heel' like a dog.

Even all this could not obliterate from Agnes's mind the love, admiration or whatever it could be called, that Amy appeared to feel for her.

Agnes was frightened of such devotion. It spoke of suffocation, control and jealousy. Even as she sat in the well-tended garden of the home – Sunset Lodge – she turned the bottle over and over in her hand. The little rattle the capsules made was unheard by Major Hayward who was getting a little deafer every time she visited him.

Agnes now had to speak really loudly to make him hear. He was at the moment telling her about the death of one of the inmates. It was the first, she believed, that had happened since the Major had been at Sunset Lodge.

'He fell out of bed. Don't know if he was dead and fell or fell and he was dead. Y'know?' He shook his head. He did not seem unduly upset about the death and shrugged his shoulders.

'Well, that's how it is, isn't it? It's what you expect.'

Agnes turned the bottle round and round. It felt quite warm in her hand. It would be so easy, so safe!

Mix the drink, take it up to Amy. Empty each capsule into the mug first.

198

She could hear herself now – sounding so convincing.

'Yes, my friend has been very depressed lately. Well, she had a lot of pain after a dental appointment. Also her brother came over from Australia, some trouble about a will. I didn't know a lot about it, but I know she was deeply affected by . . .'

No need to say too much, just the essentials as she knew them.

More would come out after Amy's death of course.

Barbara's death, Robert's visit to the doctor and lawyer. Enough to make a person like Amy take her own life.

No other way out now. Agnes felt she would never get round to removing Amy from her life in any other way, but this. The little capsules rattled again as the bottle was turned over.

'And it is good that your friend is just as fond of animals and looking after them as you are, Agnes.'

Major Hayward broke into her thoughts with these rather inappropriate words.

The white-coated nurse or helper, whatever he was, stood at the edge of the path by the big entrance door, signalling that it was time for them to come in for their meal.

All the residents obediently started for the door. Some were pushed along in wheelchairs, some had walking aids. Some, more active, used just one stick.

Agnes turned the Major's chair round and pushed him along towards the entrance, Wilma walking sedately by their side.

At the door they had to part. Dogs, even Wilma, were not allowed into the home. Major Hayward held the dog's head in both hands, stroking her grey muzzle with his thumb.

'Goodbye, old girl. I hope to see you again very soon.'

He turned to Agnes and took her hand. He retained it for a moment and looked very directly into her eyes.

'Thank you for coming, Agnes, and for bringing Wilma. I hope what you are worrying about will turn out for the best. I've never seen you worried before. I can tell when people are worried.'

Agnes was surprised, but couldn't deny it. Perhaps it was having the little bottle to finger in her pocket. She smiled, however, and shook her head in denial.

'Oh, it's nothing, Major Hayward. Nothing at all.'

She surrendered the chair to the white-coated attendant and Major Hayward raised a hand in a farewell gesture.

'It's so nice to know that your friend loves looking after animals just as much as you do, Agnes!'

He repeated the words he had said before.

Agnes would have loved to reply, if only to see his reaction, 'Even if you know she is a lesbian, Major?'

But she said nothing and he was gone through the door.

Agnes was interested by his remark. She wondered how he had sensed that something was indeed worrying her.

Seated in her car with Wilma on the passenger seat beside her, Agnes gazed across the road through the gate of Sunset Lodge, waiting for a gap in the passing traffic to let her out on to the road home.

Her resolution remained.

Amy would have to go back to her flat, but of course there was the tenant to get rid of first. It might take weeks and all the time she would be imploring Agnes to let her stay.

Tippy would miss her most of all. Perhaps she could take the little cat with her when she went.

At the traffic lights, while Agnes waited for the red light to disappear, she put her hand in her pocket and touched the little bottle of capsules. She couldn't leave it alone.

If Amy did not go, then she would use what means she had. After all, it was up to Amy to end this stupid infatuation.

'I need to be with you!'

She heard the words again coming from the tearful Amy.

She did not want to be loved, possessed by another woman. Anything, anything, but that! Agnes shivered.

It had to be resolved and sooner rather than later!

On this rather sombre note, Agnes entered the house. As she was passing through the hall, the telephone rang. She picked up the receiver.

'The Sanctuary,' she said automatically. She had got used to the new name by now.

'This is Guy Singer. That dinner, Agnes – I don't suppose you could manage Wednesday, could you?'

Agnes felt her spirits rise. She answered with pleasure.

'Yes, I could. Wednesday would be very nice.'

'About seven thirty then? I will call for you if that . . .?'

Agnes agreed, and as she put the receiver down she was conscious that her mood had taken a sea change.

Amy must be got rid of. She was all the more anxious now. Nothing must be allowed to make her new friend think that she lived with a woman because she preferred it. Amy might give him the impression that she and Agnes were very close. That must not happen.

She knew what men thought of lesbian relationships. The idea seemed to repulse all the men she had known. Young men were perhaps more tolerant about such things and were even curious as to what they got up to, but the older men were not so broad-minded.

Amy was in the enclosure. She closed the wire door behind her and came out to greet Agnes. As always at her heel walked Tippy. The black cat clearly idolized Amy, perhaps because she had been so very patient when Tippy first arrived and would not emerge from her cat carrier. Then it was only for Amy that she came half out of the box. Amy's patience and concern for Tippy was something Agnes would not easily forget.

Today, however, she was thinking of the telephone call. Should she tell Amy about her dinner date? She decided against it. She might show her disapproval by a disparaging remark or throwing a jealous tantrum.

Oh hell, Agnes thought. Why can't I enjoy the thought of a date, if one could call it that, without the addition of worry because some silly woman has a crush on me?

Agnes greeted Amy and bent down to stroke Tippy who accepted her caress but shrank back a bit. Agnes understood, as she always understood animals so well.

'She really only trusts you, Amy, and always will.'

The remark she had just made sent a little twinge through her. How would Tippy fare without Amy's love?

Agnes told Amy all about her visit to Major Hayward, Wilma's reaction to him and his reaction to Wilma. Also how one of the inmates had died and how very pretty the garden was looking. All very very boring.

But Amy listened with rapt attention to every word and even questioned her about the staff at the home and did Agnes think they were kind to him.

'Oh Agnes, it's so good of you, what you've done for that poor old man. Buying his house and taking Wilma so he didn't have to have her put down. And going to visit him – I think you're wonderful, Agnes!'

Hearing all this, Agnes could not resist a terse reply.

'For goodness sake, Amy. I got the house dirt cheap because they couldn't sell it and of course I couldn't let Wilma be . . . and I like going to see Major Hayward. He is not a poor old man, he is an intelligent well-educated man who is a real joy to have a conversation with.'

Amy was suitably put down by this and apologized.

'I didn't mean he was . . . I just meant it was nice of you to take the trouble to . . . you know, nice of you.'

Agnes let the matter drop. Amy knew she had made a gaffe and walked away, followed closely by Tippy, tail erect and making small meowing noises.

'Talking', Amy called it and Agnes was inclined to agree with her. Cats can be very vocal and chatty when they are fond of someone.

One thing Agnes could not fault was her companion's attitude to animals, all of them, even Clancy the goat. She loved them all.

Wednesday morning arrived and Agnes had still said nothing to Amy about the dinner date.

It was midday. Amy, whose turn it was to cook the evening meal, questioned her as she usually did about what she would like to eat.

'Shall I do pork chops or lamp chops this evening, Agnes? If you say which you prefer I will take them out of the freezer. I know you mostly like lamb. Which shall I do?'

Agnes was just opening her mail. It had come a little late and she had only just collected it from the mail box at the gate. There was one catalogue from Damart for Amy which she handed over.

'Oh, not another of those. That's the third this week and I never seem to buy anything. Pork or lamb?'

Amy threw the catalogue down on to the table and looked at Agnes, waiting for her answer.

'Oh, I forgot to tell you. I am going out to dinner tonight. You have whatever you like best, Amy.'

If her companion was surprised or upset in any way she certainly did not show it. She just smiled.

'Oh, good. Have a nice meal. I expect it will be better than my cooking anyway. Are you going to a hotel?'

'I don't expect so. You are a good cook and certainly better than I am. I'm having dinner with our vet. I expect it's to drum up trade.'

Agnes felt she had to justify not telling Amy before but then wondered why she had to explain herself anyway. She put out a hand to pick up the catalogue on the table. Amy made exactly the same gesture at the same time. Their hands touched. Agnes looked up. Amy's cheeks had gone pink and she withdrew her hand as if she was afraid of getting burned. She turned away and left the catalogue where it was in its shiny plastic cover. Both moved away from the table.

Agnes felt herself sighing and thinking, For goodness sake, did her face redden because she had touched my hand or because she is trying to avoid ever touching me?

She decided it was the latter reason.

Amy wanted desperately to stay. Should they talk about it or ignore it? Well, she would put the nonsense out of her mind at least for today, at least for this evening anyway. She began to wonder what she would wear. It was quite a time since she had been out with a man to dinner. Oh, except Robert of course. She had given him dinner here and pretty disastrous that had been, as she remembered.

Agnes went up to her bedroom to look through her wardrobe. Her hair was not too bad. She had gone on having it styled and cut as usual.

What kind of place would they go to, she wondered?

She took out a plain silk dress in her favourite colour, pale, pale green, and a suit, well cut and of a very slightly darker green. She hung the two on the wardrobe door and decided to make up her mind later. Suddenly she did not want to go.

Why had she accepted so readily? Just to have a man take her out again? Agnes couldn't understand her own feelings. She tipped up her bottle of Joy perfume. Very little left, but why bother? The lovely smell of the scent made her feel a little less doubtful, made her look forward to the outing a little more.

Amy appeared at the bedroom door, glanced at the two garments. She seemed still relaxed, no resentment.

'Lunch is ready. It's only soup and toast. I thought that would be enough as you're . . .'

She turned and went down the stairs.

Agnes put the stopper back in the perfume bottle. The scent still lingered round her as she made her way down to the kitchen. She felt if Amy made one remark about the perfume she would probably throw the soup over her. She hated being – how could she put it – inspected, overseen, watched. She liked to do things her own way. So she was wearing perfume, so what?

Amy put the soup on the table and said nothing at all.

But even that did not satisfy Agnes. When she was dressed ready to go out this evening Amy would be bound to say something, complimentary of course, like, 'Oh, you do look nice, Agnes, that colour really does suit you.' And when the car drew up outside, 'There he is, Agnes! On the dot, isn't he?'

Agnes did not think she could stand that.

When she spooned up the soup, made by Amy, and not out of a tin, really delicious, she wondered whether perhaps she was becoming a little paranoid. She decided she wasn't. Living with another woman was not for her, absolutely not. She finished her soup and pushed away the dish.

She must say something.

'That was very good, Amy, very good indeed. I shall miss your home-made soups when you go.'

Amy paused ever so slightly as she picked up the two dishes to put them on the draining board ready for washing up. She nodded, but once again said absolutely nothing in reply to that remark. She just went to the oven and took out the two baked apples she had prepared for, as she called it, 'afters'.

The smell of cloves drove out the smell of Joy!

Agnes looked at the small black and gold clock on her bedside table.

Twenty minutes before Guy Singer was coming to collect her.

She stood in front of her dressing-table mirror regarding herself critically. She had yet to put on the pale green dress. It hung on the outside of her wardrobe at the moment. It had been there since lunchtime, hanging to get the creases out of the rather full skirt.

Looking closely at her hair, she saw the cut was as good as ever and each strand fell back into place if she shook her head, or the wind stirred it. She had it washed, cut, and tinted, if it was necessary, every fortnight. As she leaned closer to the glass, the tinting did not look as good as usual.

Agnes parted her hair with her fingers. She had noticed some time ago one or two grey hairs and, when they were tinted, they did not take the colour as well as the rest. Some remained grey. However, she was determined, at the moment anyway, not to use a stronger tint. She would just hope it was not too noticeable.

Anyway, did it really matter?

Her figure – well, she couldn't find fault with that. She stood back a little to see more of herself in the mirror.

Yes, her figure remained good.

She never put on weight – well, hardly ever.

She had a little while she was in the flat in spite of long walks with Polly, but she could soon take the few pounds off. Maybe she had already, she had not bothered to weigh herself lately.

This dinner date was certainly making her take more notice of what getting older was doing to her, in looks anyway. Good or bad, Agnes wasn't too displeased.

Agnes had already made up her face and looking at that with her new super-critical eye, she wondered if she had put too much blusher on, or a shade too much eye shadow? She suddenly wished she was not going out to dinner at all, but as she slipped the dress over her head the skirt fell in soft silky folds round her legs and made her feel better.

Grimacing at herself, she then picked up the thin gold chain which was all the jewellery she was wearing. She fastened it securely.

As she was doing so Amy spoke, her voice coming from the bedroom door. She stood outside, but as she spoke she moved a little further into Agnes's bedroom. She was smiling, full of admiration.

'Oh, I'm so glad you are wearing that lovely dress. I remember you wearing it to one of the little drinks parties at the flats. It looks so nice on you, suits you. It's such a lovely shade of green.'

Agnes turned, full face towards Amy. She had never felt so furious. She felt her pulse rate rise. She felt almost breathless with outrage. She moved forward a little and Amy stepped back, perhaps half afraid that Agnes might approach a little nearer and strike her.

Her face paled as Agnes flushed redder.

'How long have you been standing watching me?'

Her voice was almost a hiss.

Amy's mouth opened, her hands fluttering upwards.

'I was just passing. The door was open and I just saw you slipping into your green dress. I didn't mean . . . I wasn't prying, Agnes, I was only passing your door on my way to my room.'

As she spoke, almost wailing, Agnes noticed Tippy standing close to Amy, her green eyes wide. Momentarily Agnes fused the two together.

Amy the witch or bitch. Take your pick, with her black familiar cat. The black cat always with her. Watching, wanting help. With the Bennetts, with Robert, with the dentist. What plea for help would be next?

Agnes managed to control her anger. A car hooted at the gate. Guy Singer. Here already!

Agnes glanced at the bedside clock. Two minutes early.

Amy was about to say something else but Agnes gave her no time to do so. She picked up her light coat from the bed, then her small handbag. The cat jumped on the bed, purring loudly. Agnes brushed by Amy, almost pushing her out of her way. Amy tried again to speak, to explain, and Agnes suspected also to apologize in some way.

She was already showing signs of being tearful.

'And don't shut Tippy in my bedroom, Amy.'

It was a command.

Agnes hurried downstairs and across the hall, this time

not even glancing at herself in the hall mirror. She yanked open the front door and slammed it to behind her. She heard Amy still trying to call something to her, but ignored whatever she was saying, and stood for a moment trying to compose herself, banish her anger and look pleasant.

As she approached Guy's car he got out, opened the gate and came up the path to meet her. She smiled at him. He opened the door on the passenger side, explained the mechanism of the safety strap, almost always a little different in every make of car, saw that she was safely in and closed the door. In the driver's seat he kept the door open for a moment so that the safety light shone in the car, illuminating the inside a little.

'You're looking very nice, Agnes, and your perfume is lovely. I don't often notice women's perfume, but yours is perfect.'

Agnes thanked him for his compliments and began to feel better. She could feel herself relaxing and her heart rate subsiding back to its normal rhythm. She stole a glance at her companion. He had on a dark suit and gleaming white shirt. He looked quite different without his usual corduroy trousers and rather ancient and worn-looking sports jacket which he wore at work. His after-shave too was pleasant. He started the engine and drove away from The Sanctuary.

Agnes was determined to enjoy the evening and forget Amy, though the thought of her standing there at her bedroom door, watching her, was not easily forgotten.

Chapter Twenty-One

Agnes arrived home at about twenty past eleven, rather later than she had expected, but she and Guy had sat and talked after their meal. The hotel had a very comfortable lounge with a blazing fire, a very welcome sight as the night had turned quite chilly after a lovely warm sunny day.

They had sat together on the big overstuffed settee, chatting away. Sitting drinking coffee that was as good as the food, and a liqueur, Agnes had felt relaxed and comfortable for the first time in several weeks.

As she put her key in the front door and watched Guy's car drive away she at least had to give a Brownie point to Amy for leaving the door lamp on, so she had no trouble in finding the lock and inserting her key. As she entered, she switched off the porch light and switched on the hall light.

She walked across the hall to the kitchen and was certain, or almost certain, that she heard a door closing upstairs, very softly.

Perhaps she was wrong, but it was better than her finding Amy up and waiting for her, making the excuse that she wanted to see some television programme. Still, Agnes thought, after the way she had blazed at her before she went out, maybe she had intimidated her enough to keep her out of the way, at least for a bit.

Agnes was determined not to think about or assess the evening with Guy until she was in bed and able to give all her mind to the time spent with her new friend.

Some of the evening had been good, some not quite so good, the latter largely her fault. She dismissed it all from her mind and ran a glass of water. The coffee had made her thirsty.

Then she went upstairs and listened as she passed Amy's door. Not a sound. She closed her own bedroom door behind her softly. After all, she might have misjudged Amy, thinking she heard her door close. Perhaps she was fast asleep. She was not a great one for television anyway, seldom watched for long.

Agnes sat down at her dressing table, opened the big jar of cleansing cream and cleaned off her make-up. Watching herself in the glass, she murmured to herself, her lips moving as she said the words.

'Don't think, don't think yet. Work it out later in bed.'

She took off the green dress and hung it up.

Guy had admired it, loved the gentle colour, he had said. That had been one of the good points of the evening, one of the many good points. But, the not so good, they were what she wanted to think about.

Agnes pulled up the covers, settled her head on the pillow and switched off the bedside light. The room, plunged in darkness, was the signal she had given herself to go over the evening carefully and the mistakes she had made.

It had all started so well. Guy had looked so nice, so different, and quite handsome. The hotel had been perfect too. Just outside Lewes, a country house beautifully converted into a large two-roomed restaurant.

Quite a few people were dining. All waiters, no waitresses.

They both had lobster thermidor.

She had asked him to talk about himself first. That was after he had tried to question her a little about her past, her origins, something Agnes was never particularly happy talking about.

Guy's past was quite interesting but not all that dramatic.

He had always wanted to be a veterinary surgeon.

'The training is longer than a doctor's, Agnes, because of the difference in all the species' anatomy and diseases,' he had said.

He paused while they both tackled their lobster. Not an easy dish to negotiate but one of Agnes's favourites. They decided to have their coffee and liqueur in the beautifully appointed lounge. There, beside a blazing fire, they had sat while he finished the story of his life, which he seemed to enjoy telling her.

He had married young and the marriage had not been a success, though between them they had managed to rub along for about twelve years. He didn't say much about his wife. No children, then an amicable divorce and he, as he laughingly put it, 'had gone back to Mother'.

'I was forty then and found living at home easy and comfortable. My father had died during my marriage. My mother is old now and my living at home is, I believe, a great comfort to her. She feels safer with a man about the house.' The way he had ended his little story should have made everything apparent to Agnes, but it certainly didn't.

'Now tell me about your past and how you come to be running an animal sanctuary with someone who is, I am sure, just as devoted to the strays that come to you as you are, Agnes.'

Agnes sat up in bed, put her head in her hands. Why had she told him, why had she talked about such a thing as Amy and her current predicament? First she had skated over her early life with no mention of the orphanage, just that she was brought up in a town near Oxford. Then her life as a nurse, briefly her marriage and her husband's death. Then she had started talking about Amy and how she had formed an attachment to Agnes which was proving rather irritating. Indeed she had almost asked his advice as to what he would do!

211

Agnes switched on her bedside lamp. Sleep was impossible at the moment. She couldn't have put before him a worse problem. His reserve had totally broken down as he heard Agnes's story.

'Get rid of her, Agnes, get her out of your life. My wife was seduced away from me by a woman. A lesbian. I had no idea what was going on. I should have. She had merely put up with my lovemaking, there was never much response. Then after a few years she would not tolerate me near her. She eventually went away with this woman. I made light of it when I told you about the divorce, Agnes, and I only tell you some of the truth about my marriage now. The whole thing disgusted me. Perhaps I am a naive sort of chap, innocent. When she pushed me away more and more I put it down to another man and thought she was being unfaithful to me.'

Agnes, sitting up in bed, was having some difficulty in understanding her own feelings, or were they fears, heightened perhaps by the talk with Guy? Had he really intended to frighten her so much?

He had been pretty explicit in his description of what he had seen when he had caught his wife and her female lover in bed together. Agnes supposed he thought he was talking to an ex-nurse who would have seen so many things, disgusting or horrific, that the details he was recounting would not have any effect on her. He had been wrong, very wrong. It had probably helped him to get the scene off his chest, but it had not helped Agnes.

'Get rid of her, Agnes, get her out of your life!'

She had, she supposed, intended to do just that. Tell Amy that she must move out as soon as possible. But, how soon would this be? Probably weeks before Amy could get rid of her tenant or find somewhere else to live. Then there were the animals. They both loved them so much. Polly, Wilma, Tippy, Horace and Harry even. The poor mother cat and her kittens . . .

Oh, Lord!

Agnes turned off the bedside lamp, lay down and pum-

melled the pillow into a more comfortable position, determined to get some sleep, but it didn't work. She started to
imagine what might happen, things she knew were stupid
and completely irrational. Well, she was almost certain
they were.

Amy stealing into her bedroom and trying to get into
bed with her. Amy trying to embrace her, caress her. Amy
pleading with her to let her live with her. Agnes had some
experience of lesbians making passes at her.

When she was in her early days of nursing one or two
nurses had tried. She remembered in particular one sister,
the Home Sister, as she was called in those days, bringing
her Horlicks at night. It was some time before she had
realized that this sister, about forty years old and to
Agnes ancient, was a lesbian. It was only when the
woman had put her hand on Agnes's leg outside the bedcover that Agnes caught on. Even then she had been very
afraid, though the sister had drawn back at Agnes's look of
fear and revulsion and there then had been no more
Horlicks!

Years later, when Agnes had almost forgotten the incident, she heard that Sister Matthews, the erstwhile Home
Sister, had committed suicide. Pity had taken the place of
fear in Agnes's mind, but now the same feeling of fear had
come back and in the place of that almost forgotten senior
nurse was the timid tearful Amy Horrocks!

Chapter Twenty-Two

Agnes's mood had changed when she woke in the morning. She was more determined than ever to get rid of Amy, go she must, somehow or other!

She came downstairs a little later than usual. Amy had already made coffee and was now making toast. Her back was to Agnes as she entered the kitchen. Agnes thought she was probably going to sulk and look affronted and put out, making out she was cut to the quick. She was wrong.

Amy put the toast rack in front of her with a pleasant smile. Then she poured two cups of coffee.

'Shall we walk Polly and Wilma first? I think it's going to rain, it says so on the radio weather forecast.'

Agnes took a piece of toast from the little rack and automatically reached for the butter. She did not feel too good and was honest enough to tell herself that undoubtedly she had drunk too much last night.

While she had been with Guy, maybe because it was such a long time since she had been taken out to a meal, she hadn't thought about how much wine she was drinking. Two bottles of wine. She must have got through one, maybe more, and the liqueurs, one – two? She couldn't remember. It had been so relaxed, so comfortable. Anyway, something had given her a headache. She pushed away the buttered toast and sipped the coffee. Even that tasted like cardboard. She realized Amy had said something.

'What did you say, Amy, something about the dogs, was it?'

Amy repeated her suggestion but Agnes shook her head.

'No, I'd rather take them on my own. I want to be by myself for a bit. You can get on with the others if you will.'

Amy looked shattered. She took a bite of buttered toast.

'Is it because of last evening, my interfering? I really didn't mean to be prying or anything, Agnes. I was just passing your door, truly!'

Agnes didn't reply or even look up. She just went on sipping her coffee. Amy went on eating.

Then at last Agnes felt she must make some remark.

'It's nothing to do with you, Amy. I think you were prying and I hate that. I hate being watched. It's just the way I am.' She stood up. 'I'll go now. Walkies, Polly, Wilma.'

The two dogs got up. Wilma, slowly and with her usual dignity. Polly began to rush around in circles, barking. She then rushed out into the hall to look for her lead. Wilma watched Polly, tail waving slowly to and fro. Agnes stood in the hall, looking at the two dogs. Relationships with those two, so simple. Food and a lot of love and care. They seemed to respect each other.

Men and women, always difficult. All humans were difficult.

Out on the Downs the clear breezy day made even Wilma a little skittish. She belied her grey muzzle and ageing limbs and chased Polly round for at least ten minutes. After that she came back to Agnes who was sitting on the old teak seat she always made for at the top of the first hill. Wilma leaned against her legs, panting a little with her tongue lolling out. Now and again she looked up as if to say, 'These young pups don't know when to take a rest.'

The sun shone, though not very warmly. The short grass rippled as the wind blew across it. The white clouds were scudding across the sky, followed by slightly darker ones behind them. Amy had been right about the forecast. Rain clouds were not too far distant across the gentle contour of the Downs. Agnes loved this place. She looked around her with thankfulness. What a wonderful place to live! Only one thing was spoiling it, one person. Agnes called the two dogs and went back to the car. She put two bowls of water down for them and after they had both drunk as much as they wanted, she turned the water bowls on to the grass to empty them and put them in the box which lived in the back of her car, with the bottle of fresh water.

As she put the box back on to the car seat she noticed that the leather of the seat was slightly worn. This car was eight years old. Time for a new Porsche. The dogs jumped into their places in the car. Polly, at least, jumped in, Wilma had to be helped a little. Her arthritis was apparent when she tried to jump up into the car or even on to a chair or sofa.

Agnes's headache was almost gone. She felt so much better for her walk. The thought of getting a new car also made her feel good. But, there was something she had to do before she bought a new one. She started the car engine and sat for a moment looking at the darkening clouds. Something she had to do, and soon.

Did she really want to be alone, live alone? She thought she did. Would a kennel maid coming in daily be enough? She had lived alone before but not for very long. Damn Amy and her beastly, stupid crush. But she couldn't go on with it. The solution was there, even now in her handbag beside her in the car, giving its reassuring little rattle every time she moved the bag. Could she . . . yes, she could and would!

One more confrontation perhaps with Amy re the moving out – then . . . If she didn't act quickly it would be too late. Amy must get on with moving out, or take the consequences.

When she arrived home Amy was standing waiting for her at the gate. She looked slightly apprehensive. She held something in her arms, something wrapped in a white towel which, from where Agnes looked and stood, resembled a baby. But, for goodness sake, even Amy wouldn't be so half-witted as to take in a real live child!

'What is it, Amy, what have you got there?'

Agnes drew closer and patted the white towel. As she patted, the inmate of the towel cuddled up in Amy's arms and showed its small furry, slightly pointed nose. Ginger face, little black button-like eyes, blinking as they were exposed to the light. A baby fox, a cub. Amy looked up at Agnes, her face anxious and questioning. She put the towel back.

'A teenage boy brought it. He found it in a field, just at the end of a little wood. The Hunt had got them. Mother torn to bits and two cubs as well. This one was still alive, hiding in some long grass.'

'Is he hurt in any way? He looks very very young, Amy, but you did quite right to take him in. Poor little chap, he can't help what species he is.'

Amy had given the cub some warm milk. She had no idea whether the little creature was weaned or not. Inside, Agnes tried milk as Amy had, in a bottle with a teat. Not much success. Then she had an idea. She made some porridge, put it in a little dish and offered it to the cub. Success! It could lap the porridge up and licked the plate clean, its long tongue cleaning its mouth.

Agnes decided to ring Guy Singer, thank him for the dinner and ask for a little advice about the cub, how to feed it and treat the creature. He suggested she did not pet the animal too much as when she wanted to let it loose in the country again, if she did, it would bond with her and she wouldn't be able to get rid of it. Agnes replied rather tartly. The words 'get rid of it' offended her.

You mean put it back for the Hunt again. I don't think so, Guy, she thought, but she just thanked him for his help and put the telephone down with a bit of a bang. She was disappointed in the vet, her friend. Perhaps he hunted? She had no idea.

'What did Mr Singer suggest we do, Agnes?'

'Nothing of importance, Amy. We must manage, but I don't intend to let it loose to be hunted again and torn to pieces as its mother was.'

Amy literally glowed with delight. She put out a hand and squeezed Agnes's arm in what was almost a caress.

Agnes felt herself wince away.

'Oh, you are wonderful, Agnes. I thought you might say something like that. You are really lovely. I didn't think the vet would think about a fox cub like we would. He'd just think of the chickens it might kill. Well, they are made like that, they can't help it.'

That night Agnes fed the cub again. This time it lapped up some milk as well. Whether she was treating the cub correctly she didn't know. This worried her a little. She knew that anyone or almost anyone she asked would either hunt or have had chickens killed by foxes and would not be interested in saving a fox cub. Every hand was against it.

She put the cub in a cat basket in the kitchen. It seemed sleepy and curled up on the blanket like a little puppy. Agnes went to bed hoping for the best. She was fairly tired. The day had been quite long. The mother and kittens were now active and playful and had to be let out into the enclosure where the kittens ran about, rushing back to mother cat when they felt like it or wanted feeding. They were eating kitten food now. More work.

Tippy would have none of the cat and kittens, and she spat and hissed at them. Tippy was Amy's cat and still followed her everywhere like a dog.

Agnes read a little before she settled down to sleep. As she switched off her light she thought she heard a short sharp yelp. She switched the light back on and listened and looked at Polly who was stretched out in her basket near Agnes's bed. She gave a small sleepy yelp-like sound. She often did this when she was sound asleep. Agnes used to, and still did, think that the little dog was dreaming, perhaps about being chased by a cat or big dog, or even

218

chasing a cat herself. She put the light out again and settled down. She was soon asleep.

Something woke her.

The luminous hands of her little clock showed it to be ten to two. The slight squeak which she had heard, which had awoken her, was made by the handle of her bedroom door being gently turned. Agnes froze. The red numbers on her bedside clock gave out a glow, faintly illuminating the room. She could see the old-fashioned brass door handle, part of the brass door furniture all over the round house. It turned ever so slightly, making a tiny squeaking noise.

She lay still, absolutely still, watching the door. Agnes longed to switch on her bedside light and scream out, 'What the hell do you want, Amy? Get out of my room!'

But she didn't. She lay quite still, her eyes narrowed to a slit, watching.

The door opened about a foot and even in the faint light from the little clock she could see it was Amy in her blue dressing gown. Agnes knew the dressing gown was blue, but in the rather weird red light it looked pink.

Amy's face was in shadow.

She pushed the door open a little more then just stood looking at Agnes. She did not move any further into the room. Quite still, she stood there looking. Agnes felt her heart rate increasing, but went on pretending she was asleep. Anything but a confrontation in the middle of the night. What could she do anyway? Suppose she moved, showed she was awake, would Amy cross the room and touch her, try to . . .

Amy seemed to stand there for ages, just looking. What was she expecting? Suddenly Amy backed a little and the door closed without a sound, so gently that Agnes could visualize how slowly and carefully Amy had pulled it to and let the handle rotate back, closing the latch. No squeak this time.

Agnes sat up now. She heard nothing. No sound of Amy crossing towards her own room, no sound of the door of

219

her room closing behind her. Then there was a sound. Someone crying softly. Amy. Agnes, sitting up in bed, her heart still beating a little faster than usual, listened. The crying stopped. She leant back against her pillows. Something had to be done and done soon.

Meanwhile, supposing Amy tried again?

She got up suddenly, crossed the room as quietly as she could and picked up a hardwood chair. She took it over to the door and again, as quietly as she could, wedged the back under the handle. The door had no lock so this was the best she could do, just in case Amy came back. Then, still without putting her light on, she picked up her handbag, which she kept beside her dressing table, and got back into bed. She opened the bag, took out the familiar little bottle of capsules and thrust them under her pillow, dropping her handbag down beside the bed.

The time had come!

Agnes pulled up the covers, settled her pillow and lay facing the little clock. She had a lot to think about. How to do it, when to do it. She had no fears about the task ahead. Amy was a typical suicide type. Depressed, trouble with her family. Ran a residential home where barbiturates were available. No problem there at all. Agnes played it over in her mind, bit by bit. Rehearsal was always a good thing. After a time, when it was all straightened out in her mind, and reassured by the chair wedged under the door handle, Agnes managed to get to sleep.

Chapter Twenty-Three

When she awoke the sun was shining through her curtains, yet she could hear a splattering of rain. She parted the curtains. It was raining slightly and the sun was shining. Agnes's bedroom overlooked the big wire enclosure. Over it was a beautiful rainbow. She stood looking out at it until the rainbow faded away, then she went downstairs to the kitchen to make herself tea. There was no sound in the house.

Amy must be asleep. She was always a heavy sleeper in the mornings.

Agnes sipped the tea then suddenly remembered the cub, there in the kitchen.

She could hardly forgive herself! There was no sound from the cat basket. Agnes put down her cup and went across the kitchen to see if the little animal was still alive.

It was.

The furry little face, the bright black eyes looked at her through the wire mesh door of the cat basket. Strangely, in the unlit kitchen its little face looked more fox-like. It made a noise, half whine half bark, and put a small paw up to the wire mesh.

Agnes opened the door and lifted the cub out. It was trembling. After yesterday's experiences, hiding, watching its mother torn to pieces and the other cubs killed as well, what could you expect but fear?

Agnes put it back in the cat basket, warmed some milk, then put it in the bottle with a teat. At first it made a mess of the milk and appeared not able to suck. Suddenly it seemed to catch on to the idea and began to suck ravenously.

Holding it in her arm Agnes wondered what the fox cub would have to cope with as it grew up.

Guy Singer had given her no tips as to feeding it, only how she would have to get rid of it. Being a vet, he was probably a hunting man himself, so would only think in terms of destroying it as vermin, never mind how barbarously.

Agnes looked down at the cub in her arms. It looked back at her, fear disappearing from its bright eyes. She stroked it gently and it reacted like a cat, pleased to be petted, making tiny growling noises.

'Who made you in the mould you are, foxy baby, who engineered your genes to make you a killer? A killer without even the need to eat. Not one chicken, not just enough to eat, but ten, eleven . . . fifty. Indiscriminate.'

She felt rather foolish.

She had spoken aloud but there was no one to hear her. No sign of Amy, no sound from upstairs at all. She shook her head. Perhaps her attack when she had caught Amy watching her get dressed ready to go out with Guy had . . . But that didn't explain her night visit last night. What was that all about? At that moment Amy entered the kitchen. Agnes jumped. She had not heard a sound, not Amy opening her bedroom door, nor her coming down the stairs. She was like a ghost!

'For goodness sake, Amy! What are you creeping about for?'

Amy winced at Agnes's tone, which was harsh and irritable. She had only once before heard Agnes speak to her like this. Agnes saw the reaction but did not feel the least bit sorry for what she had said. She waited for Amy to give some explanation about last night's visit to her room. There was none. Agnes decided not to bring the matter up either. After all, she had made out she was asleep, so how could she ask Amy what she was doing coming to her room at that time in the morning?

Amy sank down on to her knees beside the fox cub. Polly was very interested in the new animal and was sniffing round it. The cub showed no fear of the little dog.

'How is he, the little one? How pretty he is, Agnes!'

Tippy, of course, was in her usual place beside Amy. She had followed her into the kitchen and had probably been all night on Amy's bed, her usual sleeping place.

The cat looked at the cub with interest.

'He seems all right, Amy. We will let him have a little run outside so he can relieve himself and I'll feed him again later. I've given him some milk.'

Amy put out a tentative hand and stroked the cub's head. Agnes got up abruptly and took the little animal outside. She ignored Amy except to say, 'There's some tea there, Amy, if you want a cup.'

Well, Agnes couldn't stand the feeling that anyone adored her.

A man, perhaps. But a woman! She couldn't take it!

Hero worship, yes. She could stand that. She had once or twice experienced that from young nurses in training when she had been the all powerful 'sister' figure.

The black and white mother of the kittens greeted Agnes with a chirrup.

Her kittens had progressed quite a bit since they had been brought in. They had grown and they looked more healthy. Their eyes had opened and they sucked and nuzzled their mother's undercarriage with enthusiasm.

As Agnes opened their wire door, the mother cat stood up and the kittens fell off her. She came up to Agnes, purring, then went off to dig herself a hole in the earth surrounding the grass in the enclosure. She then settled herself down, gazing into the distance with a faraway expression that always amused Agnes.

Then the cat turned round, sniffed and covered the hole up with dainty white paws. Her kittens, meanwhile, some distance away, were sniffing and crawling about. They perhaps could not as yet see as far as the distance Mum had taken herself off to and she was in no hurry to get back to them.

She strolled round a little more, eating a little grass, sniffing the morning air. She looked now and again at Agnes, who was pouring some milk for her and putting a saucer of cat food beside it.

'Breakfast is served,' Agnes said smiling.

Agnes wondered, as she always did wonder, what was going through the little cat's mind. No language to use, at least no words that the human could understand.

'I've fallen on my feet here. Decent grub and shelter!'

Is that what her cat mind was saying?

Agnes's thoughts were interrupted by the clink of the latch on the enclosure wire door. She turned round and there stood Guy Singer.

He closed the door carefully behind him and came up to Agnes who was still watching the cub at her feet. The cub was staggering a little as if its back legs were weak. It was gazing around, puzzled.

Guy picked up the little animal before she could stop him. He held it roughly in one hand. It wriggled and began to tremble again and cry.

Guy looked at it with distaste and no pity at all.

'Shall I finish it off for you, Agnes, before it grows big enough to do any damage? It will behave like the vandal it is before much longer.'

'Do you hunt, Guy? Would you chase after this small creature and watch it torn to pieces, screaming?'

Agnes snatched the cub from the vet's hand. She hated Guy at that moment more than anything in the world. He was callous, brutal.

'This cub's mother and her other cubs were torn to pieces by the dogs. This one escaped because it hid. The participants in the Hunt would have been close enough – lucky enough, they would perhaps think – to see it all, smell the blood and guts. See the terrified look in the

224

vixen's eyes. How would you feel, Guy, what would that do to you?'

Guy Singer came forward a little and put his hand on Agnes's arm, the arm that held the cub. She flinched away from him.

'You said on Wednesday, when you were being so explicit about the antics your wife indulged in with her lover, that you could speak openly because I was a nurse. Well, now I can speak openly for the same reason.'

Guy looked at her but made no remark. Perhaps his cheeks had flushed a little. He looked down and scuffed the grass with his shoe.

'If you think of them as vermin, like rats, why don't you shoot them? No – you want to watch them being torn to pieces alive, screaming like this one's mother, just to get a sexual buzz while you watch!'

Guy looked across to where Amy stood, obviously able to hear the conversation and listening with interest.

He looked affronted, and his face reddened even more. He drew back, as if he intended to leave.

'I don't know what you mean, Agnes. Nobody feels that.'

Agnes could not be stopped now. She was saying things she had wanted to say for a long time.

'Oh, don't give me that, Guy! I was trained in a place where the Hunt was all-powerful, those men and women on horseback. The men in their pinks and the local villagers thinking they were lords. The women too, trying to get into the killing, to see the killing, to hear the screaming, see the blood.'

She went on.

'They all get a great sexual thrill out of it – the men and the women. The whole thing is barbaric and disgusting!'

In a way Guy seemed shattered by her tirade, almost as if he were half agreeing and half disagreeing.

Agnes would not give up.

'Do you ride to hounds, Guy? Can you honestly say that

you have never experienced a sexual buzz at the kill, watching?'

Guy Singer shook his head, turned on his heel and left the enclosure, closing the door carefully behind him.

Agnes watched the vet's car draw away from the gate.

She must have shocked and offended him. But she did not care!

Amy came over from the corner of the enclosure where she had been standing. She looked amazed – presumably because of the things Agnes had blurted out. Her opinion of the Hunt and its followers. Things that perhaps Amy herself was aware of, but would never have the courage to put into words.

'You poor little fox. I never knew that, Agnes. I didn't know that they got sexually aroused by things like that. It's just sadism, I suppose, isn't it? People who like torturing things?'

Agnes had no wish to discuss it with her companion. She did not answer this remark at all.

She shrugged her shoulders and cuddled the little fox cub.

'Well, I'll have to look for a new veterinary surgeon. Guy Singer won't feel inclined to look after any of my animals now. Neither would I want him to. So that's that, Amy!'

As evening approached, it started to rain big stormy drops.

The cat and her kittens had to be shut up early. Clancy was bedded down and the hedgehogs put under cover.

The rain grew heavier with the sound of thunder over the Downs. Little flashes of lightning started. Amy, Agnes knew, was rather nervous of storms. She had said so when she had been in the flats. Agnes enjoyed them, especially when they became dark and threatening over the sea and the forked lightning lit the scene with an eerie glow.

'It's my turn to make the meal, Agnes. Would you like spaghetti bolognaise or something lighter, cheesy?'

Agnes shrugged again, as if she couldn't have cared less. Again she did not answer.

Amy looked a bit crestfallen and preceded her into the house, walking quite quickly as the thunder became louder and the clouds blacker.

The door of the enclosure was securely locked behind them.

Still carrying the little cub in her arms, Agnes watched Amy. Tippy, not liking the storm much either, followed closely on Amy's heels.

Agnes herself was followed by Polly and Wilma. The big wolfhound seemed untroubled by the noise or the rain, but Polly, tail slightly down, followed closely and cast an anxious brown-eyed look now and again at her mistress as if to say, 'Is it all right, this row? I'm not used to this kind of thing and I certainly don't like it much at all.'

As the lightning flashed, her tail sank lower.

Agnes soothed her pet and when she had shut the front door of the cottage behind her, Polly shot into the kitchen and put herself to bed, unusually early in the evening.

Amy repeated the question about their meal and Agnes felt she must reply out of sheer politeness, but the incident last night and the altercation between herself and Guy Singer had left her totally without appetite. However, she did not want Amy to know this.

'Yes, spaghetti bolognaise would be very nice. White wine?'

She poured a glass for Amy and one for herself and walked out of the kitchen, still holding the little cub in her left arm. In the sitting room she turned on the news and settled on the settee. The little creature on her lap stirred as the picture and the sound came on but snuggled down again, with one paw over its eyes as if blotting everything out. Agnes was not worried about Rusty, as they had christened him. He had eaten well today. Agnes, acting without advice from anyone, was sticking to milk, porridge and a tiny bit of Whiskas kitten food. Probably not the right food for him, but he seemed to be thriving on it at the moment. The only thing that seemed to upset him was being alone, so Agnes carried him about with her, rather to Polly's indignation.

Agnes sat watching the news and not really taking it in. The pictures floated from one news story to another. She sipped her wine and thought about her outburst to the vet, not regretting it at all.

Agnes had spent four years training in Leicester, hunting country. Working as a junior in Casualty, she had heard horrific stories of sadistic cruelty to foxes, hares and deer. It had sickened her then and it sickened her now. Guy would know, a vet and a huntsman. He would know what she said was true.

Perhaps he wasn't aware, though, how many ordinary people knew what 'being in at the kill' really meant. Then her thoughts turned to Amy. She was nervous about tonight. Might Amy try again, try to get into her room? She determined to wedge the chair under the bedroom door handle, like last night.

She heard Amy rattling plates and cutlery about in the kitchen. She cooked well. Agnes felt she would miss that, but when? She had not really tackled the subject with Amy. She suddenly felt quite overcome with depression, a feeling she recognized in herself and was frightened of.

The cub, the vet, Amy and her wretched 'crush'. How had she got herself in such a mix-up? All she wanted to do was make a home, a sanctuary for the things she loved most in her life. She looked down at Rusty lying in her lap and Polly beside her on the settee, leaning rather heavily to show that she was 'top dog' but would tolerate this ginger creature who looked rather like herself.

The cub still had one paw over its eyes and was moving a little. Agnes tried to take an interest in the local news. The meal would soon be ready. They ate in the kitchen usually in the evening. She felt she could not cope with any kind of confrontation. Her old enemy depression, which had attacked her before, seemed to be dangerously near.

228

'Ready! Shall we have it out here or would you like it in there on a tray? It's just as easy, either way.'

Amy seemed very eager to please.

Agnes signalled that she would come into the kitchen. Still with the cub in her arms, she followed Amy to the table.

The meal was as good as usual and Agnes felt she had to say so. Amy's face lit up at the praise. She gathered the plates up smiling and went over to pour the coffee. Something else she always made to perfection.

'Now we've finished in here I am going to bed Rusty down. He's got to learn to be by himself sometime.'

She thought Amy looked at her rather curiously at this remark.

Agnes folded a warmed blanket into the large cat carrier, put Rusty firmly inside and closed the wire mesh door. Two black eyes, like shiny black beans, looked out at her. Then the fox gave a big, wide-mouthed yawn.

'There, you see. When we put the light out, he will sleep.'

Amy did not look completely convinced.

'Do you think he will be all right, completely by himself?'

Agnes switched off the kitchen light and they both went into the sitting room. Amy switched on the television.

Both sat down.

Agnes could feel Amy stealing a glance at her, trying to assess her mood or to learn what she was thinking. Amy was probably wondering if she had got over telling her off about the green dress incident, had forgotten about it.

Well, Agnes hadn't got over it, or over the twisting door handle last night.

She got up suddenly.

'I'm going to bed. I'm rather tired, Amy. Goodnight.'

Amy almost got up too, then seemed to think better of it and sat down again.

Once in her own room Agnes felt her depression deepening.

She knew she wouldn't sleep. She had a sleeping pill, a mild one. She thought she might take that. She creamed her face and slipped on her nightdress and then hesitated. She took the chair she had used last night and wedged it under the handle of her bedroom door. Better be safe than sorry!

Agnes got into bed and picked up her current book but couldn't be bothered with it. She then decided to take the sleeping pill with the glass of water on her bedside table and tried to settle down.

She put her hand under her pillow and it closed on the little bottle of capsules. She held it firmly.

Was it time to use them?

The thought did something to push away her depression. Maybe it was the sleeping pill, but soon she felt sleepy and her eyelids dropped.

A lovely peaceful feeling . . .

Agnes must have slept, for she woke with a start. There was a sound, a small sound.

A squeak!

She switched on her bedside light.

Polly?

No, Polly was sound asleep, upside down in her basket.

The squeak was the door handle.

Agnes watched it gently turn. The chair moved very slightly but made no sound on the carpet.

She felt sick. Sick and frightened. Her heart was hammering away and she quickly switched off the bedside light in case it should show under the door. She lay, listening intently. She heard steps, soft and slippered across the hall and then the soft, very soft, closing of a door. Amy's door.

Agnes tried to settle down again but the effect of her sleeping pill had disappeared. She looked at her bedside clock.

It was a quarter past two. She must have slept longer than she realized.

She had tried again – Amy had tried again and would not be put off. What did she want?

A love affair between the two of them?

Agnes switched on her bedside light again and took out the little bottle from under her pillow. The contents gave their usual reassuring little dry rattle. She switched off her light, clasped the bottle tightly in her hand and thrust it under the pillow, still holding the bottle. She felt she never wanted to let go of it until the contents were used to the good purpose she knew they were capable of.

It was so comforting to know the little bottle was there, ready for use.

Her depression retreated as she decided exactly what she was going to do – as soon as possible!

Chapter Twenty-Four

Next morning, Agnes stirred and opened her eyes. She felt disorientated, muzzy. She rubbed her eyes and half sat up. She could see across the room. The daylight was just seeping under her drawn curtains. Polly sat up, then apparently decided it was too early to get up or make a move and curled herself up in her basket again.

Agnes remembered she had taken a sleeping pill, or had she? Yes, she remembered the white round pill and the water she had drunk to get it down. This was why she felt muzzy and peculiar.

As a nurse, when she got out a sleeping pill to give a sleepless patient, she had always reassured them.

'Oh, don't worry. This will make you sleep and not make you feel muzzy in the morning.'

Usually they had contradicted her flatly. If they took the Mogadon or nitrazepam or whatever, they would still stick to their guns and persist in their opinions that it made them feel fuzzy in the morning. Well, according to how she felt at the moment, they were right! She closed her eyes, squeezed the lids together and was suddenly aware she had cramp in her hand. The hand, still under her pillow, was still clutching the bottle of Nembutal.

She drew it out. The bottle was quite warm. She could just see it in the pearly misty dawn light. She sat up a little further. Her mouth was dry and tasted sour. She turned over and searched for the glass of water beside her bed. It had a bathroom taste and was tepid.

The little clock read five past five. Muzzily Agnes

thought that for that time in the morning, it should be lighter. More sounds from outside, then she heard rain, hitting the glass of the window quite heavily.

Raining . . . Well, all the animals were safely in dry quarters. No need to worry about them. She was about to lie back on her pillows when the chair, wedged under the door handle, drew her eyes towards it. It looked sinister, its two legs on the floor, the other two slantwise, stuck up in the air.

Agnes remembered now, in the night when – how long ago? – it had moved, because Amy outside had twisted the door handle and given a little push which had moved the chair very slightly.

This was the second night she had tried, tried to get into her room.

What would Agnes have done if this time she had not just paused at the door and looked? Maybe this time she had realized there was something there stopping the door opening. Surely she must have?

Agnes sat up. What would she have done? Fought her off?

She remembered – and wished so much she didn't remember – the story Guy Singer had told her of the two women in bed together. Had he done that to get a sexual buzz like the beastly people at the slaughter of the fox at the kill?

Now Amy!

Agnes felt as if she were surrounded by perverts and sadists.

What to do?

She threw back the bedcover and thrust her feet into her slippers. She crossed the room and drew back the curtains. The outside world was completely obscured by the deluge of rain.

Agnes wondered why the noise of it had not wakened her. Perhaps it had?

She backed away from the window and sat for a moment on the side of the bed, thinking. Then she put on her dressing gown and put the little bottle of capsules into the pocket. She carefully removed the chair from its protective position and put it back in its place.

Agnes opened the door.

The hall was a little brighter than her bedroom. The window was bigger and the curtains drawn back.

Amy's door was shut. There was no sound.

Agnes went downstairs, very quietly, but not before she had put up a hand to Polly and signalled 'Stay' to her.

Polly, always loath to get up, obeyed.

In the kitchen she put the kettle on and drew back the blinds. She could see the puddles on the grass, the dull morning sky mirrored in them.

The kettle snapped off. Boiled.

Agnes made tea and drank a cup, all her movements careful and silent.

The capsules rattled now and again as she moved. She took a piece off the kitchen roll and stuffed it into her pocket to hold the little bottle still.

She then finished the second cup of tea, emptied the teapot, washed her cup and saucer and turned away from the sink, drying her hands.

Amy stood in the doorway, also in her robe. She looked white and strained. Her eyes strayed to the window but she made no remark about the rain, or anything else. Then she looked straight at Agnes.

'I've had a dreadful night and hardly slept at all, Agnes.'

Agnes, thinking of the movement of the chair, could believe her.

'So have I, Amy. I took a sleeping pill and it worked but only for a short time. Something woke me.'

She did not take her eyes off Amy's face as she said this.

'Perhaps it was the rain, or was there a storm again?'

'I don't think so. I didn't even realize it was pouring.'

Agnes's hand slid into her pocket and her fingers caressed the little brown bottle, almost lovingly.

'We can't do anything with the animals. They are dry and warm where they are. Go back to bed, Amy.'

Agnes looked at her watch, then at her companion.

'It's only half-past five, Amy. Go back to bed and I will make us both one of those milk and Bovril drinks that Robert made for you. He said it was your favourite. I tasted it and rather liked it too. We can sleep till eight.'

Wilma got up suddenly, distracted by the activity around her. Agnes opened the back door for her. At her age her bladder was not quite as reliable as Polly's. She went outside and stayed there a little time.

When she came in, she shook the rain off her coat and Agnes threw the big blanket they used for her over her back and dried her, much to Wilma's delight. The old dog loved notice of any kind. She went back to her bed.

Meanwhile Amy measured out two mugs of milk into a saucepan and got the Bovril out of the cupboard. She put Wilma's blanket back on to the radiator.

'Let me do it, Agnes. I'll bring it up to you. It's really nice of you to think of that. I'll do it.'

Agnes pushed this idea very firmly away. It was almost an order.

'No, you look a bit white and worn out. You haven't even got over Robert's visit yet, that's what I think, and you have had a bad tooth and all those antibiotics you had to take for quite a long time . . .'

Amy left the kitchen and went upstairs, first into the bathroom and then into her own bedroom. Agnes heard the bedroom door close behind her.

While the milk was heating Agnes did a quick check on the fox cub. He got up at her approach. She took some of the heating milk, mixed it with cold milk and put it in the teated bottle. She fed the cub and replaced the wad of newspaper on which the little animal had slept during the night. Back at the stove she brought the milk to almost boiling and poured a little into one mug. She then put her hand in her robe pocket and took out the brown bottle.

One by one she broke each capsule into the hot milk at

the bottom of Amy's mug. The white powder blended easily with the milk. At last all the capsules were emptied. She put the shells back into the bottle, screwed the cap on and put it into her pocket. She stirred and stirred the milk then filled the mug three-quarters full with steaming milk. She followed Amy's brother's instruction and spooned the correct amount of Bovril into the milk, stirring again until the Bovril had turned the milk pale fawn. Then she did the same to her own mug – this time there was no white powder to put in. The smell of the hot mixture was quite pleasant. She put both mugs on a small tray and took them upstairs. Amy's mug had two large red poppies on it. Agnes smiled to herself – rather appropriate, she thought.

Amy was in her bed, still with her robe on, her hair tied up in a hairnet that Agnes had not noticed when she had come into the kitchen. Tippy was curled up at the foot of the bed. She looked up briefly as Agnes put the mug on the little locker beside the bed. The cat opened her mouth wide in a huge yawn, showing her pink tongue and sharp white teeth, then settled back again, neat, black and comfortable.

Agnes felt a flash of sorrow. Tippy would miss Amy. She would have to make it up to her. Poor Tippy. She stroked the cat's head, and Tippy made a little purring noise. Amy looked at the mug. She smiled her thanks.

'Thank you, Agnes, how very sweet of you. It's a funny drink, I know. I must have been a funny child.'

Agnes felt the need to get out of the room as quickly as she could. She had no wish to talk to Amy about the drink or about Tippy. She just wanted to arrive at the point where she could safely call the doctor or the police and there would be no more need to put a chair as a wedge under her bedroom door handle. She would be alone.

She turned away from Amy and the cat, carrying the tray with her, and left the room.

'Thank you again, Agnes, thank you so much. I'll see

you about eight, then we'll have to get really busy and give walkies to everybody!'

That was meant as a little joke, Agnes realized. She went into her own room and shut the door, then opened it again, just a crack so that she could hear anything. She didn't quite know what she was expecting to hear. Nothing, she hoped! Anyway she felt the door was best left open.

Polly jumped on to the bed. Normally she didn't allow this, but this morning was rather an unusual morning and Agnes felt she needed the moral support that Polly's small warm firm body leaning against her gave. She sipped her drink. It was still very hot, but rather tasty. The Bovril had a strong flavour and would, Agnes hoped, completely mask the taste of the drug. She gently smoothed Polly's head and put the mug on the little table beside her. All she had to do now was wait.

The waiting was not easy. Agnes found she was unable to sit back in her bed and just listen. She tried her drink. It was about cool enough now so she sipped it and imagined Amy doing the same. How soon would the powder start to work? She had stirred and stirred it, but perhaps it would sink again to the bottom of the mixture and, unless Amy drained the mug, she would not –

Agnes's thoughts were interrupted by a cry and a clattering noise.

The noise, coming from Amy's room, made Agnes throw back her bedcover. She stood for a brief moment by her bed. She felt frozen, as if she could not move to go and investigate. This had not been how she had pictured her plan. Not at all.

She had thought that Amy, comforted by the kindness of Agnes in remembering her childhood drink, would be duped into thinking all was forgiven between them. Amy would drink the mugful, snuggle down in her bed and fall into a dreamless sleep. There had been enough Nembutal to ensure that. A picture flew through Agnes's mind as she stood there listening. Had the powder, which she had mixed and stirred so carefully, settled again in the bottom of the mug? Had Amy drunk, then tasted the white bitterness and suspected? No, that was not possible.

Another noise from Amy's bedroom, from behind the closed door, brought another picture. It was a long, drawn out 'Oh, no!' Amy's voice.

Agnes could stand it no longer. She opened her own door, switched on the light in the little hallway and crossed to Amy's door, putting her hand on the door knob. She twisted it and opened the door. There at once the scene was explained, the clattering sound and the agonized 'Oh no!'

Amy was sitting up in bed. Tippy, her green eyes wide with fright, was on the bedside locker. The little mat on the locker was askew under Tippy's claws. The front of the locker was dripping with fawn-coloured milk. The bedside rug was soaked with liquid and, just behind the rug on the pine floor, was the shattered poppy-covered mug.

Amy's eyes, as wide and frightened as the cat's, looked at Agnes. She was about to get out of bed and had already thrown back the duvet.

'Oh, Agnes, I'm sorry. Your kind thought . . . It was Tippy, she liked the smell of the drink and jumped up and . . . she didn't do it on purpose!'

The cat jumped down and hid under the bed. Agnes felt slightly sick with fear, with frustration and with regret. And Tippy – had she managed to drink any of the liquid? Probably too terrified after that loud crash . . . She must mop it all up immediately.

'Don't get out of bed, Amy, you'll cut yourself on the china. Stay there.'

Agnes rushed to the bathroom, grabbed two small towels and returned to Amy's room. Kneeling on the floor, she collected the four or five pieces of mug. The base, thicker than the rest, showed no sign of the sediment of white powder she had feared might be there. She mopped up the milky fluid and rolled up the rug, taking it into the bathroom. She put it in the bath and turned the hot tap on until the water just covered the rug.

In Amy's room, the black round-eyed cat had jumped back up on the bed and was purring as she stroked the thick black fur, no longer bristling with fright.

'It was my fault. I dozed off and the next thing the mug was on the floor and all your nice drink gone. Tippy didn't mean to do it, really she didn't, Agnes, really she didn't. She just jumped up and caught her claws in the cover. It smelled good, you see.'

Agnes did her best to calm her down. She gathered up the towels, the broken mug clunking inside their folds. She was just about to leave the room when Amy's protestations of apology began again. This time they stopped Agnes in her tracks and she turned to listen to what Amy was trying to explain.

'Two nights! Two nights, Agnes! I hadn't slept much. The little cub, little Rusty, he cried for his mother. Well, that's what I thought he was crying for. I did try two nights to come and tell you but the first night you were asleep and the next I couldn't open the door so I nursed him till he fell asleep and I . . . I should have told you, but I thought you'd be cross and you've done so much.'

Agnes turned round, still clutching the damp towels. She felt foolish to a degree she had never felt before. She looked at Amy, still holding and stroking the black cat, now lying across her knees. Amy looked up at her and smiled, rather wanly.

'Sorry about the mess, Agnes, and the rug and everything but Tippy didn't mean to do it.'

Agnes took in the scene and met Tippy's round green eyes looking at her.

'Oh, I don't know, Amy, perhaps she did.'

Suddenly she began to laugh, heartily and not at all like Agnes Turner once Carmichael.

She couldn't explain to Amy what she meant or why she was laughing.

'Animals do sometimes know a great deal more than we

239

do, you know. I've said that to you once or twice, haven't I, Amy?'

Amy nodded, and something in both women seemed to relax.

'Well, this morning I'm even more sure of it.'

Agnes left the room, closing the door behind her. She threw the wet towels into the bathroom hand basin.

She went back to her own room. This time she did not wedge the chair under the door handle. She just climbed into her bed and lay back on the pillows. As she did so, just as she was going to switch out the light, she looked at the door and smiled.

'Thanks, Tippy,' she said.